Fair Fight

Cora Leach gazed longingly at the joyful dancers. One of the soldiers noticed her and, before Cora had time to retreat, he grabbed her by the hand and pulled her out into the firelight. Seeing no sign of her husband or his brothers, she permitted herself to enjoy the reel before darting back to her place in the shadows, where she found Joe Leach waiting. Cora froze abruptly. Without a word of warning, Joe struck her with his fist, driving the hapless girl out of the shadows to crumple, dazed, to the ground.

Having seen all the abuse he was going to stand for, Jeb strode over to help Cora.

"God damn you," Joe snarled. "Get your hands off my wife!" It was all he had time to say, for Jeb whirled around and planted his fist squarely on Joe's nose. He put everything he had behind the punch, hoping to drive his fist right through the scoundrel's skull. Tanner would swear later that he heard Joe's nose crack from across the circle of wagons. Joe staggered backward before tripping over the wagon tongue and landing hard on his back.

"You're pretty damn good at beatin' on women," Jeb spat. "Let's see how you like it with somebody who'll fight back."

TANNER'S LAW

Charles G. West

BERKLEY
New York

BERKLEY

An imprint of Penguin Random House LLC

penguinrandomhouse.com

Copyright © 2008 by Charles G. West

Excerpt from *Range War in Whiskey Hill* copyright © 2008 by Charles G. West

Penguin Random House supports copyright. Copyright fuels creativity, encourages diverse voices, promotes free speech, and creates a vibrant culture. Thank you for buying an authorized edition of this book and for complying with copyright laws by not reproducing, scanning, or distributing any part of it in any form without permission. You are supporting writers and allowing Penguin Random House to continue to publish books for every reader.

BERKLEY and the BERKLEY & B colophon are registered trademarks of Penguin Random House LLC.

ISBN: 9780593441473

Signet mass-market edition / January 2008

Berkley mass-market edition / September 2022

Printed in the United States of America

1 3 5 7 9 10 8 6 4 2

For Ronda

Chapter 1

"Corporal Bland," the sergeant called out. A tall, broad-shouldered man got to his feet and stepped away from the line of weary soldiers resting on the ditch bank. When he approached, the sergeant said, "Lieutenant wants to see you." The sergeant turned on his heel and walked back toward the temporary command post near the crossroads. Tanner Bland followed without comment or question.

Lieutenant Richard Pearson looked up when the two men approached. "Thank you, Sergeant," he said, dismissing him. Turning to Tanner, he said, "Corporal Bland, I need to ask you to take on a mission of high importance." He cocked his head apologetically. "You notice, I didn't say I was ordering you. I said I'm asking you to volunteer." There was no reply from the quiet man, something that the lieutenant had come to expect from the corporal. He felt a considerable measure of guilt in sending for Tanner again. He was requested for dangerous assignments more often than any other man in his company.

Tanner waited patiently for the lieutenant to continue. Pearson looked into the dark expressionless eyes that never gave any clue to the man's thoughts. "Well, I'll get on with it," he said. He led Tanner over to a makeshift table on which a map had been spread. "Here's where we are, at this crossroads." Using his finger, he identified points on the map. "Here's Waynesboro, and this is where the Union's main body is camped on the other side. Now our scouts tell us a whole regiment of cavalry left the main body late this afternoon, heading east on the Charlottesville road. We suspect Sheridan is going to launch his offensive tomorrow morning, and General Early needs to know where that cavalry regiment is going. He's ordering me to send a scout tonight to find out."

He paused for Tanner's reaction. As he suspected, there was hardly any. After a moment, when it was obvious the lieutenant was waiting for an answer, Tanner said, "Yes, sir. I'll try to find 'em."

"Good man," Pearson said. "I knew I could count on you. How long will it take you to get ready to leave?"

"I reckon I'm ready now."

"Good man," Pearson repeated. "I can get you a horse if you want."

Tanner looked at the map again to fix the Charlottesville road in his mind. "No, sir. I'll just go on foot."

He set out immediately, passing the picket line, and entered the forest beyond the dusty road. Making his way up through the hills with nothing but the moon to light his path, he cut directly across the ridges south of the town. Away from the controlled chaos of the army, he was at home in the forest, having spent a great deal of his young life in the hills of Alleghany County, hunting and trapping.

In less than two hours' time, he had crossed the hills east of Waynesboro to arrive at a creek that ran along the Charlottesville Pike. After stopping momentarily to drink from the creek, he started out along the road, heading east. Even in the moonlight, the tracks of the cavalry horses were easily seen. He had not walked a mile when the tracks left the road, crossed the creek, and followed a valley back toward the south. It told him that a flanking maneuver was what the Union cavalry had in mind. That was as much information as the lieutenant expected, but Tanner decided to see how far they had gotten before making camp.

The Union troops were not difficult to follow. They left a wide trail through the plowed fields of the valley. Tanner could smell the freshly turned soil beneath his feet. No doubt the owner of the field had started his spring plowing recently. After crossing the field, he followed the tracks into a forest of hardwoods. Soon he saw the glow of campfires flickering through the dense growth of trees and vines, and he knew he needed to exercise a little more caution.

Moving with the quiet ease of a natural-born hunter, he made his way closer to the Union bivouac until he could see the soldiers sitting around their fires. After a moment, he thought, *The lieutenant was right. There must be a whole regiment camped here. Our right flank is going to catch hell if we aren't ready for them in the morning. I best get back and tell Lieutenant Pearson.* He quickly turned to leave.

"Who goes there?" a voice challenged from out of the darkness.

Damn, Tanner thought. *A Union picket.* He had inadvertently gotten so close to the camp that he was inside the picket line. There wasn't much time to think. If he made a run for it, the sentry would alert the whole regiment. If he shot him, the sound would have the same result.

"Who goes there?" the sentry repeated, this time with considerably more authority.

"For Pete's sake," Tanner replied, "can't a man have a little privacy to take a dump?"

The sentry stepped out from behind a large poplar trunk, his rifle held in position to fire quickly. "You must need a helluva lot of privacy," he said. "Who the hell are you?"

"Bland. Tanner Bland," Tanner answered honestly, hoping it was too dark for the guard to see his Confederate uniform.

The guard thought for a moment, but could not recognize the name. "Well, Bland, get on back to your unit. You ain't got no business out this far."

"I'm done, anyway," Tanner replied as casually as he could. He took a couple of steps in the direction of the camp before turning away from it again, hoping the picket wasn't paying close attention.

"Where the hell are you goin'?" the sentry asked impatiently. "Hey, hold it right there!" he exclaimed when a flicker of firelight through the trees cast a faint light on the gray uniform Tanner wore.

Tanner acted instantly. Holding his rifle by the barrel, he swung it as hard as he could, catching the sentry beside his ear with the butt. Staggering backward, too stunned to cry out, the sentry tripped over a bramble bush, crashing to the ground with Tanner right on top of him. A desperate struggle ensued as each man fought for his life. The guard tried to yell for help, but Tanner's grip on his throat rendered him incapable of more than a gasp for air. He clawed at Tanner's face in a frantic attempt to break the viselike grip, but Tanner would not yield, knowing that to do so would mean his death. It seemed an eternity before the sentry's struggles ceased and he fell back unconscious.

Tanner wasted no time extracting himself from the brambles and diving into the darkness of the forest. There was no thought of killing the guard. He didn't want to take the time. There was no point in it, anyway. Either way, the Union soldiers would find out that he had been there. His only thought now was to be sure he was long gone when they did. He hoped his information would be of value to Pearson—it looked to Tanner like all hell was going to break loose when morning came.

I'm in a helluva fix now, Tanner Bland thought as he slid along a muddy ditch bank on his belly. A few scant yards beyond the edge of the deep drainage ditch, he could hear the hollow drumming of hooves as a Union cavalry company passed by him, looking for stray survivors from the battle. In reality, it hadn't been much of a battle. There was little left of General Jubal Early's Valley Army. No more than fifteen hundred or so could be mustered to repel General Sheridan's fourteen thousand cavalry troops that fell into line at Waynesboro. *Hell, we held them for a little while,* Tanner thought, *until they rolled up our right flank and scattered us all to hell and gone.* It was the regiment he'd scouted the night before that had hit the Confederate flank the hardest.

It had not been a pretty sight, watching the men he had fought with for the last seven months lay down their weapons in surrender. It was hard to cast blame, however, for to stand and fight was suicide. As he lay still for a few moments, listening, the sounds of a horse's hooves came dangerously close to the edge of the ditch. The horse stopped right above him, and then there was silence. Had he been discovered, lying as still as a corpse? He held his breath and waited for the shot that would pronounce his decision not to surrender a mistake. The stillness of the moment rang in his ears like a whirlwind. And he thought of Ellie. Why, he wondered, in this moment of peril, would the image of the woman he loved suddenly appear in his mind? He could almost feel the gaze of the Union soldier upon his back. Whatever happened in the next few seconds might determine whether or not he would return to his home and to Eleanor Marshall.

Lying facedown in the muddy ditch, Tanner considered the odds of rolling over quickly enough to bring his rifle up and get off a shot before the Union soldier fired. He decided they were not in his favor. *Maybe he just doesn't see me,* he thought. *His damn horse knows I'm here. It's been blowing and snorting ever since he stopped above me.* After several more agonizing seconds, however, the rider moved on, either having not seen him or concluding that he was dead. Tanner exhaled slowly, realizing that his entire body had been so tense that it probably looked like it was in rigor mortis.

He continued his painfully slow crawl along the muddy ditch, dragging his rifle and haversack in the cold slime as he inched his way toward a bridge about thirty yards away. Several minutes passed without the sound of horses on the bank above his head, so he increased his pace a little. Once he reached the cover of the bridge, he decided it would be safe enough to raise his head above the edge of the ditch to see where he was going. The sight that met his eyes was disheartening, to say the least.

There on the main street of Waynesboro, milling aimlessly about like so many sheep in a pen, were the remnants of General Early's Army of the Valley. With an army that numbered only fourteen thousand at its peak, they had tied up Union forces of forty or fifty thousand for seven months, delaying them from attacking Lee's army at Petersburg and Richmond. Now, shattered and depleted, they stood in pitiful profile, the shadow of a once proud army.

He supposed that the Valley Army had done its job as well as could have been expected against such superior forces. And now that they were so badly outnumbered, maybe surrender was justifiable. But Tanner didn't squander a moment contemplating the decision. He had no intention of sitting out the rest of the war in a federal prison. He was at home in the forest and hills and he would take his chances on avoiding the Union patrols.

Since no one took a shot at him when he raised his head above the ditch bank, he took a few moments more to assess his situation. Behind him, on the other side of the ditch, was a low building that appeared to be a warehouse of some sort. He considered scrambling out of the ditch and taking refuge in the building, but changed his mind when a company of Union cavalry suddenly appeared around the end of it. *Searching for strays,* he thought. *Strays like me.* He crouched back down in the ditch and waited until the soldiers completed their search of the abandoned building. They were soon in the saddle again and moving down toward the congregation of prisoners. He could see other units performing the same kind of search missions, too many to risk exposing himself. So he dropped back down to the bottom of the ditch and continued to crawl along through the mud.

After covering approximately seventy-five yards more, he reached a point where the ditch deepened, allowing him to risk running in a crouch. Taking one last look behind him to make sure he had not been spotted, he checked his weapon. Wiping mud from the breech and barrel of the Enfield rifle he carried, he silently congratulated himself for the forethought to give the barrel a coating of lard the night before to prevent rust.

He had by now progressed to a point adjacent to the edge of the woods where his company had made their last attempt to hold the Union forces amassed against them. Concerned till then with no thoughts beyond removing himself from harm's way, he now realized that quite by accident he had chosen the best route of escape. He was retreating in the direction from which the enemy had advanced, and at the moment he liked the idea that he was going one way while the enemy was going the opposite.

When he was sure there was no one else about, he scrambled out of the ditch and ran for the cover of the trees, almost stumbling over the body of a Confederate soldier sitting with its back against a large gum tree.

"Damn!" he swore after catching himself on the tree trunk to avoid falling. "Sorry," he then muttered contritely under his breath. Staring with dull sightless eyes was the corpse of a young boy, his chest torn apart by shrapnel, probably K-shot or some other deadly canister round. Tanner speculated that the unfortunate young man had sat patiently waiting for the life to bleed out of him. He hurriedly looked closely to see if the boy had been a member of his company. He decided not.

Pausing then to look around him, he took in the grim scene of a beaten army. Here and there lay other bodies, a testament to the fierce, though brief, battle that had taken place. In the heat of the fighting, when they were being pushed back into the town, he had been aware of comrades falling on both sides. Seeing the aftermath now, it struck him as a miracle that any had survived to surrender.

He'd had no time available to think as he crawled through the muddy ditch, but now he knelt on one knee deciding what to do. While he considered his circumstances, he continued to look around him at the carnage left by the battle—the lifeless lumps that were once his brothers in arms, the discarded pieces of equipment. He could smell the rancid odor of gunpowder that still hung over the forest. Glancing up at the trees, he saw the tattered lower leaves and branches shredded by minié balls, evidence of triggers pulled before rifles were aimed properly, the result of a panic to fire quickly and reload in the face of a charging enemy. He shook his head sadly when he thought about the wholesale slaughter about him.

Casting sorrowful thoughts aside, he turned his focus back to his primary concern at the moment. Taking a minute to get his bearings, he found the sun through the canopy of oak leaves above him, and turned to the west. Starting out at a lope, he made his way through the trees, avoiding the silent bodies. He gave no thought toward searching any of the fallen for usable items, though he would not hesitate to take from the dead, especially his comrades. He certainly would not begrudge their taking something of his if the situation were reversed. But now he knew that because of the debilitating lack of supplies, no one in his company had anything worth taking. During the weeks leading up to the battle, the men of his regiment had foraged farms and villages for food, but there was nothing left to forage. Even the population of rabbits and squirrels seemed to be depleted. The only thing he might gain from his dead comrades was possibly a few extra cartridges for the Enfield he carried.

Approaching the western edge of the forest, he slowed to a cautious walk before emerging into an open field, a dozen or more acres wide. It was across this field that the Union cavalry had charged and his unit had stood to repel them. Looking out over the open space, he could see the scattered bodies of Union soldiers, seeming small and pathetic in their eternal sleep. Here and there, the larger lumps that were the slain horses appeared like random boulders in the level field. He was still trying to decide whether to strike out straight across the field or to circle it, when he heard someone call out.

Reacting instantly, he dropped to one knee and swung his rifle around to aim at the point from which he thought the voice had come. "Corporal Bland." The voice came again. Instinctively shifting his rifle to aim at a clump of briar bushes several feet to the right of the first target, he still could not locate the source. "Don't shoot, Corporal. It's me, Jeb Hawkins."

"Jeb Hawkins," Tanner echoed in surprise. "Where the hell are you?"

"I'm down here in this damn hole," the man replied.

Still Tanner did not spot him right away, but in a few seconds' time, he saw branches parting no more than ten feet before him to reveal the head and shoulders of Jeb Hawkins, a man from his company. Upon moving to help Jeb up, he discovered the bushes hid an old stump hole. Grasping Jeb's wrists, Tanner hauled him up through the brambles. His tunic was spattered with blood. "Damn, Jeb," Tanner exclaimed, "how bad are you hurt?"

Jeb replied with a grin. "I ain't hurt bad a'tall. Just some little cuts and scratches." He went on to explain that he received his injuries when he split the barrel of his rifle. "When them Yankees charged, we was firin' so fast, and all the guns goin' off right and left of me, I didn't even know that I hadn't pulled the trigger, and I rammed another load down the barrel, right on top of the first one. When I pulled the trigger that time, it knocked me plumb over backward, and I landed in that stump hole. Landed on my head, I reckon, and by the time I started to crawl outta there, our boys had started re-treatin'. I was gonna scramble out and catch up with 'em, but Billy Thacker fell right in my arms, with a hole in his chest the size of my fist. We both wound up in the bottom of the hole."

"You sure you aren't hurt? There's a helluva lot of blood all over you."

"That's mostly Billy's," Jeb replied. "They got him right through the heart, I guess. I thought he never was gonna stop bleedin' before he finally just quit breathin'. He was still layin' on top of me. I started to crawl out again, but the Yankees were already movin' up through the bushes." He displayed another grin. "So I figured I'd just lay right where I was, with ol' Billy." He paused, then asked, "How come you're slippin' through the woods by yourself? Where's the rest of the boys?"

Tanner painted the somber picture for him. "I don't know how many others got away," he concluded, "but it looked like damn near the whole bunch of survivors surrendered."

"So it's just you and me then," Jeb said, scratching his head thoughtfully. "What are you aimin' to do?"

"I'm aimin' to get the hell away from here," Tanner replied. "That's the first thing I'm gonna do. This valley is crawlin' with Union troops, and I don't plan to spend any time in a Yankee prison."

"That's damn sure my feelin's as well. Whaddaya say we team up?"

"Suit yourself," Tanner replied. "I'm thinkin' maybe we can head up in those mountains west of the pike. It oughta be easy enough to stay outta sight in those hills. Then maybe we can work our way back down the valley, and cut across to Lynchburg or somewhere. We're bound to run into some of our army between there and Richmond."

Jeb didn't reply at once, nodding slowly while he thought the prospects over. He apparently thought the matter of rejoining the army worthy of considerable speculation. Tanner studied the man in the meantime, realizing he knew very little about Jeb Hawkins. He had never spent any off-duty time with him. From a little town in Kansas, Jeb had traveled to Virginia to join General Jubal Early's army. Tanner knew that much—that and the fact that Jeb, a tall, rangy man with a shock of sandy red hair, soon established a reputation as a hard-drinking, quick-tempered hell-raiser anytime he was off duty. As far as soldiering, from what Tanner had seen, Jeb Hawkins never hesitated when given an order, even though he usually looked as if he was considering questioning it.

"Well, hell," Jeb said, his decision finally made. "That's what we'll do then. Maybe we'll find ol' Robert E. Lee hisself." Before Tanner could take a step, Jeb added, "I need me a gun, though. My rifle barrel's split like a cherry tree."

"There's Thacker's," Tanner said, pointing toward the dead man's weapon.

"I'm thinkin' more about pickin' up one of them Spencer repeatin' carbines those Yankee cavalry boys carry. If we hustle our asses, we oughta have time to find us a couple of rifles before they come back to pick up their dead."

"That makes sense to me." Tanner readily agreed, wondering why he hadn't thought of it himself. Without further comment, the two hurried out of the trees and into the open field. "There's gotta be some stray horses around here somewhere, too," he called out as he headed for a Union body.

"I'm gonna leave you this bullet sack of .58-caliber cartridges," Jeb said to the corpse of a young man whose head was half blown away. "I wouldn't wanna just take this fine carbine of yours without tradin' you somethin' for it." He laughed at his macabre humor as he relieved the body of its ammunition pouch of rimfire cartridges. "Look here, Corporal, this feller has one of them Blakeslee cartridge boxes."

"So has this one," Tanner said, in the process of equipping himself from another unfortunate soldier. He was well familiar with the cartridge boxes fashioned by a man named Blakeslee. The Spencer held seven cartridges in its magazine, and Blakeslee had built a carrying case that held anywhere from six to thirteen tubes loaded with the cartridges. The rifle was loaded through the butt, and these tubes could be quickly inserted, loading all seven bullets at once. It was a hell of an advantage in a hot firefight.

Well equipped, and loaded down with extra ammunition for their confiscated weapons, the new partners stayed to scavenge the enemy dead as long as they dared before deciding it best to remove themselves from the open field.

"Damn, Corporal, I wonder what happened to the horses," Jeb said, panting as they ran toward the lower end of the field.

Breathing rapidly himself, Tanner answered, "My name's Tanner. That looks like a creek runnin' along the bottom of the hill. If they're anywhere around, that's the place we'll find 'em."

Tanner's prediction proved to be accurate. Just past the lower end of the field, the creek wound its way into a heavy forest of oaks and poplars. About thirty yards into the trees, it almost doubled back on itself, forming a narrow glen. It was here that half a dozen cavalry horses had gathered to graze on the tender grass within the double bend of the creek. Curious, but not frightened, all six horses bobbed their heads up to study the two men approaching.

"Well, would you look at that," Jeb commented. "All bunched up and waitin' for us to come get 'em." He chuckled at the thought. "By God, I reckon I ain't in the infantry no more. 'Course, I never figured I'd be in the Yankee cavalry."

Tanner merely grunted in response, his mind already evaluating the choice of horseflesh before him. "Looks to me like the gray and that sorrel beside him are the best of the bunch," he offered. Of the six, those two appeared to be more broad-chested and built for stamina. "I'm not holdin' myself up as being an expert on horses.

I'm just sayin' I figure on takin' one or the other of those two."

"Yeah, I reckon," Jeb allowed, although he was eyeing a hand-tooled saddle on one of the other horses. It looked to be of Mexican origin and had the initials *JW* tooled on the apron. "That black sure is sportin' a fine-lookin' saddle. I bet it was an officer's horse."

Tanner took another look at the black mare. "If you were to ask me, which you didn't, I'd say take the saddle, but throw it on one of the other horses. That horse may look pretty, but she's too narrow in the chest, and her legs are too long. The gray or the sorrel would likely run her into the ground. But that's just my opinion."

Jeb thought that over for a few moments, then decided Tanner was probably right. "I expect that's true," he said. "Which one of them two do you favor?"

"Either one."

Jeb speculated a moment more before speaking. "I reckon you favor that fancy saddle yourself, and you outrank me." He studied Tanner intently, awaiting his answer.

Tanner was not looking at him when he answered. Instead, he was gazing out toward the field they had just left. When he spoke, his voice was quiet and calm. "Right now, we ain't worried about rank. You fancy that saddle, you take it. Take your pick of the horses. But be quick about it. There's a Union patrol on the road on the other side of that field, and they look like they're fixin' to cut into the field."

"Damn!" Jeb exclaimed, becoming immediately alert. At the same time, a grin appeared upon his face when he realized Tanner wasn't concerned about rank. "Fair enough," he said. "I'll take the saddle, so you take first pick of the horses."

More concerned with expediting a quick withdrawal, Tanner said, "All right, I'll take the gray." He walked slowly up to the two horses he had selected and caught the reins of both. Looping the reins over a laurel branch, he prepared to remove the cavalry saddle from the sorrel while Jeb approached the black mare. He hesitated with his hand on the girth strap, however, when the black bolted, leaving Jeb to chase wildly after her.

The horse, somehow spooked by Jeb's manner, splashed through the creek with Jeb right behind her. Under less dire circumstances, it might have been amusing, with the exasperated redhead struggling up the bank, arms waving frantically, running after the frightened horse.

Tanner took one more glance back toward the field to check on the Union patrol's progress. When he was sure they had not spotted the two Confederate soldiers, he calmly stepped up on the gray. Taking the sorrel's reins as well, he started out after his new partner, figuring they might both be sitting cavalry saddles. Jeb appeared to be pretty physically fit, but Tanner felt fairly confident that he wasn't going to outrun a horse. He gave the cantankerous horse a run for her money, however, before giving up the chase. The contest ended with the black standing, watching warily, on a pine knob some fifty yards from the winded Confederate infantryman. If, indeed, Jeb had been correct in assuming the black was an officer's mount, the horse had no doubt recognized the two as enlisted men and apparently deemed it highly improper for Jeb to presume to climb on her back.

A somewhat impatient observer to all this, Tanner guided the horses along behind the haphazard chase through the trees. In spite of the potential danger of the Union patrol now searching the open field behind him, he was not overly concerned as long as Jeb and the black continued moving in a westerly direction, away from the patrol. Even though it was only the second day of March, the woods were fairly dense, and he felt certain they had not been spotted by the soldiers.

Pulling up beside Jeb, who was bent over, hands on knees, gasping for breath, Tanner handed the sorrel's reins to the frustrated man. "If you really fancy that saddle that much, I'll try to get it for you." He left Jeb holding the sorrel and gave the gray a touch of his heels. The big horse responded immediately, crossing the creek again and climbing up the pine knob toward the waiting mare. Tanner had a notion that the mare was only spooked by the red-haired Rebel chasing her. That turned out to be the case, for the black stood patiently waiting while Tanner rode up beside her and took her reins. He dismounted, and unbuckled her girth strap. "You can go ahead and jerk the saddle off of that sorrel," he called out to Jeb as he pulled the hand-tooled saddle off.

"Well, I'll be double-dogged damned," Jeb exclaimed, scarcely able to believe his eyes. From that day forward, he would always believe that Tanner had a special way with horses, a belief that Tanner didn't embrace himself, but never bothered to refute.

When the transfer of saddles was completed, Tanner said, "Let's get movin'. I wanna get up in the hills on the other side of the pike before dark."

Chapter 2

Now mounted, with plenty of ammunition for their newly confiscated carbines, and a small supply of salt, coffee, and hardtack, all courtesy of the Union army, Tanner and Jeb made camp by a narrow stream that wound its way down a wooded ravine from the mountain above. From their position high up on a ridge west of Waynesboro, they could watch the activity on the valley pike. The main body of the Union army didn't linger in the little town very long. After defeating General Early, Sheridan crossed over the Blue Ridge and headed toward Charlottesville.

The new partners sat on a boulder that offered a clear view of the road out of Waynesboro and discussed their options. Though neither man voiced it, it was clear to both that the Southern cause was lost as far as the war was concerned. Their regiment having been destroyed, they now had the feeling that they were fugitives. The thought of simply giving up and going home had crossed both their minds. But Tanner had never started anything important that he didn't finish, so he knew his conscience would dictate his decision in the end. Jeb was never bothered by conscience, but he had come a long way to fight in this war, and it was a long ride back to Kansas. Still undecided, he waited for Tanner to make his decision.

"Well," Tanner finally said, "there's still a few patrols running around down there. Speakin' for myself, I'm thinkin' to wait it out right here for a day or two more and see if the rest of those Yankees clear out and follow Sheridan to Richmond. Then I figure we'll be in the clear. We can cross back over the pike, and head south toward Lynchburg, and join up with another unit."

Jeb thought about it for a few moments before making up his mind. "Hell, that plan sounds as good as any," he said.

It was two full days before the last stragglers of Sheridan's army left the town to recover what it could of life before its encounter with the fiery Union general. In groups of two or three, the townsfolk returned to the streets, emerging from hiding places to fearfully contemplate homes stripped of food and supplies. It was a grieving community that Tanner and Jeb rode into on the third day after the battle.

Their scant rations already depleted, they decided to see if any of the people had hidden away supplies that they might be willing to sell to two Confederate soldiers. Of the buildings left standing, one appeared to be a general store and seemed as good a place to look as any. When the two riders approached, they were met by the owner on the front step. His eyes sparked in anger as he announced, "There ain't no use lookin' in here. Your friends have already stole everything off the shelves." Taking a closer look then, he realized that the two were not Union soldiers. "Sorry, boys," he said in apology. "I thought you were some more of them thievin' Yankees."

"No harm done," Tanner replied. "We've been hidin' out in the hills since the rest of our regiment got whipped. We're on our way south to try to join up with Lee's army."

Without having to be told what they sought, the store owner volunteered, "What I just said was the truth. The Yankees cleaned everything off my shelves. There ain't a scrap of bread in this town, nor the flour to make more. They even found the cornmeal and coffee I'd hid under the floorboards. I'm sorry I can't help you boys out."

"Thanks just the same," Tanner said. "I reckon we'll all have to make it on rabbits and squirrels. Good day to you, sir."

"Good luck to you, son," the store owner said. As Tanner started to turn to follow Jeb, the man asked one more question. "Where is your home, young fellow?"

Tanner reined his horse back. "Alleghany County," he answered, "not far from a little town called Covington. My father's got a farm there."

"Covington—I know the town," the store owner said, smiling. "Well, I hope you get back there soon, and we can get this war behind us."

"Yessir," Tanner replied. "Well, good day to you," he said again, and wheeled his horse to follow Jeb, who was already fifty yards ahead of him. He was about to urge the gray forward but then he quickly hauled back on the reins. At the end of the street Jeb was abruptly halted by a patrol of six Union cavalry that appeared suddenly from around the corner of the bank building. Realizing in that instant that the soldiers had not spotted him as yet, Tanner immediately guided the big horse into the alley beside the general store.

With no time to react, Jeb was caught with no chance of escape. He was instantly surrounded. "Well, lookee here, boys," a heavyset man wearing sergeant's stripes chortled. "I do believe we caught us a Johnnie Reb." He pulled his horse up almost nose to nose with Jeb's sorrel. "And he's ridin' a U.S. Army branded horse, and carryin' a Spencer carbine." He directed one of the other soldiers to relieve Jeb of the rifle. "I expect you killed the man they belonged to, and from the looks of that fancy saddle, he was most likely an officer."

"I didn't kill him," Jeb replied defiantly. "I found the horse and the rifle back yonder in that field. I'm just sorry it wasn't me that did shoot him." He took a quick glance behind him to see if Tanner had escaped detection.

"Is that so?" the sergeant responded. "Well, boys," he said, addressing his men then, "murder, horse thievin', stolen government property. We got us a hangin' to tend to."

Jeb started to back the sorrel away, but was stopped before he could move. With five rifles leveled at him, he relinquished the reins. "Well, that's about right," he spat. "Takes about six Yankees to hang one Reb."

"You suppose we ought to take him back and turn him

in with all those other prisoners?" one of the Union privates asked.

"Shit, no," the sergeant snapped back. "We got other things to worry about without havin' to look after him. He's done plenty to warrant a hangin'. We'll string him up on that hickory yonder—be a good sign for any more Rebs that might be hidin' out around here, thinkin' to steal government property."

Moving cautiously behind the buildings, Tanner made his way to the back of the bank building. He dismounted and tied the reins to a porch post. Pulling his carbine from the saddle sling, he checked to make sure it was fully loaded before moving to the corner of the building. On one knee, he peered around the corner in time to see the six Union soldiers lead Jeb's horse to a tall hickory tree on the other side of the street. *Son of a bitch!* he thought. *They mean to hang him!* Even as he thought it, one of the soldiers took a short piece of rope and tied Jeb's hands behind his back. Another took a longer coil of rope and began fashioning a noose. Thinking out his first move, Tanner tried to quickly assess his situation. *That leaves three with rifles trained on Jeb,* he thought, for like the men with the ropes, the sergeant's weapon was still holstered. He had seven shots. Every shot had to count, because there would be no time for reloading.

There was some doubt in his mind, but he saw no other choice open to him. He was going to fire the Spencer carbine for the very first time. All he had to go on was the rifle's reputation. He didn't know if the particular weapon in his hand was going to shoot high, low, or to one side or the other. *It's a helluva time to find out,* he worried, but it was at close range. That would improve his odds some, and it figured to be Jeb's only chance. Resolved to do the best he could, he stepped out from behind the building and moved quickly along the side to a low watering trough opposite the corner.

Undetected by the lynching party to that point, he lay on his belly and pulled his rifle up beside him. Inching over to the end of the trough, he readied the weapon to fire. He peered around the trough to picture the attack in his mind one final time. The actions of the patrol had attracted the attention of a handful of the town's citizens, who stood horrified by the blatant execution about to be performed. *Three still mounted with rifles on Jeb,* he recorded silently, *the other two busy with the ropes, and the sergeant with no weapon drawn.* He was going to have to be quick.

He picked the closest mounted soldier as his first target. Just as the soldier with the noose held it up for the sergeant's approval, Tanner squeezed off the first round. It caught his target squarely between the shoulder blades. The man dropped his rifle and slid off his horse. Knowing it was not yet the moment to rush his shot, Tanner cranked the trigger guard down to eject the spent cartridge and pull another into the chamber. As he had hoped, the hanging party was stunned momentarily, with no idea where the shot had come from. When a second shot rang out, and another soldier fell to the ground, panic overcame the four remaining.

The lynching became immediately secondary in importance to the three privates. Finding cover outweighed

it. They scattered, along with the few spectators that had
gathered, to find protection. With no less fondness for his
own hide, the burly sergeant wheeled his horse to escape.
Then, determined to prevent his prisoner from cheating
death, he wheeled his horse back to face Jeb again,
pulling his pistol from his holster as he did. Before
he could aim it, a third shot from Tanner's Spencer
slammed into his chest, causing him to drop the revolver.
Having some confidence in the Spencer's tendencies
then, Tanner put another round neatly in the center of the
sergeant's forehead to make sure he was dead.

In the midst of the sudden attack, Jeb was as stunned
as his captors. With his hands tied behind his back, he
was holding on for dear life with his knees, trying to remain in the saddle while the frightened sorrel reacted to
the sudden retreat of the other horses. He was saved from
possibly coming off the horse by one of the spectators.
The man, a blacksmith, ran up to take the sorrel's reins,
and quickly calmed the nervous animal. When the horse
was under control, the blacksmith produced a pocketknife
and cut Jeb's bonds. No words were spoken between
them, but the look in Jeb's eyes expressed gratitude to the
blacksmith's satisfaction. Once again, Jeb found himself
without a rifle. He dismounted to retrieve one of the
weapons lying in the street. He nodded toward the blacksmith. The smithy, understanding, picked up the other
rifle and immediately departed to hide it away in his
shop. Seeing Tanner standing by the trough then, Jeb led
his horse to join him.

Looking back over his shoulder to be sure that what
he was about to declare was accurate, Jeb grinned

broadly and exclaimed, "I don't think them other three are gonna stop till they get to the Potomac." Tanner nodded agreement in reply. "Partner," Jeb announced, "I knew I could count on you." In truth, he had not been certain, but he would be from that moment forward. "That was a fine piece of work you did back there. Those boys were aimin' to send me to hell to see my daddy. Yessir, a fine piece of shootin'."

"I expect we'd best be on our way before we run into another patrol," Tanner replied and turned to fetch his horse.

When he rounded the back corner of the bank, he discovered a committee of three men standing by his horse, waiting to greet him. Two of the faces were familiar. One was the storekeeper, the second was the blacksmith, the third was a dark-haired stranger with only one arm. Startled, Tanner stopped in his tracks and quickly brought his carbine up, ready to fire.

"Hold on, son," the store owner said. "We're on the same side." When Tanner stood silent, eyeing the three cautiously, the store owner continued, pausing only to nod to Jeb when he appeared around the corner. "My name's Horace Stanley. This here's Bob Wilson," he said, nodding toward the blacksmith. "We thought you oughta talk to Leland Forrest here," he continued, referring to the man standing beside him.

Not waiting for questions from Tanner and Jeb, Forrest took it from there. "Horace told me I should talk to you boys, and from what I just saw, I think he was right." With long black shoulder-length hair and a full beard streaked with gray, the man introduced as Leland

Forrest resembled a fire-and-brimstone preacher, wearing a black frock coat, the left sleeve pinned up just above the elbow.

Tanner exchanged a puzzled glance with Jeb before asking, "What about?"

"Horace says you're aiming to join Lee at Richmond," Forrest replied. He received a slight nod in return. "Well, fighting men like yourselves might do the South a helluva lot more good right here in the valley. Lee's holed up in the trenches around Richmond and Petersburg. He can't go anywhere. Grant's got him treed, and if the Yankees succeed in cutting the South Side Railroad, Lee won't have any supply line. He'll likely have to evacuate Richmond. You two fellows won't make much of a difference there, but you could make a helluva difference right here."

"Doin' what?" Jeb interjected.

Forrest favored him with a smile. "Fighting Yankees," he replied. "We've organized a company of men to harass the Union detachments that have followed General Sheridan into the valley. I won't lie to you. We're mostly made up of older men and those wounded in the war, like myself. But we're eighteen in number—you two would make it an even twenty—and we're all from right around these parts. So we know the country, where to strike and where to hide. We could sure use you two."

Tanner didn't know what to say for a few moments. He looked at Jeb, but Jeb was looking to him to respond. Not sure what his feelings about the proposition were, he said, "We're still in the army. It's our duty to report back."

"Sure it is," Forrest said. "And I understand that. And I admire your stand on your responsibility. But what I'm trying to say is that you will be doing the South a lot more good in a unit where you can hit and run, give the enemy fits, and in the long run delay their siege of Richmond because they'll have to deal with us here."

Tanner glanced again at Jeb, and received a wide grin in response. The rangy redhead looked to be receptive to the notion. Tanner had to admit the proposition had merit. Indeed, it might offer an opportunity to contribute more to the Southern cause than to fade back into the ranks of an infantry regiment. "Hell, why not?" he finally decided. He and Jeb were immediately greeted with wide smiles and handshakes.

"We're mighty glad to have you boys," Horace Stanley said after Tanner and Jeb introduced themselves. "It ain't possible for me to ride with Leland, what with the store and family and all, but I help in any way I can with supplies and whatnot. Bob helps out the same way. He's got a family to look after, too."

Leland Forrest spoke up again. "I expect we'd best get you fellows outta town right now. There's bound to be a Yankee patrol back here as soon as one of those three that ran off can find somebody to report to." After shaking hands briefly with Stanley and Wilson, he motioned for Tanner and Jeb to follow him. "My horse is tied up behind Bob's forge. Follow me, and we'll head up to our camp."

Once his horse was retrieved, Forrest led them along a creek that backed the blacksmith shop, then entered a hole in the thick wild hedge that lined the bank to a hidden trail leading down to a deep ravine. "From now on," he explained to his new recruits, "if you have to come to town, this is the safest way to come."

The one-armed leader of the valley raiders had not lied when he told Tanner and Jeb that the group was made up of old men and cripples. The first time they rode with the gang, they could not help but question their decision to join up. More than half of the eighteen were gray-haired men, some already suffering with nature's afflictions of age. The balance of the gang was made up of veterans of the war, sent home because of wounds too severe to remain in the active army. But Tanner found that all were experienced hunters, and at home in the heavily wooded hills of the Shenandoah. So Tanner and Jeb rode on more than a dozen raids on Union supply wagons and rear-action work details, causing little more than minor irritation during the next month. In between raids, they camped in the mountains, and lived mostly off the wild game plentiful there. Many times Tanner thought about going home for a short visit. Their range of operation was seldom more than a single day's journey from his home in Alleghany County, but the need to protect the secrecy of their little group kept him from risking a visit. Finally, on one of the sorties, an attack on a Union woodcutting detail, Leland Forrest was mortally wounded while leading the charge. That loss seemed to sap the desire from most of the elderly members of the gang, and with that added to the disappointing news that Lee had been forced to evacuate Richmond, the little unit began to unravel. Tanner and Jeb were thinking they had already stayed too long. "I'm thinkin' more and more about sayin' good-bye to this sorry war and headin' on out west," Jeb announced one evening while watching a pitiful little rabbit's carcass roast over the fire. Tanner didn't answer, but looked up from cleaning his Spencer carbine to give Jeb his attention. "Hell," Jeb continued, "what good are we doin' here, anyway? Our little raidin' parties don't amount to a bucket of piss in the Atlantic Ocean."

Tanner laid his rifle aside and looked around him at the ragtag camp. After Leland's death, the soul of most of the older men seemed to have died with him, and already several of the original party had offered weak apologies and left for home. Those remaining, mostly men wounded in the war before joining Leland's raiders, tended to look to Tanner and Jeb for guidance. Thinking now of Jeb's comments, Tanner understood the reasoning behind them. There was no Union unit of any importance left to fight in the valley. The last sortie they had ridden on took them almost forty miles toward Charlottesville to attack a train depot. When they got there, they found that the information they had received was inaccurate. They found no company of Union soldiers, and no supply depot. They were left with a long, hungry ride back to their camp in the hills. It was hard to disagree with Jeb's assessment of the group's value to the cause.

"I expect you may be right," Tanner finally responded. "There's not much use in tryin' to keep this up. I've been thinkin' a lot about goin' home, myself."

They didn't take it any further than that for the time being, primarily because, deep down, neither man liked the idea of quitting. A few days later, the decision became moot with a visit from Horace Stanley.

It was the eleventh of April when Horace made his way up to their camp with the sorrowful news that Lee had surrendered two days before at the little town of Appomattox Court House.

The war was over. It was difficult to believe after so many years of fighting that it was time for every soldier to go home. Tanner and Jeb sat before their campfire late into the night talking about their plans.

"Why don't you come on back to Kansas with me?" Jeb suggested. "We'll push on west of there, head up to Montana, up to them goldfields maybe." Reacting to the noncommittal expression on Tanner's face, he added, "I've got a grubstake stashed at home if that's concernin' you. Whaddaya say, Tanner? You know Virginia ain't gonna be no place to live with all the Union army and regulators takin' over everything."

Tanner smiled and shook his head. It was going to be hard to part with Jeb. The two had become as close as friends could get in the short time since Tanner had found Jeb in the blown-out stump hole. "I swear, Jeb, I'd be tempted to take you up on that, but I've got a little gal waitin' for me back in Alleghany County. And I promised her I'd be back." He was being truthful when he said he was tempted, for he had always been fascinated by reports of the big sky country. But he could not deny the longing in his heart for Ellie.

Jeb grunted his disappointment, then said, "Why, hell, go on back and marry her, and bring her with you."

Tanner paused to picture Eleanor Marshall's likely

response to such a proposition. She would probably not
relish the idea of leaving the comfort of her father's
expansive house to take to the gold prospector's trail.
The thought caused Tanner to chuckle. He and Ellie had
known from their school days that they would marry and
Tanner would take over the management of her father's
many acres. The thought of her now caused an aching in
his heart to see her. He pictured her face on the day he'd
left, tears streaming down her cheeks to drop softly upon
her lace bodice.

"I reckon I'd best go back home, Jeb. I'm gonna be
expected to help run her daddy's farm now that he's gettin' on in years. I've got my own land to look after, too,
my father's place. We'll need both my brothers and me
to run both places."

Jeb grinned, disappointed. "Hell, I don't blame you,
partner. It sounds like you've got it all set up for you. I
wish I had a little gal waitin' for me to come back."

There was limited conversation between the two
friends as each man prepared to depart the secluded
ravine in the mountains above Waynesboro. It had been
a meager camp due to scant supplies, but it had never
been discovered by the Union patrols sent out to put
a stop to the harassing raids. Jeb, usually talkative, was
strangely silent on this crisp morning. Tanner understood. Men who fought wars together came to depend
upon each other. Parting company now, after the battles
they had survived, made each man feel as if his back was
suddenly vulnerable. When both saddle packs and
bedrolls were secured, the two partners turned to shake
hands.

"You'd best be careful about showing that U.S. brand on that horse," Jeb cautioned with a slow grin.

"I aim to," Tanner replied. "I'm figurin' on stayin' off the main roads. I can find my way home through the mountains." He gave Jeb a light slap on the back, and teased, "That horse is in for some sufferin', since you've got nobody to talk to all the way back to Kansas. What was the name of that town?"

"Mound City," Jeb said. "It's a short piece above Fort Scott, not far over the Missouri line, if you change your mind."

"I ain't likely to," Tanner replied. "I guess I'm too partial to Virginia." Once again his mind focused on Ellie, and he knew right then he would never see Kansas.

"That little gal's got you hog-tied right enough," Jeb said, a grin spreading across his ruddy face. He put a foot in the stirrup then and grabbed the saddle horn. "Take care of yourself, Tanner," he said as he climbed aboard the sorrel and turned the animal's head toward the west.

"You as well," Tanner replied. He watched Jeb's back for a few moments before stepping up in the saddle. With parting words for a few members of the raiders still packing up to leave, he made his way through the abandoned camp, up toward the top of the ravine. Pausing at the crest of the hill, he glanced back briefly before striking a course across the mountain ridge to the southwest.

Chapter 3

The big gray gelding followed the deer trail down the western slope of the mountain, moving along without any direction from Tanner. The game trail was one Tanner was quite familiar with, having followed it on many occasions when hunting. He looked around him, taking in the forest that had yielded more than a few bucks and does in the years since he and his brothers first started sneaking his father's rifle from the pegs over the fireplace. He was trying to determine if anything looked different since he had gone away to war. It didn't. As far as he had been able to tell, the war had not touched much of the county. Still, he was anxious to see his father's house to make sure it had suffered no damage. *I wonder if Travis is home yet,* he thought. His older brother had gone off to war a few weeks before him. Last he heard of him he was with Lee's army in Richmond. It was left to his younger brother, Trenton, to stay home to help his father manage the farm.

Down from the slope and onto the narrow road that led past Ellie's house, he passed over the log bridge where he had pulled the cow out of the flooding creek. He smiled to himself when he pictured it. The damn thing slid on the logs and would have drowned had he not gotten a rope around her head and held her above water until Ellie's father had come to help him. He was twelve years old at the time. Even at that age, he knew he was going to marry Ellie. The thought caused his smile to widen.

He felt his heart pick up an extra beat when he rounded the curve in the road, and could see Arthur Marshall's two-story house nestled firmly in an oak grove. Then he noticed the buggies and saddle horses lining the lane from the road to the house, but no people. A few yards closer and he could hear the hum generated by a crowd of people. He realized then that they were behind the house. Puzzled, he wondered what was going on. He thought for a second, *What day is this?* Then he remembered. It was a Sunday. *A funeral?* The thought caused him to worry. Was he arriving on a sorrowful occasion?

He nudged the gray and picked up the pace, covering the last few yards at a comfortable lope. Turning onto the lane, he encountered Albert Thompkins, a neighbor who had a small farm on the other side of the river.

Thompkins recognized Tanner at the same time. Startled, he blurted, "Tanner?" and almost dropped a bucket he had just gotten from his buggy. He stood staring as if seeing a ghost.

"Howdy, Mr. Thompkins," Tanner greeted the stunned man. "What's goin' on? I hope it ain't a funeral."

"Tanner . . ." was all Thompkins could say at that moment.

The old man's reaction was astonishing to Tanner, and he was about to ask if he was feeling all right when Mrs. Thompkins came around the side of the house on her way to help her husband. Like Albert, she stopped in her tracks, her jaw dropping, to gape at the returning soldier.

"Martha, it's Tanner," Thompkins announced unnecessarily.

"Tanner Bland," Martha gasped. "We thought you were dead."

Tanner smiled at that, realizing then the reason for his strange reception. "Ah, no ma'am, I ain't dead," he said.

Finding his voice then, Albert Thompkins spoke. "When Jubal Early's troops were defeated at Waynesboro, we saw a roster of all them that surrendered. There was another list of those that were dead or missing. You were on that list. A month went by, and most everybody on that list was accounted for. Everybody else was presumed dead."

"Well, sir," Tanner said with a chuckle, "I ain't dead." He motioned toward the house then. "Did somebody die?"

There was no answer from either of them for a long moment. Then Mr. Thompkins spoke softly. "No. Somebody got married."

An immediate sensation of blood draining down to his feet caused Tanner to grasp the saddle horn to steady himself. A wedding in Arthur Marshall's house could mean only one thing. He did not want to believe what he feared. "Ellie?" he asked, his voice shaking.

"Oh, Lord," Martha Thompkins wailed. "Tanner, we all thought you were dead."

"Who's the groom?" Tanner asked, his voice stern and leaden. His initial reaction was to fight for what was always rightfully his.

The horrified man and wife exchanged woeful glances, and then Albert answered. "Your brother, Trenton." There was no response from the stunned young man. Unable to form words to reply, he stood there dazed by the devastating blow to his sense of reason. "They were married a couple of hours ago," Albert added.

Tanner sat in the saddle, utterly unable to make himself think. He had known since he was a boy that he would marry Eleanor Marshall. Conflicting emotions battled within him, whirling around in his brain—anger, injury, dismay, despair, all within a matter of a few short seconds. Trenton, younger than Tanner by a year and a half, married to Ellie, *his* Ellie? Surely this was a nightmare that only seemed real. He gazed at Martha Thompkins with pleading eyes, hoping she would suddenly disappear and he would awaken. She simply stood gazing back at him, shaking her head sadly.

Realizing the reality of his nightmare, he at last gained control of his emotions. Slowly and deliberately, he dismounted, not certain whether or not he wanted to face the bride and groom. He was hurt, injured to his mental core, and he didn't know what to do. Both Albert and Martha Thompkins continued to stare at the devastated young man, at a loss for words. What *could* one say in this situation? They both breathed a sigh of relief when Tanner finally spoke again.

"I reckon I should welcome Ellie into the family," he said softly. He paused to think about that for a second, then added, "And give Trenton my blessings."

"Why, that would be a real Christian thing to do," Martha said and stepped back to let him pass. She and her husband then followed along behind him when he took the gray's reins and led the horse toward the backyard.

Rounding the corner of the house, Tanner walked into a gathering of a dozen or more wedding guests as they celebrated the happy occasion with food and drink. The buzz of conversation and laughter ended abruptly as the guests were suddenly struck dumb by the unexpected appearance of an apparition. Seated at the center of the table was his Ellie, dressed in a flowing white gown, Trenton at her side. Her eyes open wide in shock, she looked as if she was trying to get to her feet. But in the next instant, her eyes rolled toward the top of her head, and she fainted dead away. Trenton jumped to his feet, knocking his chair over in the process, not knowing what to do—help his bride or go to greet his brother. "Tanner . . . ," he blurted, just as Albert Thompkins had.

Tanner, still undecided if he should be angry or understanding, stood transfixed for a long moment, his eyes focused on the woman he had longed to see for so long. Several of the women closest to her rushed to help the stricken bride while Trenton stood helplessly lost. Dazed by the confusion that his arrival had created, Tanner's gaze fell on Ellie's mother as she rushed to her daughter's side. Then he glanced at the distraught face of her father. He realized that he might as well have dropped a grenade in the midst of the celebration. Unable to cope with the situation at that point, Tanner shot a quick glance in his brother's direction and muttered, "Congratulations." When he turned to leave, he came eye to eye with his father.

John Bland had stood speechless at the end of the long table as the awkward scene played out between his two sons. Relieved to discover his son was alive, yet overcome with the shocking turn of events, he did not know what to say. When Tanner broke the painful silence with a simple one-word greeting, "Pa," his father stepped forward to embrace his son.

"Tanner," he said, "I don't know what to tell you, but thank God you made it back."

"I'll be on my way," Tanner said softly, talking only to his father. "I'm sorry I put a damper on the wedding party." He turned his horse around then and climbed up in the saddle.

Alarmed, John Bland asked, "Where are you goin'?"

"I'm goin' on home," Tanner answered. "I want to pick up a few of my things." Not wishing to discuss it further, he nudged his horse, leaving the devastated wedding party behind him.

It was a somber and thoroughly shaken soldier who returned home from the war on that warm April afternoon. At the particular moment he turned the gray in at the gate, he felt that his world had ended. All the plans and dreams he had nurtured, the future for Ellie and him, everything he cared about, had come crashing down upon him. And the sickening thought occurred to him that he had ruined things for everyone by not getting killed.

Riding up the path to the house, he was met by three barking dogs. Two of them he recognized as his father's hounds. The third was evidently a new addition since he had been gone. Yapping and snarling, the dogs challenged the big gray gelding's right to access the house. Tanner yelled at them, calling the two by name, but they did not stop until he dismounted. Then, content that they had adequately performed their duties as watchdogs, they slinked back to the shade under the porch. Tanner led his horse to the trough by the well. After the gray had drunk, Tanner led him to the barn. He was in the process of feeding the horse some oats when he heard his father's horse coming up the path from the road.

"Has the weddin' party broke up already?" Tanner asked, unable to think of anything else to say.

"Tanner, what are you gonna do?" his father asked, ignoring the question.

"Whaddaya mean, what am I gonna do?" Tanner responded. "There ain't much I can do about Trenton and Ellie, is there? No use talkin' about that. It's a done thing." As much as he wanted to be finished with the subject, he still could not help wondering how it happened. "She didn't wait very long after news of my death, did she? And Trenton . . . how long have they been . . ." He didn't bother to finish, feeling disgusted just thinking about it. "Aw, to hell with it," he concluded, then quickly changed the subject. "How you makin' out, Pa? Everything all right with you?"

"I'm doin' all right, but this thing today is one of the

worst things that's happened to me since your mother died. I swear, son, we all thought you were dead. Don't take it out on your brother."

"I'm not. I wish 'em both well," Tanner said, realizing that his father was caught in the middle between his two sons. "I'll be leavin' here just as soon as I get a few things together." His father started to protest, but he silenced him with the one statement he knew to be true. "I wish 'em well, happiness and all that, but I'll be damned if I can stay around to watch it."

"Where are you goin'?" John Bland implored, realizing that he was about to lose his son for the second time.

"I don't know . . . Kansas, I reckon."

"Kansas? Why? What's in Kansas?"

Tanner cocked his head to one side and frowned. "I reckon it's what ain't in Kansas that matters," he answered, still picturing Trenton and Ellie together. "I wanna get out of this damn uniform just as quick as I can." He paused to glance at his father. "You didn't get rid of all my clothes after I died, did you?"

His father simply answered, "No," not missing the barb intended. "Son, I don't blame you for feelin' the way you do, but nobody meant to do you any harm. Listen, don't go ridin' off mad as hell. It'll be dark in a couple of hours. If you're still hell-bent on leavin', you might as well wait till mornin'." Seeing the question in Tanner's eyes, he said, "Ain't nobody here tonight but me. They'll be stayin' at the Marshalls' for a couple of days." He waited for a moment when he saw that Tanner was thinking it over. "You look like you ain't been eatin' much. I can at least give you somethin' to eat."

"I guess I could use a good night's sleep," Tanner said after a few minutes had passed with no reply. It occurred to him then that he owed his father at least a short visit after having been gone for so long. "I'm sorry, Pa. Of course I'll stay till mornin'—give us a chance to talk a little." It just occurred to him then that he had not seen his older brother at the reception. "Pa, I didn't see Travis. Is he . . ." He hesitated to finish the question.

"He's all right," John Bland quickly assured him. "He's still in Richmond—something to do with provost marshals."

"Thank God he made it through," Tanner said.

Maybe one of the important things about living in a remote part of the state, if not the most important, was the fact that fields and livestock were not devastated in the war. Consequently, John Bland was able to provide a hearty meal for his son. After supper, they were even able to steer the conversation away from the events of the tragic afternoon. His father was interested to know where Tanner had been in the fighting before Waynesboro, the details of each battle he fought in, and in general, what it was like to be in the infantry. They talked about the war until well past dark. "I see you got yourself a horse," John commented, and Tanner told him of the circumstances that led to the acquisition of the gray. "Well, that ain't too bad. You went off to war on foot, and came home ridin' a horse. I reckon you'd have to call that a profit."

"Yeah, I reckon," Tanner answered, "till you figure in my loss." The quip served to revive his melancholy once more, and he felt a need to be alone with his thoughts. "I need to get some fresh air before I turn in. I reckon I'll take a little walk outside." His father nodded. It was obvious that Tanner wanted to be alone.

Whether by design, or accident—Tanner didn't consciously think about it—he found himself on the footbridge across the creek that led to the path through the poplars and oaks to a mossy glade encircled with rhododendron where the creek branched out to form a Y. The glade was halfway between his house and Eleanor's, and it had been their special place where they would meet. They had been slipping off to meet there since in their teens. This was where many hopes and dreams had been created. This was also the place where he had told her that he had volunteered to go to war. And this was the place where he had promised to come back and she had promised to wait.

Why he had come here on this most sorrowful of nights, he couldn't explain. Maybe he just wanted to be where happy memories dwelt, to see it just once more before he left Virginia for good. Even in the darkness of the evening, he could make out familiar trees and rocks. He sat down on a large oak limb that ran horizontally for about five feet before turning up toward the sky. He remained there for at least half an hour, listening to the night sounds of the glade.

He sighed and was preparing to start back to the house when suddenly a slight rustle of leaves behind him made him pause. A raccoon or possum most likely, he thought, and stood still to listen. Then he heard it again, but this time the sound was distinctly that of footsteps. His reactions were more instinctive now, and the thought that came to mind was that he had no weapons with him. With nothing but his hands for defense, he stood prepared to fight. Within seconds, the rhododendron branches parted and she appeared, as she had appeared many times before in dreams. But this time it was no dream.

"I hoped you'd be here," she said, her voice shaking with emotion. "I knew you had to be here. I prayed to God you would be here." She ran to him, and he caught her in his arms. They clung tightly to each other while she cried uncontrollably. "Tanner . . . Tanner," she pleaded between sobs. "It isn't fair! They said you were dead."

It was several minutes before his spinning brain could regain control again and he could speak. "Ellie, what are you doin' here? Where's Trenton?" He forced her away from his chest so he could look into her eyes.

Like a child unable to stem her tears, she tried to answer. "Asleep . . . drunk," she choked out. Then after a pause to catch her breath, she calmed down. "I had to see you. Trenton drank himself into a stupor. I left him asleep across the foot of the bed. I was afraid you'd gone away again."

"This isn't right," Tanner forced himself to say. "They'll miss you back at the house."

"I don't care," Eleanor insisted. "It isn't fair! I've waited for this night all my life, but it was supposed to be with you." She pressed her body close against his again. "They said you were dead. I didn't know what to do. Trenton asked me to marry him. He has been so attentive to me the whole time you were away, always offering to help, always stopping in to see me. When they said you were dead, it almost killed me as well. I didn't care anymore, about anything, so I told him I'd marry him."

She held him even closer, her face turned up to him, inviting. "I'll go away with you if you want. We'll find another place to live where nobody knows us."

"We can't do that, Ellie. Trenton's my brother. And it would not only hurt him. What about your folks? My father? We just can't do it. What's done is done."

"I know," she confessed reluctantly. "You're right, but I would do it if you wanted me to." Her chin dropped, her eyes closed tightly for a few moments while she thought about what she was about to say. Her mind made up then, she spoke, her words solemn and direct. "I have dreamed of my wedding night for so many years, and it has always been you in that dream. This is my wedding night. We're here in our special place together. I want you to take me now, as it should have been."

Tanner wanted to roar out against his crippling frustration. He knew that he simply could not do what she asked, no matter how much he wanted to. It was wrong. "Ellie, I can't. No matter what we have felt for each other, you're my brother's wife."

"I swear he will never know," she pleaded.

"I'll know," Tanner said softly, "and later on you'll know, and regret it." He gently pushed her away from him then. "Now, before anyone misses you, go on back to your bed and your husband. Trenton's a good man. I wish you both health and happiness." Without giving her time to protest, he turned and walked away before she had a chance to see the gleam of a tear in his eye.

Shortly after sunup the next morning, Tanner Bland bade his father farewell and left Alleghany County and Virginia behind him for good.

Chapter 4

The remaining days of June and most of the month of July were spent in the saddle as Tanner Bland made his journey across the country. With no knowledge of the land he crossed, and with limited contact with anyone along the way, he had only the sun to guide him. He figured that if he simply held the big gray gelding to a steady western course, he would eventually hit Kansas. He had very little hope of finding Jeb Hawkins, even if he found Kansas, but he remembered that Jeb had often spoken of his home in Mound City. His ultimate intention was to ride on farther west, into Montana Territory, as Jeb had suggested. But he decided he might as well see if he could find Jeb on the way.

It was a long journey, with few stops, although he had found it necessary to spend a couple of extra days by a river in Kentucky because the gray was beginning to show signs of weariness. Although the horse was big and strong, it was still trying to survive on grass when it had been accustomed to periodic portions of oats.

There were long days in the saddle, passing through

the hills of West Virginia and Kentucky, skirting mountains and crossing countless rivers. Some of the rivers he identified, the Ohio, and the Mississippi, because he found it necessary to part with some of the small amount of money his father gave him to be ferried across. Being a sizable man, and well armed, he was not subject to many questions from the strangers he met.

By this time horse and rider were becoming well acquainted with each other's moods and habits. Tanner decided it was going to be a workable partnership, so he thought it time he gave the gray a proper name. For lack of a better idea, he called the horse Ashes, since its color reminded him of the gray-white ashes of a campfire. "Ashes," he said aloud, trying it on for sound. "Ashes," he repeated. "Suit you?" The big horse jerked his head up and down and snorted. "Good. I thought it would."

Since he figured to keep the horse for a long time, there was one other chore that he deemed necessary, one that the gray might not appreciate. He took the bayonet he had retained when he discarded his Enfield rifle and placed it in the coals of his campfire. While he waited for the bayonet to turn cherry red, he made sure Ashes' reins were tied securely to a tree. When the bayonet was glowing hot, he wrapped one corner of his blanket around the shank and withdrew it from the fire. Taking but a moment to study the US brand on Ashes' flank, he decided there was only one way to alter it. The gelding was not at all pleased with the alteration, and would have bolted, leaving its master on foot, if Tanner had not hobbled it. Working as quickly as he could, he burned over the Union army brand, turning the US into 08. He speculated on the possibility of adding a 1 in front, but the gray was not willing to tolerate further abuse, so Tanner settled for the two-digit brand. When the branding was completed, he slapped a handful of wet mud on it, hoping to ease Ashes' discomfort.

Under way again, the big gray kept a cautious eye on its master for the next day or so. But after a while, the sting of the new tattoo was forgotten, and horse and rider became partners again.

Tanner was well adjusted to living off the land, eating what food was provided in the form of game. His nights, lonely and painful at first, became less and less contaminated with poisonous thoughts of Trenton and Ellie. By the time he struck the Marais des Cygnes River, he was able to sleep at night, free of troubling dreams of her and what might have been.

He knew when he struck the river that he had been in Missouri for at least five or six days, but he had no idea how far he was from Kansas. Jeb had told him that Mound City was not far over the Missouri border. Tanner had no notion if he was north or south of the town. For no good reason, other than a whim, he decided to follow the river's northwest course, since it seemed to be the right general direction.

After riding a mile or so along the river, he encountered a young boy of twelve or thirteen fishing from the bank. In answer to Tanner's question, the lad informed him that it was the Marais des Cygnes River, and if he followed it for another twelve miles, he would come to a little settlement called Trading Post. "Then you'll be in Kansas," the boy said.

Tanner thanked him and continued on. "Helluva name for a river," he muttered to Ashes as he left the boy staring after him. Once he reached Trading Post the following day, he was given directions to Mound City.

Spotting the stable as he rode into town, he guided Ashes toward it. The owner, a wiry little man with a bald pate and a full set of whiskers, laid his tools aside to greet the stranger. "Evenin'," he said, getting up from the feed box he was building. "The name's Porter. I own the place."

"Evenin'," Tanner returned. "I'd like to leave my horse for the night and get a double portion of oats." It had been a while since the gray had eaten anything but grass, so he thought the horse would appreciate it. He dismounted and led Ashes into the stable, where he started to remove the saddle.

"Cavalry saddle," Porter commented. "Been seein' a few of them since the end of the war."

"I reckon," Tanner replied, hesitating before pulling the saddle from Ashes' back.

"You musta been in the Confederate army," Porter said.

The comment caused Tanner's eyebrows to rise, and he turned to look at the man. "How do you know that?"

"That aught-eight brand," Porter said confidently. "Jeb Hawkins come back from the war a week or so ago, and his horse had the same brand. He said the Confederates didn't put a regular brand on their horses. They just numbered 'em." Then he paused to scratch his head, as he thought about what he had just said. "How come your horse has got the same number as his?"

Tanner turned his head back to his horse to keep the stable owner from seeing the grin on his face. "That's because he was in a different company than I was. He had number eight in his company. I had number eight in mine. I'll bet he didn't have the same color horse as mine, did he?"

"No. That's right, he didn't. His was a sorrel."

"There, you see, he had the number eight sorrel. I had the number eight gray." Tanner's explanation appeared to satisfactorily explain the puzzle for Porter. "You wouldn't happen to know where I could find Jeb, would you? I know him."

"Sure, I know where he is," Porter replied. "Where he's been most of the time since he come back—in jail."

Even knowing Jeb for no longer than he had, Tanner could not honestly say he was surprised to find that his friend had already gotten himself in some kind of trouble. "What did he do to get thrown in jail?" he asked.

Porter did not give Tanner an answer right away. Instead, he studied the broad-shouldered young stranger for a few moments as if deciding whether or not he should trust him. Finally he made his decision. "You say you served with Jeb in the Confederate army?"

"That's a fact."

"Well, it's obvious to me that you ain't been around these parts before, so I'm gonna tell you the way things are. You're in Linn County, son. There's been a helluva lot of blood shed in this county between Free-Soilers and pro-slavers. It started a long time before the war, and it ain't cooled down now that the war's over. Jeb's daddy was shot down dead in a barroom fight between three pro-slavers and a couple of Free-Soilers. 'Course old man Hawkins didn't have any slaves, but he believed in the right of the state to decide whether we was gonna be a slave state or not. I doubt if young Jeb cared one way or the other, but them killin' his pap sure as hell put him on the side of the Confederacy." He paused to relight his corncob pipe before continuing.

"I'm tellin' you all this so's you'll know to watch what you say around here. I supported the Confederacy, just like Jeb's pa, so I don't want you to get to talkin' to the wrong people in town. You come ridin' in here on a Union horse with the brand worked over . . ." He paused and winked an eye at Tanner. "I ain't as dumb as I look. Some folks around here might ask you some questions about that. One of 'em is most likely gonna be Jeff Yates. He's the sheriff, and he rode with the Kansas Jayhawkers, so he ain't got no love for you Southern boys."

"Ain't you folks heard? The war's over."

"That may be, but there's still some bad blood around here. I'm just tellin' you how things are. Just figured you'd want to know."

"Much obliged, Mr. Porter," Tanner said. "I'll try to stay outta trouble. You never told me what they've got Jeb in jail for."

"Disorderly conduct, disturbin' the peace, resistin' arrest, assaultin' a peace officer, and I think they're considerin' chargin' him with stealin' that horse."

"Damn!" Tanner grunted. "How long is he in jail for?"

"For as long as they want to keep him, I reckon,"

Porter said with a shrug. "Or if they charge him as a horse thief, till they hang him."

Tanner thought Porter's words over for a long minute before inquiring, "Where's the jail?" It was time to hear what had happened from Jeb's mouth.

"Down at the end of this street," Porter said, nodding his head to emphasize. "It ain't much more than a shack, a little two-room log cabin. You'll see it. They're talkin' about building a new jail outta stone, but all we've got now is a shack."

"Much obliged," Tanner said, tightening the cinch under Ashes' belly again. "I think I'll go see Jeb. I'll be back to leave my horse." He turned to leave, but Porter stopped him before he got to the door.

"I ain't got any idea if you're interested or not, but Jeb's horse is in the corral out back. And that fancy saddle is in the tack room. I'm supposed to keep an eye on 'em, but like I told the sheriff, ain't nobody here when I go home to supper." He turned then and walked toward the back of the stable before Tanner could thank him again. "You watch yourself, young feller," he called back as he disappeared from view.

It was a lot to think about. Jeb had made casual reference to the divided passions over the war in his county, but in mentioning his father's death, he had simply stated that it was in a saloon fight. Keeping Porter's advice in mind, especially his comments on the 08 brand, Tanner rode down to the end of the street to the jail. As the owner of the stable had said, the jail was little more than a log cabin with a sign over the door that read SHERIFF. There were no horses tied out front, and when he pulled up at the steps, he saw that there was a padlock on the door.

Tanner dismounted and looped Ashes' reins over the hitching post. There was a window on the side of the cabin, so he walked around the building to look inside. Peering through the iron bars, he saw a small room with a desk and a single chair, evidently the sheriff's office. At the rear of the room, there was a closed door that apparently led to the cells. Moving to the rear of the building, he found a second window, this one smaller and a few feet higher than the one on the side.

Looking around for something to stand on, he could find nothing in the way of a bucket, a box, or even a log. So he went back for Ashes. Looking up and down the street, he saw no one but a couple of men passing the time of day in front of a saloon about fifty yards away. They seemed to pay him no mind, so he climbed in the saddle and rode around to the rear of the jail. Seated in the saddle, he could easily see in the tiny window. "Jeb?" he called, even though he could not see anyone in the room. "Are you in there?"

"Tanner! Is that you?" The reply came from directly below the window.

"Yeah, it's me," Tanner answered. "Where the hell are you?"

"I'm right here," Jeb said and stood up on the bunk that was right under the window. The bed was close against the wall, which was the reason Tanner had not seen it from outside. Jeb's smiling face appeared up next to the bars. "I swear, I never thought I'd see you again," he gushed, obviously delighted. "What the hell are you doin' here? Did you get run outta Virginia?" He chuckled in response to his gibe.

"I came lookin' for you," Tanner said. "I was hopin' I'd catch up with you before you set off for the goldfields in Montana." He laughed then. "Looks like there was no need to hurry. What the hell did you do to get thrown in jail?"

"Got drunk. That was what I suppose started it all. But, hell, Tanner, I wasn't lookin' for no trouble. Matter of fact, I was feelin' like I was everybody's friend until that son of a bitch behind the bar said somethin' about my pa. Said I was fixin' to end up like he did, or somethin' like that. I don't remember exactly what he said. I was drunk. Anyway, Jeff Yates, he's the sheriff, he said I broke a whiskey bottle over the bartender's head. I reckon I did. I don't remember. Yates sneaked up behind me and hit me up side of the head with a gun butt, and dragged my ass in here. That's how I got here." He ended his story with a wide grin. "Ain't that a fine way to treat a hero home from the war?"

Tanner shook his head in mock dismay, then turned dead serious. "Jeb, that fellow, Porter, over at the stables, told me they were tryin' to charge you as a horse thief because of that sorrel you borrowed from the Union army."

"I heard about that. Hell, I told 'em I bought that horse at an army auction. Same as you," he added, "if they ask you."

"It didn't do you much good," Tanner said.

Jeb laughed. "Nah, I reckon it didn't, did it?" Then he abruptly changed the subject. "But I still don't understand what you're doin' here. I thought you was goin' home to get hitched. What happened? Did you bring her with you, or did she meet another feller?"

"Yeah, my brother," Tanner replied. Jeb's question had been asked as a joke. When he realized that his friend was serious, he sputtered over an apology. Tanner shrugged it off, saying they all thought he was dead. He went on to tell Jeb the story of his homecoming.

"Well, I'll be damned," Jeb muttered slowly when Tanner finished. "There's a bright side to it, though," he said cheerfully. "Now we can go to Montana, and find us a fortune—get us enough money to buy a couple of high-class wives. Hell, we might turn Mormon and have a couple of wives apiece."

"There's not but one small detail that needs to be worked out," Tanner reminded him. "You're in jail."

"Ah, hell," Jeb snorted. "They ain't gonna keep me here long. It'd cost too much to feed me. I probably woulda done been out if it was anybody but me. Ol' Jeff Yates don't like me much. He didn't like my old man, so I reckon it was natural he wanted to throw me in jail for a spell. That horse-stealin' talk is just that—talk, trying to throw a scare into me."

"Maybe so. I hope you're right. That fellow, Porter, thought they might be serious about it. I'll go back and see if I can sleep in the stable for a couple of days till they let you outta here. Maybe I can find the sheriff and get some idea from him. Is he ever in the office?"

"Not much of the time," Jeb said. "He's got a farm, like ever'body else around this town. So he just padlocks the door and drops by whenever he feels like it. The good part of it is I don't have to see his ugly face but now and then. Annie Whatley from over to the saloon brings me two meals a day, so I ain't been sufferin' none." He favored Tanner with a wry smile then. "Besides, I knew you'd come rescue me."

Tanner left with the hope that he might find out more regarding the length of Jeb's stay in the crude jail. Jeb advised him to steer clear of Jeff Yates. He further advised him not to let on that he was Jeb's friend. Tanner figured the best place to get information was the saloon, so after making arrangements with Mr. Porter to sleep in the stall with Ashes, he walked down the street to the Statesman.

The evening crowd of patrons had already begun to gather in the dimly lit saloon. When Tanner opened the door, he paused in the entrance to take a look around the room before stepping inside. Off to one side, and a few paces from the door, there was a table with a sign requesting that saloon patrons leave all weapons there. A few men stood at the bar, exchanging conversation over their beer mugs. It was not a large room, but big enough to crowd in four tables beyond the bar. On this evening, only the table in the back corner seemed to be occupied, but there was a group of seven men gathered around it, having borrowed chairs from the vacant tables. Tanner figured that the table no doubt represented the saloon's regulars.

He paused at the weapons table to leave his Spencer carbine before proceeding to the bar. His appearance caused a brief lull in the din of conversation in the noisy room as most everyone eyed the stranger. After only a moment, however, the talk resumed its prior level.

"Howdy, mister," the bartender, a stocky man sporting a handlebar mustache and wearing a bandanna around his head, greeted him. "What'll it be?"

"I'll have two shots of your best whiskey," Tanner replied and grinned to himself when he realized the bandanna was, in fact, a bandage. It had been a long time since he had taken a drink, and he figured it would probably be a long time before he had another. So he figured he might as well have the best.

The bartender looked him over while he poured from a bottle taken from beneath the counter. "Ain't seen you in here before," he said. "Just get into town?"

"Yep," Tanner replied as he paid for his drinks. "I'm just passin' through." He tossed the first drink down, grimacing as the fiery liquid scorched his throat. Then he placed the empty shot glass back on the bar, nodded to the bartender, picked it up again when it was refilled, and carried it over to the empty table next to the one in the corner. He pulled up one of the few empty chairs and sat down facing the occupied table.

His plan was to strike up a conversation with one of the locals and possibly guide it toward the prisoner in the jail. He cautioned himself to avoid being too obvious in seeking information. As it turned out, he found out what he wanted to know without having to question anyone. Jeb became the general topic of conversation at the crowded table when another man joined the group.

Pulling up a chair, the newcomer squeezed in between two at the table. From the round of greetings the man received, Tanner gathered that he had been away from town for a while. After acknowledging the greetings, he leveled a question at a heavyset man with a dark beard and eyes buried deep beneath a brooding forehead. "So, Jeff, I hear you got ol' Zack Hawkins' boy locked up in the jail."

"That's a fact," the heavyset man replied.

"I expect there's folks around here that was hopin' he wouldn't make it back from the war." He shook his head as if puzzled. "I swear, I don't know why that boy would wanna come back to Mound City."

"Probably just to spite us," another man interjected.

The heavyset man snorted in disgust. "Well, it didn't do him a helluva lot of good, did it? Just to come back here to get hisself hung."

"What did he do to get himself hung?" the newcomer asked.

"Stole a horse is what they were talkin' about," one at the table commented. "Ain't that right, Sheriff?"

"We're done talkin' about it," the sheriff informed them. "Judge Harris is fixin' to rule on it tomorrow, and I expect we'll have a hangin' the next day after that."

Seated at the next table, Tanner slowly sipped his drink. He had heard all he needed to hear. The sheriff sounded pretty confident about what the judge's ruling would be. They were going to railroad Jeb. It wasn't a prosecution of a crime. It was simple extermination that the good folk of Mound City had in mind. Tanner had heard stories, some from Jeb, about the Kansas-Missouri border wars between the Free-Soilers and the pro-slavers that led up to the war just ended. According to Jeb, there were plenty of folks in Mound City who held Southern sympathies. Sitting in this saloon now, Tanner wondered where those people were, and if they were apt to come out in support of one who'd fought for the Confederacy. The sheriff certainly was confident that Jeb's trial was merely a formality before the hanging.

It was pretty clear what he had to do. Tossing back the last few drops of the strong whiskey, he placed the empty glass on the table, and stood up. When he did, he found the sheriff's gaze focused upon him. Tanner looked at the fleshy brute of a man for a few long seconds before turning and slowly walking toward the door. Behind him, he heard the scraping sound of the sheriff's chair being pushed back from the table. He continued to walk toward the table where the weapons were deposited.

"Hold on there a minute, mister," Jeff Yates called out, his voice brusque and commanding.

Tanner casually reached down and picked up his rifle before turning slowly to face the sheriff. Yates halted a couple of steps from him and looked him up and down before speaking again. "I'm the sheriff in this town, and I like to know what business strangers like you have in Mound City."

"I don't have any business in Mound City," Tanner said. "I'm just passin' through. I ain't broke any laws, have I?"

"Why, none that you've been caught at yet," Yates replied with a smirk. "We've been seein' a fair number of drifters comin' through here since the war, and that ain't what the folks here wanna see." He gave Tanner another hard look. "You fight in the war?"

"Maybe," Tanner replied.

"If I was to guess, I'd say it wasn't on the Union side," Yates said. When Tanner answered with only a smile, the sheriff snorted. "I thought so." He nodded toward the rifle in Tanner's hand. "I don't believe you Rebs were issued Spencer carbines. I might have to order you to hand that over. That's government property."

The last thing Tanner wanted was a confrontation with the sheriff, but he had had enough of the surly lawman's attitude. "I took this rifle off a dead man. The next man that gets it is gonna have to take it the same way."

The noisy barroom suddenly got quiet, with no sound except the scraping of chairs on the plank floor as the patrons pushed back from the table. Yates was stopped momentarily, not expecting the defiance he encountered. His eyes locked on Tanner's, measuring the depth of the stranger's resolve. Something he saw there told him that there was cold steel behind the gaze. "Mister," he warned, "you're fixin' to make the biggest mistake of your life." His hand dropped to rest on the handle of his pistol. "Now, hand that rifle to me butt first."

Tanner brought the Spencer up chest high and cocked it, loading a round in the chamber. He suspected that the sheriff not only wanted the rifle, but also meant to throw him in jail with Jeb. A smattering of hushed comments filled the room behind the sheriff as his friends watched the confrontation. They went silent again when Tanner leveled the rifle at Yates. "Sheriff," he said, his voice soft and deadly, "I ain't broke no laws in your town, but if your hand comes up with that pistol in it, you're a dead man."

Yates was stopped cold for a few moments, unsure of himself and uncertain if the brash young man actually had the nerve to follow through with his threat. His hand lingered on the handle of his revolver, but he hesitated to grip it. "Are you that big a fool?" he finally snarled. "Threatenin' a lawman?" Tanner made no reply, simply staring coldly into the sheriff's eyes. "Look around you," Yates said. "You're outnumbered about seven to one. You pull that trigger and there'll be half a dozen on you before you can cock that rifle again."

"I reckon there'd be only two dead then," Tanner replied. "But one of 'em's gonna be you. So it's your call. I walk outta here and no harm done. Or you and I can catch the evenin' train to hell together."

"I've got him covered, Jeff," the bartender sang out and pulled a double-barreled shotgun from under the counter.

This was not good news to Tanner. He hadn't figured the bartender to get involved in the standoff. He wondered why the man hadn't shot first and talked later, but his unblinking gaze never left Yates' face. "My finger's gettin' awfully damn itchy," he said. "If that shotgun goes off, you're a dead man. Tell him to put the gun away, and I'll not waste any time ridin' outta your friendly little town."

One could almost hear the crackle of tension in the room as the standoff continued. Yates glanced at the weapons on the table behind Tanner, wishing at this point that he had never insisted on the ordinance that caused them to be there. The bartender was holding a gun on the stranger, and was sure to get him. But Yates was staring at the barrel of Tanner's rifle, and he didn't know if Tanner would automatically squeeze the trigger if the bartender fired. He wasn't ready to take the risk.

"Put it away, Lonnie," the sheriff finally said. When the bartender lowered the shotgun, Yates turned back to Tanner. "All right, I'm gonna let you go, so these innocent bystanders don't get hurt. But I want you outta my town, and I don't mean maybe. I ain't likely to be in such a good mood next time I see you."

Not influenced by the sheriff's attempt to save face, Tanner said, "Reach across with your left hand and lift that pistol outta the holster real slow. Do it, dammit!" he roared when Yates hesitated. "All right, drop it on the floor and kick it over here." Becoming more and more flushed by the moment, the sheriff did as he was told. Tanner stooped to pick up the weapon, being careful to keep the rifle trained on the sheriff.

Backing slowly toward the door, Tanner watched the crowd of uneasy citizens of Mound City carefully, lest anyone try to make a run for the weapons table. None was heroic to the extent of testing the tall stranger. Tanner opened the door and paused in the doorway for a moment. Then he suddenly stepped outside, slammed the door, and jammed the sheriff's pistol barrel through the door handle, wedging it against the doorframe. It wouldn't hold for long, but it might delay the pursuit enough to let him get a head start. Running as fast as he could, he darted between the saloon and the dry goods store. Turning the corner, he sprinted along behind the buildings, heading for the stable.

John Porter was startled when Tanner suddenly

appeared at the back of the stable at a dead run. "What tha—" was all he managed to get out as Tanner rushed by him, going straight to the tack room where his saddle was stored. In a moment, he reappeared with the saddle on his shoulder, heading for the corral.

"I reckon I won't be stayin' the night after all," Tanner blurted as he passed the astonished stable owner. "How much do I owe you?" he called over his shoulder as he cornered his horse against the rail.

"Nothin'," Porter replied while Tanner slipped the bit in Ashes' mouth and pulled the bridle on. "You done paid me for the oats." He stood gaping as Tanner threw the saddle on the big gray horse. "You sure seem to be in one helluva hurry. Is somebody after you?"

Busy with the girth strap, Tanner answered without pausing, "I don't know, but I expect it's a possibility." He figured that the first thing that happened when he slammed the saloon door was a rush for the table and the weapons. Then he was counting on the pistol holding for a little while, and when it was finally dislodged and they could open the door, they wouldn't know for sure which way he had run. Of the men at the table with Yates, he wondered how many, if any, would come after him with the sheriff. *No matter,* he decided as he stepped up in the saddle. *One or a hundred, I'd best get the hell outta here.* He turned to tell Porter to open the gate, but the stable owner was already ahead of him. Tanner nodded his thanks as he passed through. Once clear of the gate, he called on the gray for speed, leaving the little town at a gallop.

In the clear so far, he thought, looking back over his

shoulder for signs of pursuit. The big gray's hooves pounded the hard clay as he drove for a bend in the road that would take him out of sight of the buildings. Lying low on Ashes' neck, he waited for the snap of bullets to overtake him, but there was none, and soon he gained the shield of a grove of hardwoods at a curve in the road. Riding on, he eased up on the gray a bit as he quickly looked about him for the best place to leave the road. Knowing he didn't have much time to decide, he took the easiest route of escape. Pulling hard on the reins, he swung the gray to his left, jumped a shallow ditch, and followed a faint drainage trail down through a stand of hickories and oaks. Weaving between dark trunks, he made his way through the trees until coming to a creek bordered by chokecherry thickets and buckthorn.

Behind him he heard the sound of several horses on the road he had just left. He pulled the gray up to listen. He could not see the road, but from the sound, he knew that they had continued on, evidently failing to see where he had plunged into the trees. This, he decided, was as good a place as any to wait out the remaining daylight. The sheriff had to figure that he had fled the town, anxious to put Mound City far behind him. So Tanner reasoned that the lawman would not think to search for him close to town. The problem to be solved now was how to get Jeb out of jail. He looked up at the late-afternoon sun. "Well, I've got plenty of time to figure out how I'm gonna do it," he said.

While he pictured the tiny jail in his mind, and tried to think of his best chance of breaking Jeb out, he took a look around the woods he had picked as his hiding place.

Leaving Ashes to graze by the creek, he pushed through a thicket on the other side to discover a cleared field of perhaps five or six acres. At the far end of the field, a small farmhouse sat between two sizable oak trees. Tanner stood in the cover of the thicket for a while, watching to see if there was any activity around the house. Seeing none, he felt reasonably safe in assuming there would be no one venturing across the field in his direction. He returned to the creek to wait out the daylight.

A little before dusk, he heard the sheriff's posse returning to town. Sitting up to become more alert, he listened hard to make sure the sound of hoofbeats on the road continued on past. He settled back and waited. Finally, darkness settled in around the chokecherry bushes, and Tanner determined it was time to act. The fact that he was about to embark on his first ever act that was against the law never entered his mind. As far as he was concerned, he was planning to free a comrade in arms from an enemy prison. It was a matter of right or wrong, and he couldn't leave Jeb there to be hung.

"Your supper's a mite cold," Jeff Yates said as he pushed the door open with his foot. Entering the cell room carrying a plate of food, he pretended to be apologetic. Jeb knew the sheriff was merely entertaining himself. "I weren't here to unlock the door for Annie, so she had to leave it on the stoop. She put a cloth over it, but the flies got to it anyway. I sure feel bad about that, but I had to chase one of your Reb friends outta town." He slid the plate under the bars, knocking a biscuit off on the floor. "A little dirt won't hurt'cha," he said, tapping the biscuit under the bars with the toe of his boot.

Jeb held his tongue, determined not to let the sheriff get his goat. He picked up the plate and shooed a couple of flies from the cold bacon before stuffing a slice into his mouth. "Why, Sheriff, I'm just about overcome with gratitude. I wouldn't have expected you back at all tonight, after such a hard day of settin' on your ass in the saddle."

Yates didn't reply right away, staring at Jeb with a sly smirk on his face. Then after a moment or two, he said, "You've always had a sassy mouth on you, ain't you?" The smirk slowly transformed into a wide smile. "We'll see how sassy you can talk day after tomorrow when I hang your sorry ass."

"Ha," Jeb snorted. "Hang me for what? Disturbin' the peace?"

"Horse thievin'," Yates replied.

"Horse thievin'!" Jeb exclaimed. "I ain't stole no horse." Then his eyes opened wide and a broad smile formed on his face.

Puzzled by Jeb's sudden transformation, as if he had just heard good news, Yates stared dumbly at his prisoner for a few moments. Then, realizing that Jeb was looking at something behind him, he turned to find himself staring into the muzzle of a Spencer rifle. His hand immediately fell to rest on the handle of his pistol. "It would be a mistake," he was calmly warned.

"Howdy, partner," Jeb gleefully greeted Tanner. "I reckon it must be time for me to get outta here—and just when I was beginning to feel right at home."

"I knew you wasn't just passin' through." Yates spat out the words with a scowl. "By God, you're gonna end up at the bottom of a rope for this."

"Maybe," Tanner replied, reaching over to relieve the sheriff of his pistol for the second time in one day. "I expect you'd best take that key ring off your belt, too." With a look that would scorch a frightened man, the sheriff complied, taking the ring off and tossing it on the floor. "Pick it up," Tanner commanded.

"You pick it up," Yates shot back. "You gonna shoot me if I don't?" He sneered. "I don't think you got the guts to shoot me."

Without hesitating, Tanner lowered the muzzle of the rifle and squeezed the trigger, putting a bullet through Yates' boot. "Jesus!" the sheriff screamed in shocked disbelief. "You shot me, you son of a bitch!" He hopped backward on his good foot, staring wide-eyed at the black hole in his boot.

"I know," Tanner replied softly. "If you don't pick up those keys and unlock that cell, I'm gonna shoot the other foot." He aimed the rifle at the sheriff's foot.

"Hold on, dammit!" Yates howled. The shock of Tanner's first shot had a numbing effect on the wounded man. Now blood began oozing through the hole in his boot, accompanied by a throbbing pain. "Wait a minute!" he pleaded again. "I'm gettin' 'em." Unable to maintain his balance on one foot, he dropped to the floor, and crawled over to retrieve the keys. On hands and knees, he moved to the cell door and began to fumble with the lock.

When the door was unlocked, Jeb pushed it open and held it wide. "Come on in, Sheriff," he gestured grandly.

When Yates balked at entering the jail cell, Tanner administered a heavy boot to his backside, providing the proper motivation. "We ain't got all night," he complained. "Come on, Jeb. We'd best get on over the border to Missouri."

Jeb stepped out of the cell, slammed the door shut, and locked it. Then he tossed the keys through the open door to the office. "They're right there, whenever you're ready to get out," he said. "And you can have the rest of my supper. It's right there on the floor where you left it. I don't expect anybody will be comin' around to bother you tonight. That tick on the bunk could use a little more straw, but I managed to sleep on it."

Yates grew bolder with confidence that Tanner had no intention of killing him, and his temper began to boil. "You two are gonna be hangin' from the same tree," he threatened. "I'll be outta here in no time, and I'll be comin' after you."

"It'll be a waste of time, Sheriff," Tanner informed him. "We'll be in Missouri before mornin', and you've got no jurisdiction there."

His anger sufficiently riled at this point, Yates snarled, "You think that'll stop me? I'll run you bastards down. You ain't gettin' away with this." Then he started to yell. "Help! Help! Somebody help!"

Tanner said nothing as he solemnly gazed at the wounded lawman. After a moment, he raised his rifle again, and sighting through the bars, shot the sheriff in the other foot. Yates' yells for help turned at once into howls of pain, and he sat on the floor, rocking back and forth, holding his throbbing feet in his hands.

Outside, Jeb discovered his horse saddled and waiting beside Tanner's. When Tanner told him that the owner of the stable had saddled the horse himself, Jeb laughed and remarked, "Damn, you've been right busy, ain't you? You sure as hell ruined a good pair of boots back there, though." He stepped up in the saddle. "I knew there musta been a reason my pa thought John Porter was a good man." Reining the sorrel's head around, he said, "If we're gonna cross the Missouri border before mornin', we'd best get goin'."

"What the hell do you wanna go to Missouri for?" Tanner stopped him. "Hell, I wanna see Montana."

"You said in there—" Jeb began, but broke off. "Oh, you just said that for Yates' ears, so's he'll head in the wrong direction."

Tanner shrugged, not really convinced. "If he's dumb enough," he said.

Jeb threw back his head and chuckled. "He's dumb enough. I reckon they'll be callin' him Ol' Leadfoot now." The thought caused him to chuckle once more. "Let's go to Montana!" Then he pulled his horse up short, as if just remembering something. "There's one more thing I've gotta do before we leave." With no explanation beyond that, he kicked the sorrel into a gallop, heading for the back of the building, leaving Tanner no choice but to follow.

The two fugitives raced along behind the buildings until Jeb pulled his horse to a sliding stop behind the saloon. Leaping from the saddle, he burst through the

kitchen door to totally stun a Chinese cook and a flabber-
gasted Annie Whatley. Sweeping Annie off her feet, he
planted a kiss on her mouth, holding it so long that the
poor girl gasped for breath when finally released.

With her feet on the floor again, she staggered back a
couple of steps before gaining her balance. "You crazy
son of a bitch," she blurted.

"I know," Jeb hurriedly replied. "I said I was gonna
marry you when I got outta jail, but I'm afraid I'll have
to disappoint you." As suddenly as he had arrived, he
was out the back door again and in the saddle.

As baffled as Annie and the cook, Tanner hesitated a
moment when the woman appeared on the back step and
shouted at Jeb's back, "You crazy son of a bitch, I've already got a husband!" She looked then at Tanner.

Wasting no time to attempt to explain his friend's actions, Tanner tipped his hat, said, "Good evenin' to you,
ma'am," and galloped away after Jeb.

They left Mound City behind, Jeb leading the way.
Before striking out toward the northwest, however, Jeb
had to make one more stop. After galloping out of town,
they doubled back south of the town, where Jeb led them
up through hills thick with sugar maples to an abandoned
shack nestled close beside a busy stream.

"Home, sweet home," Jeb announced in answer to
Tanner's puzzled expression when they pulled up before
the shack. "This is where my pap and me was livin' before they shot him." He quickly dismounted. "I gotta get
my things," he explained.

Tanner dismounted and followed him inside, looking
around at the dusky interior of the shack. It struck him as

little wonder that Jeb had chosen to ride off to join the army. There was nothing left to suggest that anyone had ever lived there—only a table, a couple of chairs, and a small potbellied stove. While Tanner watched, Jeb rolled up a blanket that had been spread for a bed, grabbed a haversack containing some extra clothes and his razor, then turned to face Tanner.

"One more thing," he said, "and then we'd best get outta here. If Ol' Leadfoot gets out, this'll be the first place he'll look." That said, he lifted his foot and kicked the little stove over on its side. Then he immediately removed several stones from the base the stove had rested upon, revealing a heavy canvas sack. He took a quick look inside to make sure of the contents before giving Tanner a wide grin. "I wasn't about to leave without this," he said. "This'll take us to Montana." He went on to explain how the gold coins happened to be there. "A few years back, my pap rode with a gang that held up a Yankee paymaster's wagon. This sack of coins was hid under the wagon seat. Pap couldn't spend it without everybody around here knowing where it came from." He grinned broadly again. "So I reckon the Union army is payin' our way to Montana." Stepping up in the saddle, he cocked his head at Tanner and winked. "I told you back in Virginia I had somethin' hid back for a grubstake. I bet you thought I was lying."

"It crossed my mind," Tanner replied.

Chapter 5

"By God, you was talkin' a helluva lot bigger last night when you was soakin' up most of my likker," Garth Leach growled. "Maybe that was just the likker talkin'." He glared down at the nervous young man in the army uniform, his eyes threatening.

Private Benjamin H. Wilkes glanced around him cautiously, as if afraid someone might see him talking to the dark hulk of a man. He was already regretting the contract he had made with the brooding bully and his three brothers the night before over a bottle in the saloon. What he had bragged about was not totally untrue. He did, in fact, have access to cases of old surplus Springfield rifles. Assigned to the quartermaster section that was responsible for warehousing the surplus weapons until they could be reissued or auctioned off, he had boasted about how easily he could short the inventory. "I ain't sayin' I can't do it," he pleaded. "I'm just sayin' I have to be careful. It could be my ass if I get caught."

Garth's eyes narrowed, his thick black eyebrows closing

down into an angry frown. "It's damn shore gonna be your ass if I don't get them rifles we agreed on last night."

"We don't cotton much to men who can't back up their talk," Ike Leach put in, adding to the threat. Standing behind his brother, he stepped up to look Wilkes in the eye. The frightened soldier looked anxiously from one menacing brother to the other, wishing he had never accepted their offer of a drink the night before.

"I'm gonna pull a wagon up to that back door tonight at midnight, right after the guard makes his circle around the building," Garth said. "We'll load them rifles in no time and be gone, and you'll be a hundred dollars richer, just like I promised." He forced a smile for emphasis, which quickly returned to a frown as he threatened, "If that back door ain't open, and you ain't there, the army is gonna be less one soldier-boy."

"I wasn't sayin' I wasn't gonna be there," Wilkes insisted, doing his best to hide his fear. Looking into those cruel eyes, he had no doubt that the hulking bear of a man made no idle boasts. "I'll be there, all right," he stammered. "A deal's a deal." He glanced at Ike, who was grinning then. In contrast to Garth's imposing size, his brother was tall and razor thin, but no less intimidating with his evil gaze. "Yessir," the private emphasized, "I'll be there, just like I said."

A few minutes before midnight, a team of mules pulled an empty wagon slowly along a back alley that separated the quartermaster warehouse from the main armory. Stopping the wagon short under the branches of two old hickory trees that screened them from the back door of the warehouse, the five occupants sat quietly while waiting for the guard to walk his post past the building.

"Hold them mules still," Garth ordered his brother Jesse, who was driving the wagon. Jesse was the third of the Leach brothers, after Garth and Ike. He had inherited much of Garth's bulk and size, but had traded them for a shortage in mental capacity. "Joe," Garth commanded, "hop down off that wagon and go see where that damn guard is."

Joe, the youngest of the clan, hesitated for a moment to look at the young girl sitting in the back of the wagon at his side. When Garth looked around to see why Joe hadn't obeyed, Joe quickly got off the wagon. "I'm goin'," he protested. Then turning to the girl, he said, "Don't you move till I get back."

Jesse snickered at that. "Ain't nobody gonna mess with your little wife," he teased. "At least not with no more time to diddle than we got right now."

"Why didn't you leave Cora back there with the other wagon and the horses?" Garth scolded.

"He's afraid she'd run off on him, that's why," Jesse said. "Ain't that right, Joe?"

Joe turned to direct his reply to the frightened young girl huddled against the side of the wagon. "She knows I'd come after her if she did. I'm goin'," he said then, when Garth was about to scold him.

In a short time, Joe returned to report. "He's on the

side of the building right now, fixin' to come around the
back."

"All right," Garth said. "Ever'body be quiet."

From the deep shadows of the hickory trees, they
watched silently as the sentinel plodded slowly around
the corner of the warehouse. Moving along the back of
the building, he paused momentarily to try the back door
to make sure it was locked, then proceeded unhurriedly
on to disappear around the opposite corner.

"Let's go," Garth commanded. "Pull the wagon up to
the door. Ike, you go to that corner. Joe, you go to the
other'n. Sing out if you see anybody comin'. Me and
Jesse can load the rifles. Cora, when we get to the door,
you get up here and hold these mules."

Before the wagon came to a complete stop, Garth
dropped to the ground. Tapping softly on the door, he
waited for a response. He heard nothing from inside right
away, and his anger flared. He was just about to kick the
door in when he heard the crossbar being lifted. A moment later, the door opened to reveal a thoroughly frightened Private Wilkes. The sight of the shivering young
man caused Garth to chuckle. "I see you ain't lost your
good sense," he said.

"Have you g-got my m-money?" Wilkes stammered.

"Sure I got your money," Garth replied. "We'll load
up them rifles first before we worry about your money."

"How do I know you'll pay me?" Wilkes protested.
"I'm takin' one helluva chance here."

"You're wastin' my time," Garth shot back. He
reached out and with one hand shoved Wilkes aside. "Is
that them?" he asked, spotting a flat cart loaded with

wooden crates. "Jesse, pull that cart up to the door and start loadin'." Turning back to the bewildered private, he ordered, "Get me a crowbar or somethin'. I wanna see there's rifles in them crates."

"I ain't got no crowbar," Wilkes said. "I ain't crazy enough to cheat you. They're rifles, all right, and you ain't got but about twenty minutes before the guard makes another turn around the building."

Garth seared the man with his gaze for a few tense seconds before deciding he was too frightened to lie about it. "All right," he said softly, "we'll go ahead and load 'em, but, friend, there better be Springfield rifles in them boxes. Nobody cheats Garth Leach—and lives to talk about it."

In less than fifteen minutes, they'd loaded all the rifles on the cart. "We've got room for a couple more crates," Jesse said. Wilkes was about to protest, but was saved the effort when Joe ran back to report that he had spotted the sentry turning the far corner of the building next to the warehouse.

"All right," Garth said. "Let's get outta here. We'll pick Ike up at the corner."

"What about my money?" Wilkes demanded.

"Hurry up," Garth ordered Jesse, ignoring Wilkes. "Pull on out. I'll catch up." Turning then to the private, he said, "Step inside the door and I'll pay you."

"Hurry," Wilkes pleaded as he stepped back inside the warehouse. "He's gonna be here any minute."

"You don't have to worry about that," Garth said, smiling. "Here's your pay." Wilkes reached out for his money, but the object Garth pulled from behind him was a ten-inch hunting knife. The massive bully quickly grabbed Wilkes' outstretched hand and yanked the unsuspecting soldier toward him, burying the knife deep in Wilkes' belly. Emitting a low scream, Wilkes tried to back away from the blade tearing at his stomach, but Garth was too powerful for the weaker man. He backed the gasping soldier up against the wall, forcing the knife deeper and deeper until Wilkes sank to his knees. Garth withdrew the knife and let his victim fall over on the floor. Then to make sure he was dead, he sliced Wilkes' throat open. His business finished, he left the warehouse, closing the door behind him, and trotted unhurriedly toward the wagon waiting at the corner of the building.

"I don't reckon we'll be doin' no more business with Private Wilkes," Ike commented when he saw the knife still in his older brother's hand.

"Let's get outta here," Garth said before responding to Ike's comment. Of his three brothers, Ike was the only one whose ideas and criticisms were tolerated by the heavy-handed oldest brother. "There ain't no chance he'll tell anybody who got the guns."

"He most likely wouldn't of told anybody he'd sold the guns, and we mighta got some more from him," Ike said. "I just hope that guard don't try the door again. We might have somebody hot on our trail."

"I killed him because I just didn't like the son of a bitch," Garth replied, getting a little heated. "We ain't likely to be back in this part of the country anyway." Upon giving his actions more thought, he knew Ike was probably right, but he didn't regret killing the man.

Ike, knowing it unwise to push the issue, changed the

subject. "Well, ol' Yellow Calf can quit his moanin' about wantin' guns for his Kiowas now. We've got enough rifles in this wagon for half his band, and whiskey enough so's the other half won't care."

Garth laughed. "That's a fact."

Slipping in a word of advice, Ike offered another bit of caution. "When them soldiers find ol' Wilkes back there, and suspect they're missin' some rifles, they're gonna be out lookin' for 'em. I'm thinkin' it might be smart to see if we can hook up with one of those wagon trains passin' through Council Grove. They ain't likely to suspect a wagon train like they would two wagons alone headin' out toward Injun territory."

"By God, that's just what I was thinkin'," Garth responded, even though it had not crossed his mind as yet.

Tanner Bland had never seen the ocean, but his father had told him of a trip to the Carolina coast when he was a young man. His father had said that it was a sight that confused his mind. There was no end to it, stretching from horizon to horizon and constantly rolling like there was some great discomfort in its belly. Gazing out upon the seemingly endless expanse of tallgrass prairie on this summer day, Tanner was reminded of his father's description of the sea. From horizon to horizon, the panorama stretched endlessly before them. The steady breeze combed the long stems of grass, causing a swaying much like he imagined the ocean might exhibit. Here and there, wildflowers sprinkled the prairie with vivid colors, making it appear docile and friendly, welcoming the two travelers.

With Jeb as the guide, they left Mound City behind them, heading for Council Grove, a town on the Neosho River. According to Jeb, it had long been a favorite rendezvous spot for travelers on the Santa Fe Trail, with plenty of good water and grass, and wood from the groves of hardwood trees. "Once you pass Diamond Springs," Jeb said, "you're in cottonwood country. No more hardwood, and accordin' to my old man, cottonwood's too soft to use to repair wagons."

Council Grove was also a favorite river crossing for the long wagon trains that traveled the Santa Fe because of the Neosho's natural rock-bed river bottom. It was a meeting place for all manner of travelers, not just wagon trains. Gold seekers on their way to California often passed through, as well as army supply wagons on their way to southwestern forts. This seemingly endless parade of pilgrims was witnessed with more than a little interest by Kaw Indians settled close by.

It was close to evening when the two travelers walked their horses past the stage company's corral. "There's been talk that the stage is gonna move out of Council Grove and go over to Junction City," Jeb said as they passed. "I doubt there's anything to it. Hell, folks been comin' through here for about forty years."

Enjoying his role as guide, Jeb continued his enlightening commentary. "That over there is Malcolm Conn's store. That's where we'll get our supplies tomorrow." Then he pointed to a building farther down the street. "That there is the Hays House. I'm gonna buy you as fine a supper as you'll find anywhere right there." He grinned at Tanner. "Courtesy of the Union army," he said, and patted his saddlebag where the sack of gold coins was packed.

"Maybe you'd best hold on to that money," Tanner said. "It's a long way to Montana."

"Don't worry," Jeb immediately replied. "I aim to use this money for a grubstake. But we ain't got much for supper tonight, and anyway, we deserve one good meal before we start out on bacon and beans."

"It's your money," Tanner replied, knowing it was useless to argue.

"It's *our* money, partner," Jeb insisted.

Tanner had to agree, supper at the Hays House was a fine meal. "Now all we need is a little drink before we turn in," Jeb announced. "There's a saloon down the street where some right friendly ladies used to hang around. 'Course, that was before I went off to war, but I'd like to see if the place has changed any."

The early-evening crowd had thinned out somewhat by the time Jeb and Tanner walked into Brannan's Saloon. "Brannan's?" Jeb asked the bartender. "The place has changed names, ain't it?"

"How long's it been since you was here?" the bartender returned. "It's changed names two or three times in the last two years. I own it now. My name's John Brannan."

"Well, Mr. Brannan, pour us a couple of shots of your best. Me and my partner are headin' for Montana in the mornin', and this might be the last drink we have for a spell." Jeb looked around the narrow barroom for a few seconds before making his decision. "Hell, might as well leave us the bottle," he said.

There were only four tables in the saloon, and only one of them occupied. Grabbing the bottle by the neck, Jeb moved to a table close to the door. Feeling himself a guest of his partner's generosity, Tanner followed. "Am I gonna have to haul you outta bed in the mornin' and tote you to Montana on a packhorse?" he asked.

Jeb laughed. "Ol' steady Tanner," he teased. "Don't worry. Hell, there ain't that much left in this bottle. We'll just finish it off, and then we'll go to bed."

Just as Jeb had promised, the two partners sat enjoying an evening drink with no distractions other than an occasional outburst of laughter from the other table, where three men were playing cards. It appeared to be a friendly game between locals who knew each other. After about half an hour, the door to the back room opened and a woman entered the barroom. She paused to exchange some brief conversation with the three men at the back table before moving on to Tanner and Jeb.

"Evening, gents," she greeted them, a wide smile, bordered by a heavy application of lipstick, adorning her face. "You fellows ain't been in before, have you?"

She was not a pretty woman, probably well into her thirties, her pale face already etched with hardship lines, but she was female. Consequently, she had the qualifications necessary to ignite the perpetual glow that burned inside the core of Jeb Hawkins. "Well, good evenin' to you, ma'am," Jeb immediately responded. "You're right, we ain't been in before, but if we'd known about you, we'da sure been in here sooner." He favored her with a boyish grin while unabashedly looking her up and down.

She responded to his flattery with a return smile, and introduced herself. "I'm Myra Brannan," she said. "My husband is the owner." The broad smile that remained in place fairly told Jeb that she appreciated the attention, but warned him to watch his step.

"I'm pleased to meet you, Myra," Jeb replied. "My name's Jeb. This is my partner, Tanner." Tanner nodded when she released her gaze from Jeb for a brief moment before returning it to him. "So you're the bartender's wife," Jeb continued. He glanced in the direction of the bar. "He's a big feller, ain't he?"

Enjoying what appeared to be a flirtation with the young man, something that Tanner suspected happened quite infrequently, Myra replied demurely, "Yes, and he's got a jealous streak a mile wide." Her gaze still locked on his eyes, she waited for his response.

"Well, I can see why," Jeb said. "If I was married to a fine-lookin' woman like you, I'd most likely keep her locked up."

By this time, the conversation between his wife and the young stranger had captured the attention of John Brannan. Tanner glanced over toward the bar and noticed the big man's dark frown as he stared in their direction. Marveling at Jeb's infatuation with all things female, Tanner was about to caution him of the husband's interest when Myra ended the flirtation.

"Well, it was nice to meet you fellows," she said in a voice louder than necessary. Without glancing in her husband's direction, she added, "I've got some things to take care of out back." With that, she turned and left through the same door she had come in.

Barely five minutes passed before Jeb announced that he badly needed to empty his bladder. "I'll be back in a minute," he told Tanner. He got up and went to the bar, where a scowling John Brannan awaited. "I might as well go ahead and pay you for that bottle," he said and put some money on the counter. "I don't suppose you've got an outhouse out back, do you?"

Still scowling as he accepted Jeb's money, Brannan replied, "Not for customers I don't."

"I expect I'll have to use the alley then," Jeb said with a shake of his head, and out the front door he went.

Brannan was undecided. He waited for a while, polishing some whiskey glasses, the scowl in place while he watched the door, shifting his gaze occasionally toward Tanner, who was still seated at the table. Finally, when too much time had passed with no sign of the brash young stranger, Brannan dropped his towel on the counter, pulled a shotgun from under it, and went out the door.

There was no one in the alley next to the saloon. Brannan paused to look up and down the dark passageway for a few seconds. Then he heard voices and the sound of a woman's laughter. Knowing with certainty whose laughter it was, he ran toward the back of the building. Rounding the corner, he came upon the very thing he'd suspected. There on the back step of the saloon, he found his wife leaning casually against the doorframe, giggling girlishly at something the stranger had just said.

"By God!" Brannan roared. "I thought so, you son of a bitch!" He brought his shotgun up and aimed it at Jeb. "You don't pussyfoot around my wife and get away with it."

Jeb was stunned. He heard the hammers click back on the shotgun leveled at his head, and knew he had no chance to reach for the pistol on his belt. "Whoa! Wait a minute," was all he could come out with.

"John!" Myra shrieked. "He didn't do nothin'. He just thought he could get back in the bar this way."

Brannan hesitated, but only for a moment. "You'd best put it down." He heard a steady voice behind him, and felt the light tap of a rifle barrel on the back of his head. He froze. "Just a little misunderstandin'," the voice said. "We apologize if there was any offense to you or your wife. Ease those hammers back down, and we'll be on our way, and no harm done."

"He's right, John," Myra Brannan pleaded. "No harm done. Just a misunderstanding."

Still feeling the rifle barrel against his skull, Brannan decided it best to do as he was told. "All right." He finally gave in, and released the hammers on his shotgun. Turning to face Tanner, he issued a final bluster. "But I don't wanna see the likes of you two around my place again."

"You won't," Tanner said. "Come on, Jeb."

Without wasting another word, they turned and walked up the alley, leaving the bartender and his wife to work out their differences. "I knew you'd watch my back," Jeb said cheerfully, not at all concerned that he had come perilously close to getting his head blown off.

"One of these days, I might not be there," Tanner replied. "What the hell did you wanna go after that woman for?"

"Hell, she wasn't that bad. Besides, she had a kind of sad look about her. I figured she needed a little attention."

They passed up the hotel, preferring to bed down in the stable with their horses. Tanner awakened in the middle of the night to find Jeb missing. He awakened again hours later when Jeb returned.

"Took you a long time to piss," Tanner remarked dryly.

"I knew she needed some attention," Jeb replied. "She wasn't gettin' what she needed. I'm glad I could help her out. That husband of hers is a helluva heavy sleeper, though." Tanner shook his head, hardly believing, then turned over and went back to sleep.

Bright and early the next morning, none the worse for wear after their visit to the saloon, they spent some of Jeb's money for a packhorse to carry the supplies that were later purchased at Conn's store.

Ready to bid Council Grove farewell then, they loped out of town following the Santa Fe Trail. Although it had been their original intention to set out straight to the northwest, on the advice of Malcolm Conn they changed their plans. There were numerous reports of hostile Indian activity along the old Oregon Trail to the north, so it made better sense to follow the Santa Fe, at least to Fort Larned, then head north. That way, they could get information on the hostile situation beyond that point. Neither of the two had any real experience with Indians, but they agreed that if Santa Fe was the safer route, why not take advantage of it for part of their journey?

As near as they could estimate, Fort Larned was a hundred and fifty miles or more from Council Grove, and they held to the Santa Fe Trail, even though it bothered them that it seemed to lead them farther south than they cared to go. After traveling three days and figuring they had only one full day's ride before reaching the fort, they came to the point where the Walnut River joined the Arkansas and discovered a wagon train camped there.

Jacob Freeman walked to the edge of the circle of wagons, and with one foot propped on a wagon tongue, watched the two riders and a packhorse. As the leader of the train, he was keenly interested in strangers approaching his company of settlers bound for the northwest, whether they be Indians or white drifters. In the twilight of the evening, it was difficult to determine the nature of the two men until they had come within a few dozen yards. "Well, they ain't Injuns," he finally called over his shoulder to Floyd Reece, who was standing by his wagon, equally interested in the identity of the visitors.

"Watch 'em just the same, Jacob," Floyd returned, one hand resting on the barrel of his rifle.

"Hello the camp!" Jeb yelled when he saw several more of the men of the camp gathering to meet them.

Although cautious, since his train was made up of peaceful Christian folk, Jacob was bound to be charitable by nature. "Welcome, gentlemen," he answered. "You're welcome to come on in and rest a spell. You're a mite late for supper, but my missus might scare up some coffee."

"We're obliged," Tanner said, "but we won't put you out any. We can camp down the river a ways."

"Why, no need to do that," Jacob replied. "There's plenty of room here, and we've already got fires goin'. We'd be glad to have your company." When Floyd Reece cocked an eye at him, Jacob whispered, "It's the Christian thing to do, and anyway, I'd rather have them where we can keep an eye on 'em." Only thirty miles short of Fort Larned, he didn't like the thought of two strange men lurking around the fringes of his camp.

Jeb looked at Tanner and Tanner shrugged. Looking back at Jacob, Jeb said, "That's mighty neighborly of you. I reckon we'll take you up on it."

They dismounted and led their horses within the circle of wagons. The rest of the people in the train gathered to greet their guests, the men in frank appraisal, the women hanging back initially, the children pressing close to get a better look.

"I'm Jacob Freeman," the wagon master offered, extending his hand.

Jeb took it. "I'm Jeb Hawkins. This here's my partner, Tanner Bland." Tanner nodded. Jeb asked, "Where you folks headed? Santa Fe?"

Several people started to answer at once, but Jacob took the floor. "No, sir, we're planning to stay with the trail along the Arkansas into Colorado to Bent's Fort. Then we're set on turning north to strike the South Platte and Fort Laramie. California's our destination."

"How about you fellers?" Floyd Reece asked. "Where are you heading?"

"Montana," Jeb replied. "Lord and the Injuns willin'."

"I expect we'd best unsaddle these horses and water 'em," Tanner reminded Jeb.

"You can just turn 'em out with our stock after you water 'em," Jacob said. "Plenty of good grass here—best we've seen at a campsite the past week."

"Much obliged," Tanner replied.

After the horses were taken care of, Tanner and Jeb set up their camp. They spread their bedrolls next to their saddles, under the watchful eyes of the members of the wagon train, and were in the process of preparing to fry some bacon for their supper when Ida Freeman saun-tered up with a coffeepot in hand. "There's a little left in the pot if you'd like some coffee," she offered. "Sorry there's no beans left."

"Why, thank you, ma'am," Tanner replied, "but we've got food for ourselves."

Ida's offer of hospitality seemed to be the spark that dissolved the cloud of caution that hovered over the two strangers, and many of the others promptly crowded around to extend greetings of welcome. Within minutes, the two guests felt right at home, exchanging news and answering questions. While Jeb made most of the con-versation from their side, Tanner watched in silent amusement at his partner's gift of small talk. By the time they finished their supper, they were practically old friends of the people of the train, thanks to Jeb's natural gregarious personality. Those who had not as yet learned the strangers' names referred to them as "the talker" and "the silent one."

Always with an eye for the women, Jeb fixed his gaze on a slender dark-haired girl who inched up close to the fire to listen to the gossip swapped back and forth between Jacob and Jeb. Her name was Cora Abbott Leach, and she wasn't there long before Jeb made it a point to personally introduce himself. "Howdy, miss, my name's Jeb Hawkins. I'm pleased to make your acquaintance."

"It's *missus*," a gruff voice behind her answered before the girl could reply, and Joe Leach moved up behind Cora. His hand placed firmly on her shoulder, he informed Jeb, "I'm her husband."

Jeb's smile broadened perceptibly as he studied the scowling face of the sullen husband. "Well, then, my compliments to you, sir." After a closer inspection of the man confronting him, Jeb added, "Looks to me like you married over your head."

Deep-set eyes that glowered out from under heavy eyebrows glared unblinking at the outspoken stranger for a few long seconds as Leach's hand clamped down harder on his wife's shoulder, causing her to wince. "Get yourself back to the wagon," he growled to Cora, and pulled her roughly around. There was a silent pause in the crowd as the young woman dutifully did as she was ordered.

Studying the sympathetic faces, Tanner surmised that Cora's rough treatment was not unusual. He felt sorry for the woman. Leach looked like a hardhanded brute, and he was still smoldering as he continued to glare at Jeb. Of more than casual interest were the three men who stood close behind Leach. All seemed cut from the same rough stock as the young woman's husband, and hardly fit in with the rest of the wagon train company. Tanner guessed that they might be brothers, and he saw that the glint in their eyes as they stared at Jeb was far from cordial. Glancing around at the faces in the gathering, Tanner noted that Jeb was the only person chuckling over his attempt to make a joke.

Knowing his partner by now, Tanner was certain that Jeb would not intentionally shine up to a married woman unless he thought she craved the attention. He hoped that Jeb hadn't caused any trouble for her. As for Jeb, he blithely ignored Leach's threatening gaze, already having shifted his interest toward seeking out other likely looking prospects in the gathering. After a brief period, Leach turned and followed his wife to his wagon. The three other sullen men followed him. Tanner noticed an immediate relaxation in the crowd's mood, as if a dark cloud had drifted from overhead.

As the evening wore on, the people dispersed. Morning came early on a wagon train, and most of the folks had already stayed late to visit with the two guests. Two of the last to leave were Jacob Freeman and Floyd Reece. Standing to one side of the dying fire, Jacob asked his friend, "Are you thinkin' what I'm thinkin'?"

"I expect I might be," Floyd answered. "Them two might be the Lord's way of solvin' our little problem. Might be too much of a coincidence otherwise."

Less than a week before, the wagon train had met with an army patrol out of Fort Larned. The lieutenant commanding the patrol informed them of a new requirement set by the government because of increased hostile activity between Fort Larned and Fort Lyon in Colorado. There were new restrictions on wagon trains that traveled beyond Fort Larned, since the post did not have the manpower to escort every group of settlers that came through. Each train was required to have at least twenty wagons and thirty men. For the last few days, Jacob and Floyd had talked over the problem. They had twenty-two wagons but only twenty-eight men, including the four Leach brothers. They had almost decided to bypass Fort Larned in order not to be detained. It did indeed seem a stroke of luck, if not a favor from God, that the two young strangers showed up just before the wagon train reached Fort Larned. Jacob and Floyd were agreed.

The proposition was offered to Tanner and Jeb the following morning as the camp was breaking up for the day's journey. "We'd be much obliged if you fellers would consider it," Jacob Freeman said after explaining their predicament. "We don't expect to be at Fort Larned for more than a day or two. We're got a few folks that need some blacksmith work and some wagon repairs. Then we're for moving right along. All we'd need from you is to count you as part of our company, just to satisfy the new rule."

"Whaddaya say, Tanner?" Jeb asked. "I don't reckon a day or two will make much difference to us. And if we can help these folks get on their way . . ."

"I suppose it couldn't hurt us to hang back for a day or two," Tanner replied. He grinned at Jacob Freeman. "If you folks can stand us . . ." He figured that he and Jeb could make Fort Larned in one more day's ride. Tagging along with the wagon train would change that to two days, but he felt in no particular hurry.

"Fine," Jacob responded. "We appreciate it." He and Floyd exchanged nods, satisfied that one problem had been solved. "You fellers are welcome to camp by my wagon tonight if you like," Jacob offered. "My wife might even make up some pan biscuits to go with your supper."

"I surely wouldn't turn that down," Jeb immediately responded. "I ain't had a good biscuit in I don't know when." He nodded toward his partner. "Tanner there ain't made me no biscuits since we partnered up," he joked. He was rewarded for his humor with a patient smile from Tanner.

After the day's travel, the wagon train made camp by a narrow creek with steep banks where it emptied into the Arkansas. As promised, Ida Freeman broke out her big iron skillet and worked up dough for a large batch of pan biscuits. Tanner, a hunter since he was a small boy, took the packhorse and rode off across the prairie in search of meat. With the slow pace of travel, there had been ample opportunity to scout out away from the wagons, and he had discovered evidence of abundant game along the way.

"Want me to go with you?" Jeb asked when Tanner had prepared to leave.

It was plain to see that Jeb was already in the process of unsaddling his horse and looking forward to socializing with the wagon company. "No, reckon not," Tanner answered, noting the immediate relief in his partner's face. "I'm just gonna ride out a ways and see if I get a shot at some meat."

"All right, then," Jeb said. "You watch yourself, Tanner. There's Injuns about these parts." He dropped his saddle beside Jacob's wagon. Then, seeing Ida Freeman getting a bucket from the wagon, he stepped up to offer his help. "Here, ma'am, let me fetch that water for you."

"Why, thank you, sir," Ida responded with a sunny smile gracing her chubby cheeks. She handed the bucket to Jeb, brushed a stray strand of graying hair from her forehead, and gave the cheerful young man a long looking over. She decided that she liked him. He seemed as carefree and fun-loving as his partner was serious and soft-spoken. The two men were a decided contrast in personality. She turned then when her husband returned from the creek bank with an armload of wood for a fire.

Jeb arrived at the creek just as a woman started to make her way down to the water. He recognized her as the pretty young girl he had spoken to the night before and had been abruptly informed that she was married. Upon seeing him approaching, Cora Leach ducked her head to avoid his gaze. Jeb didn't speak, but seconds later, he moved quickly to catch her arm when her foot slid on the steep bank and she was about to fall.

"Careful, there, missy," he said, holding her up by her elbow. "I wouldn't want a pretty young lady like yourself to go head over heels into the creek."

Looking embarrassed and frightened, Cora regained her balance and was quick to remove her elbow from Jeb's grasp. "Thank you," she managed, barely above a squeak.

Jeb noticed a fairly fresh bruise beside her right eye and almost commented on it, but decided to hold his tongue. Instead he said, "Here, why don't you let me fill that bucket for you?"

"No. Thank you, sir, but I can get it," she replied, looking around as if afraid someone might see them talking.

"No trouble a'tall," he said, taking the bucket from her hand. "I've gotta fill this one anyway. It'll be easier to fill both of 'em—keep my balance better with two coming up this bank." He descended the bank before she could protest further. "I'd be glad to carry it back for you," Jeb said when he returned to the top of the bank with full buckets.

"No, no," Cora protested fearfully. "I'll get in trouble."

She reached for the bucket, but it was already too late. "Cora!" an angry voice bellowed.

Jeb turned toward the voice. It was not her husband's. Standing near the closest wagon, one of the three men who had backed Cora's husband the night before glared menacingly at the frightened girl. She grabbed the bucket, almost spilling it, and hurried back toward the camp. As Jeb watched, she hung her head when she passed by the man. Jeb could not hear the words spoken, but she was obviously scolded as she went by him. *Damn*, he thought, sorry that he had evidently caused her trouble.

Aware that the man was still standing there, now glaring at him, Jeb turned and started back to camp with his bucket of water. Standing beside her wagon, Ida

Freeman paused in her supper preparations when she saw the incident taking place by the creek bank. Though it was a minor thing, and seemingly of little significance, she deemed it important to warn Jeb about paying any attention to Cora Leach.

"I thank you, sir," Ida said when Jeb set the bucket down by the wagon wheel.

"No trouble a'tall," Jeb replied. "Always glad to help a fine-lookin' woman." He grinned as he added, "Especially one that makes such fine biscuits."

Ida cocked her head and grunted. "Don't go wastin' your charm on me," she said, brushing the ever-present wisp of gray hair from her face. Jeb threw his head back and chuckled. Ida's smile faded then and a frown appeared to take its place. "Young man, it appears to me that you're possessed of a fun-lovin' spirit, and I reckon that's your business. But I need to warn you about having any to-do with the Leach brothers, especially Garth. That's the big fellow that was just down at the creek when you were talking to Cora. Garth's the oldest of the four brothers, and Jacob can tell you that he's the most dangerous of the bunch, although they're all pretty ornery." Her warning surprised Jeb, causing him to give her a questioning look.

"Ida's right," Jacob Freeman said, overhearing his wife's comments. "Them boys is bad business, and no doubt about it."

Still puzzled by the unexpected word of caution, Jeb said, "Why, I ain't lookin' to cause anybody trouble. All I did was get a bucket of water for the lady. Same's I did for you," he added, looking at Ida. He was beginning to wonder how the four happened to be traveling with a train of obviously peaceful Christian folks. Jacob went on to explain.

"They joined up with us back at Council Grove," he said. "Two wagons, Joe and Cora in one, and Garth, Ike, and Jesse in the other. We found out about two days outta Council Grove that we'd made a mistake in lettin' them join us." Again there was a questioning look from Jeb. "They just ain't our kind of folks," Jacob went on.

"Fightin' and cussin'," Ida interjected. "You never heard such a fuss. We were kinda hopin' they'd kill each other off, after we saw what kind of people they were. The thing that bothers me most is the way they treat that poor little girl Joe's married to. I swear, she comes out with a new bruise or cut every mornin'. Janie Reece asked her what happened to her eye one mornin', and that weasel she's married to told Janie to mind her own business."

"Well, there's that," Jacob said. "But there's also the fact that the wagon three of the brothers are drivin' is loaded down with something. Fred Lister got a peek into that wagon one day when he was lookin' for his son. The little feller's about three years old, and he'd run off somewhere. Fred was just lookin' to keep the young'un from pesterin' anybody. But he got told pretty quick to keep his nose outta their wagons. Fred said he didn't get to see much, but there were some wood crates that look like the kind rifles are shipped in, and he saw one whiskey barrel. Everything else was covered up. They're up to no good, that bunch. They tagged on to us for protection, and I reckon they figure the soldiers won't bother lookin' in their wagons as long as they're traveling with respectable folks like us."

"Why don't you tell them to quit the train?" Jeb asked.

"We intend to," Jacob replied. "But up to now we haven't, for the same reason we asked you and your partner to join up. We'll wait till we get clear of Fort Larned. Then, by thunder, we'll come to a partin' of the ways quick enough."

Jeb shook his head thoughtfully. Considering the makeup of the people in the train, he could understand a reluctance to confront the likes of Garth Leach and his brothers—a pack of wolves traveling with a flock of sheep. "Well, any trouble they get from me, they'll bring it on theirselves," he said. "When the time comes, me and Tanner will back you."

"I appreciate it," Jacob said. "I'm afraid they ain't gonna like it when I tell 'em to git."

Jeb left the Freemans then to tend to his horse, but he was still thinking about what they had told him. *A wagon full of guns and whiskey,* he thought. *That doesn't sound like typical settlers, for damn sure.* "Well, I reckon it's their business and I don't need to make it none of mine," he announced, and turned his attention to the horses grazing near the river.

It was close to sundown when Tanner returned to camp with two antelope carcasses tied on his packhorse. He was a welcome sight, since he offered to share the meat with the entire train, and several of the men quickly volunteered to help him butcher the animals. The arrival of fresh meat served to spawn a festive air about the camp, and soon the cook fires were rekindled and burning brightly. Jacob Freeman announced it a cause for celebration on the eve of reaching Fort Larned. "We can make the fort with our bellies full of fresh meat, instead of salt pork," he proclaimed. Spits of green cottonwood limbs were fashioned over a couple of the fires, and soon the aroma of sizzling antelope haunches filled the air.

Off to one side of the circle of wagons, the four Leach brothers stood watching. Sullen and scornful, they stared at the festive scene like coyotes on the fringe of a buffalo herd. Only Cora sneaked a hint of a smile as she watched the children darting close to the fire to snatch a sliver of roasted meat.

Noticing the longing gaze of the dark-eyed girl, Ida Freeman walked over and spoke to her. "Don't hang back here in the shadows, honey. Come on over to the fire and join us."

Cora looked quickly at her husband, seeking his permission, and was met with a deep frown. "We already et our supper," Joe Leach replied gruffly. "Cora don't need no wild meat."

Ignoring the surly response, Ida directed her invitation to Cora. "We don't see enough of you, young lady. Why don't you come join the fun?"

"I done told you—" Joe flared, about to tell Ida to mind her own business.

"No, no thank you, Miz Freeman," Cora quickly interrupted. "I've still got chores to do before bedtime. But thank you just the same."

Ida shook her head slowly as she read the sadness in

the young girl's eyes. Then she glared at Joe for a second before turning on her heel.

Cora felt the iron grip of her husband's hand on her shoulder again. "Get yourself back to the wagon," he growled. With no word of protest, she turned and obeyed, walking back to the wagon without a backward glance at the cheerful celebration.

Close by Jacob's campfire, Jeb stood watching the incident between Ida Freeman and Joe Leach. At some thirty yards away, he could barely make out a word or two of the conversation, but enough to determine the gist of it. He said nothing for a few moments, thinking of the fresh bruise on Cora's face. Finally, he muttered, "That ain't no way to treat a woman."

Hearing his partner's low growl, Tanner turned to see what had caused the comment. Following Jeb's gaze, he immediately saw the reason. "I reckon there's a lot of men that don't deserve a wife," he said. "It doesn't seem right, but I guess it's between the two of them and none of our business."

"Just the same," Jeb replied, "I hate to see a woman treated like that."

"I know, but maybe she doesn't think it's that bad, or she would have run off and left him."

"Maybe," Jeb allowed. "Unless she's too scared of him to run."

In an attempt to take his partner's mind off the unfortunate girl, Tanner sliced off a generous slab of haunch and handed it to Jeb. "Try this," he said. "It's pretty good eatin'. As fast as these critters run, I'm surprised the meat ain't tough as nails." He went on to describe his hunt. "I've hunted all kinds of game, but I ain't ever seen anything move as fast as antelope. A man has to time his shot just right, 'cause there ain't a chance for a second shot." Jeb reluctantly pulled his concentration away from the slight young woman and joined Tanner beside the fire. Across the clearing, the four Leach brothers tired of the celebration and returned to their wagons.

Chapter 6

In the early afternoon of the following day, the wagon train reached Pawnee Fork Crossing on the Arkansas, where the original fort had been built. Continuing on two and a half miles up Pawnee Creek, they sighted the adobe buildings of Fort Larned on the south side of the creek. Jacob and Floyd debated the best location to establish camp, then decided upon a site a few hundred yards upstream from the fort where there was plenty of grass for the animals.

Lieutenant Jack Puckett rode out to inspect the newly arrived wagon train and to familiarize the travelers with the services available at the fort, which turned out to be little more than wagon and harness repair. He informed them again of the restrictions on wagon trains traveling past Fort Larned and was satisfied that they met the requirements of twenty wagons, thirty men. After the lieutenant left, Jacob talked to his people. "Those of you who need repairs best get about it right away, and maybe we can get started again day after tomorrow. I don't see much use in wastin' any more time than that around here.

It don't seem like there's much they can do in the way of supplies. It may be better when we get to Fort Lyon."

"Tanner, dammit, let's go find us a drink of whiskey," Jeb suddenly blurted. "I swear, it's been a while since I've had a drink, and I know there's some somewhere on an army post."

Tanner looked up from the rifle he was in the process of cleaning. A drink would be enjoyable after the long ride from Council Grove, he thought. "All right," he said. "I expect the best place to start lookin' might be the stables." He figured it was a good chance some enlisted man might be assigned stable duty as punishment, and most likely for drunkenness.

"Let's go, then," Jeb quickly replied. It was no more than a quarter mile back to the post, so they decided to walk. "It might be best to leave these 08-branded horses here in camp in case they come down with a case of homesickness," he said with a chuckle.

Just as they figured, there were two soldiers mucking out the stables when they walked in the open end of the building. They both paused to lean on their pitchforks when Tanner and Jeb approached. "What in blazes did you two do to draw this kind of duty?" Jeb called out in greeting.

There was no response from either at first, as both men looked the strangers over. Then one of the soldiers, a slight man with a scraggly mustache, answered. "Too much applejack, I reckon. It don't take much when Lieutenant Puckett is the officer of the day."

The other soldier, a short pudgy man in contrast to his

bony partner, spoke then. "If you fellers are lookin' for horse feed or hay, this here's for army use only."

"Hell, we're needin' the same stuff that landed you in the stables this mornin'," Jeb said. "Maybe you can tell us where a feller might find a drink of whiskey around here."

"It's against regulations to have strong spirits on the post," the skinny private announced.

Jeb took a brief moment to aim an exasperated look in Tanner's direction before turning back to the soldier. "We were both in the army. We know army regulations don't mean a damn thing when it comes to havin' a little drink. Just tell me who to see to get a little whiskey we can take back to camp."

The two soldiers exchanged cautious glances before the stocky one shrugged and said, "There's two barracks. Go to the one closest to the hospital. One end of it is a storeroom. See Sergeant Crowder, and maybe you can talk him outta some whiskey—if there's any left, which I doubt. They smuggled some in under a wagonload of hay day before yesterday."

"Much obliged," Jeb said, flashing a wide grin at Tanner. "Maybe we'll bring you back a drink."

"Maybe you'd better not," the slight soldier lamented. "Puckett'll smell a man's breath. Stable duty this time, it'll be the guardhouse next time."

"What can I do for you boys?" Sergeant Ben Crowder asked when Tanner and Jeb walked in the door of the storeroom.

"We're lookin' to buy a little whiskey," Jeb replied, "and we were told this is the place to get it."

"Whiskey?" Crowder responded as if amazed. "This is an army supply room. I don't sell no whiskey here. Look around you. Does this look like a saloon to you?"

Jeb gave the sergeant a wink. "Come on, Sarge, all we're lookin' for is a little jar of whiskey, enough for us to have a couple of drinks apiece."

"Who told you you could get whiskey here?"

"Feller over at the stable," Jeb replied. Tanner walked over and propped an elbow on the counter. Jeb never needed help talking, so Tanner was content to remain an observer.

"McIntyre?" Crowder blurted. "That little weasel never could keep his mouth shut."

"Didn't catch his name," Jeb replied. "But he was a charitable man who took pity on a couple of thirsty travelers. We were hopin' you'd be the same."

The sergeant studied the two men for a long moment before asking, "You two come in with that wagon train yesterday?" Jeb nodded. "And you come in here looking for a drink?" Again Jeb nodded. "Why the hell didn't you just get it from that feller Leach?"

Tanner and Jeb exchanged startled expressions. Jacob Freeman had told of someone seeing what looked like a whiskey keg in Garth Leach's wagon. "Well, I'll be damned," Jeb allowed. "The son of a bitch *is* sellin' it. I just figured he had a powerful thirst."

Crowder couldn't help but chuckle. "You fellers don't know much about the folks you're traveling with, do you?"

"Reckon not," Tanner answered. He didn't bother to tell Crowder that they had only joined the train two days ago.

Not to be sidetracked from the purpose of his mission, Jeb pressed for an answer. "Well, are you gonna sell us some whiskey or not?"

"Sure," the sergeant said, the grin still on his face. "I believe you boys do need a drink. Did you bring anything to put it in?" When Jeb shook his head, Crowder said, "How much you aimin' to buy? I've got some pint jars. You want more'n that?"

"No, that's enough," Tanner said, answering for them.

Crowder went back into a smaller room off the main storeroom. After a few minutes, he returned with a jar of whiskey, and Jeb made the payment. Tanner was curious about the transaction between Leach and the sergeant. "The fellow at the stables said the whiskey came in under a load of hay. Leach didn't have a load of hay on his wagon." He was not concerned with the legality of Leach's dealings with the sergeant, even though he had no use for the surly eldest of the four brothers. Soldiers were going to drink if they could get it. That was just the way of things.

"Well, that's how I usually get it. But this was brought in last night through the tunnel." When it was obvious to the sergeant that his remark created questions, he went on to explain. "The water tunnel," he said. "We have to get drinkin' water from the creek. We tried to dig wells, went down forty feet tryin' to get good water, but it tasted like sulfur. That's why you see those water barrels beside each barracks. We have to haul it up from the creek. They dug a tunnel to the creek so we can get water if the fort's under attack."

Jeb screwed the lid off the jar and sniffed the liquid, bringing a quick retort from the sergeant. "Hey, don't open that jar in here! Take it back to your camp to drink it, and don't let nobody see you carryin' it out of my storeroom."

"All right, all right," Jeb replied. "We won't let nobody see it." Grinning broadly, he walked out the door. Just outside, he paused on the top step to sample the spirit, unconcerned with being seen. "Damn, that stuff's rank," he said, smacking his lips. "Here, give her a try."

"I reckon I'll wait," Tanner said. "I wouldn't wanna get the sergeant in trouble for sellin' it to us."

"I reckon you're right," Jeb said, and slipped the jar inside his shirt. They walked back toward the train, Jeb with a not so inconspicuous bulge hanging over his belt.

All the families had taken advantage of the day's layover at Fort Larned to make necessary repairs to wagons and harness, and were prepared to start out for Fort Lyon again the next morning. Floyd Reece brought out his fiddle, sat down by the fire, and sawed away on a couple of old-time favorites. The music soon attracted folks from other wagons, and before long a small crowd had gathered. Attracted by the mournful rasping of Floyd's strings, a few soldiers from the fort came over to visit the train. Seeing Floyd set up with his fiddle, one of the soldiers went back to the barracks to fetch his squeeze-box accordion. In no time at all, there was a lively little gathering, keeping time by clapping hands and tapping toes.

Having finished most of the pint jar of whiskey by himself, Jeb was in a carefree sense of being, and he was in the mood to dance. As his partner he picked the seven-year-old daughter of Fred Lister to shuffle through the steps of an improvised buck dance, much to the delight of the giggling youngster. It didn't take long before other couples took to the grassy dance floor. The dancing went on for a while before someone organized a reel, and most of the spectators joined in. Floyd and the soldier with the squeeze-box knew only three tunes they could play together, but they kept repeating them over and over.

Off to one side of the circle, Tanner Bland sat with his back against a wagon wheel, a silent spectator of the dance. He smiled as he watched Jeb Hawkins' ungainly, high-stepping attempts to follow the music, as he changed partners—to Ida Freeman, to another of the children, then back to Lister's daughter again. He envied his partner's free spirit. It wasn't all due to the whiskey he had just downed. Jeb was just naturally fun-loving, and it didn't take much to bring that nature to the surface. Tanner's smile faded for a moment when he remembered the last dance he had attended. It was a week before he left to join the army. It had been a bittersweet occasion, for he was there with his intended, but their wedding plans were postponed. The recollection was the first time he had thought about Ellie for a few days. He had tried to discipline his mind to avoid thoughts of her, but he could not help but wonder if she and Trenton were happy, and if she had put him out of her mind. Maybe it was a good marriage. Maybe they already had a baby on the way. That last thought brought an image to his mind that he did not want to think about, and he cursed silently, admonishing himself to put it out of his head. A movement out of the corner of his eye snagged his attention, pulling his thoughts away from Eleanor Marshall.

In the darkening shadows of the evening, she was almost unnoticeable as she stood between two of the wagons on the far side of the circle. Like a starving waif watching a noble feast, Cora Leach gazed longingly at the joyful dancers. Tanner could not help but pity her. He wondered how she had had the misfortune to be bound to a weasel like Joe Leach. *I wonder how she got away from her husband to watch the dancing,* he thought. He had no sooner generated the thought than the first signs of trouble appeared.

One of the soldiers in the crowd of spectators noticed the shy young woman standing in the shadows, her foot tapping in time with the music. Before Cora had time to retreat, the soldier grabbed her by the hand and pulled her out into the firelight. Protesting desperately, she tried to free herself, but he wasn't taking no for an answer. Looking anxiously from side to side, afraid of being seen, she had no choice but to be swept into the circle of dancers. Seeing no sign of her husband or his brothers, she permitted herself to enjoy a couple of rounds of the reel before darting back to her place in the shadows. But fortune apparently seldom smiled upon the unfortunate young woman, and she found Joe Leach waiting for her between the wagons.

Cora froze abruptly when she saw her husband standing in her way. He said nothing, but the anger in his eyes lashed out at her. Without a word of warning, he struck her with his fist, driving the hapless girl out of the shadows to crumple, dazed, to the ground at the feet of one of the couples. The music stopped instantly, and a hush enveloped the celebration. All were stunned—with the exception of one.

Having seen all of the marital abuse to the helpless girl that he was going to stand for, Jeb strode over to help Cora up. "God damn you," Joe snarled. "Get your hands off my wife!" It was all he had time to say, for Jeb whirled around and planted his fist squarely on Joe's nose. He put everything he had behind the punch, hoping to drive his fist right through the scoundrel's skull. Tanner would almost swear later that he heard Joe's nose crack from across the circle of wagons.

Joe staggered backward before tripping over the wagon tongue and landing hard on his back. "You're pretty damn good at beatin' on women," Jeb snarled. "Let's see how you like it with somebody who'll fight back."

Joe didn't move at once. His nose flattened, with blood streaming down into his mustache, he was too stunned to mount a defense. Finding that he could not breathe through his nose, he could only gasp for air with his mouth hanging open. With the crowd closing in around the altercation, he tried to get to his feet, but was still dazed from Jeb's haymaker.

Terrified to a state of panic, Cora stood helpless, not knowing what to do. Afraid of what Joe might do to her if she didn't help him, she started to go to his side. Jeb caught her elbow. "Don't go back with that son of a bitch. He ain't fit to have a wife," he said.

She looked at him with frightened eyes, afraid she had no choice. "He'll kill me if I don't," she replied, knowing she had no place to go.

"He's right, honey." Ida Freeman spoke up. "You can't go back with that man. You can stay with Jacob and me."

Her statement caused a look of surprise on Jacob's face, but he rose to the Christian moment. "That's right, Cora. You can stay with us."

"Here, honey," Ida said. "Let me take a look at that cut beside your eye." She shook her head in disgust. "There's gonna be a right nasty bruise there. You're gonna ride with us. No woman oughta put up with trash like Joe Leach."

As Joe Leach crawled to the wagon wheel, struggling to help himself up, he looked furtively at the faces in the crowd, all staring at him accusingly. From the other side of the circle, Tanner Bland walked almost casually over to stand a few yards behind the spectators. He knew Jeb needed no help with Joe. He was concerned about Joe's three brothers, however, wondering why they had not responded. They were nowhere in sight. Turning his gaze back to Joe again, he watched with interest as the stunned bully steadied himself on the wagon wheel, obviously trying to decide if he should meet Jeb's challenge or retreat to lick his wounds. In a rare moment of sanity, he decided upon the latter and turned on his heel, the sound of a growing swell of muttering in the crowd of spectators ringing in his ears.

"Bad business, this," Jacob Freeman mumbled to Floyd Reece, who had come to stand beside him.

"I expect so," Floyd agreed, shaking his head solemnly. "There's liable to be hell to pay." The two leaders of the wagon train had tiptoed around the four violent brothers ever since they joined them in Council Grove. What they had hoped to avoid might now have been triggered by Jeb Hawkins' actions. "I don't reckon we can blame the young feller for what he did. We all knew how that no-good son of a bitch was treatin' his wife. But we figured it wouldn't be our problem once we left Fort Larned. We'd be shed of 'em."

Jacob glanced at the two women still standing near the campfire, Ida obviously trying to talk the frightened young girl out of going back to her abusive husband. While he knew that what Ida did was the right thing, he would have been a lot more comfortable had she not. "Well," he decided, "I don't think they're liable to do much while we're camped here by the fort, but when we leave here, I don't know. . . ." He paused when Tanner Bland joined them.

"I guess my partner might have stirred up some trouble," Tanner said. "That Leach crowd doesn't look like the kind to turn the other cheek. I expect Jeb and I will ride along with you a bit farther tomorrow, in case you need some extra help."

"I appreciate it," Jacob replied. He was about to say more, but his wife interrupted at that point.

"Cora's gonna ride in our wagon, Jacob. Right now, I need to have somebody go with us to get her things."

Overhearing, Jeb at once volunteered. "I'll go with you," he said.

Ida paused a moment, looking at Tanner standing

silently by. She sensed that of the two partners, Tanner might prove to be the more formidable, but Jeb had already demonstrated his ability to stand up to challenge. Turning back to Jeb, she said, "Thank you, sir." Taking Cora by the arm, she started toward Joe's wagon. Jeb stepped in on the other side of Cora.

Joe was not in the wagon when Jeb and the two women approached. Cora, not wishing to spend an instant longer than necessary, quickly went to a trunk near the front of the wagon. It didn't take but a moment or two to collect her simple belongings, and she soon climbed down with everything she owned in her two arms. Jeb was quick to help her, taking her elbow to steady her, unaware of the shadowy figure suddenly moving up to the front of the wagon.

Burning with shame and indignation, his nose and cheek already swelling and bruised, Joe carefully pulled the wagon sheet aside to peer through at his antagonist standing at the rear of the wagon. His hand dropped slowly to rest on the handle of his pistol. As his fingers closed around the handle, he heard the warning behind him.

"I wouldn't if I was you," Tanner Bland cautioned softly. Joe froze with his hand still on the weapon. "All you got so far is a bloody nose. You'd best settle for that. A rifle slug is gonna hurt a helluva lot more."

At the front of the wagon, Jeb quickly reached for his revolver when he heard the warning. He stepped in front of Ida and Cora, prepared to defend them. At the other end of the wagon he heard Tanner tell Joe to back away.

A moment later, Tanner called out, "You'd best escort the ladies on back now, Jeb."

Realizing then just how close they had come to a violent reprisal from Cora's husband, Ida grabbed Cora by the arm and hurried the trembling girl away. Looking quickly at Jeb as she passed him, she remarked, "I didn't even know your friend was back there."

Jeb grinned as he replied, "Tanner's always back there."

"What the hell—" Ike Leach stopped in midsentence. He pulled the wagon sheet back all the way to get a closer look, then turned his head to call back over his shoulder. "Garth, come take a look at this!" Turning back to his younger brother who was sitting in the front corner of the wagon, he blurted, "What the hell happened to you?"

Joe, who had until that moment been sitting with his head tilted back, trying to find a position that eased the throbbing in his face, gazed at his brother through swollen eyes. He did not answer the question at once, dreading the berating he was bound to receive from Garth. Garth did not disappoint.

Pushing Ike aside, the huge man stared at Joe for a long moment before speaking. "I figure the man that done the job on your face is dead. If he ain't, then I expect you'd best be explainin' why he ain't, little brother."

"Where's Cora?" Jesse asked.

Realizing then that the girl was missing, Garth stepped back from the wagon and looked left and right before sticking his head back inside. "Where *is* Cora?" he insisted.

"They took her," Joe replied.

Failing to understand, Garth demanded, "Who took her?"

"They did," was all Joe answered, nodding toward the center of the circle of wagons.

"Freeman and that bunch?" Ike asked, obviously surprised.

"Well, it weren't Jacob, but his wife was the one that talked Cora into it," Joe meekly explained.

Garth could not believe what he was hearing. "You let that old biddy take your wife away from you? You still ain't told me who made a buffalo wallow outta your face. Did Ida Freeman do that?" Impatient with his brother's lack of backbone, he said, "Crawl on outta that wagon and tell me what the hell happened here while we was over at the fort."

Dutifully, Joe crawled out of the wagon. His three brothers crowded up close to him to inspect the damage to his face. "It was them two new fellers," Joe offered in explanation. "That one, the one that's been shining up to Cora, hit me when I wasn't lookin'. I think he broke my nose. Then that Freeman bitch run off with Cora. I was fixin' to go back and take care of that bastard, but I'm waitin' till I can see straight."

"What did he hit you with?" Jesse wanted to know. "A rifle butt?"

"I don't know," Joe lied. "I told you, he hit me when I wasn't lookin'."

"Well, he's a dead man," Garth fumed, his anger rising now. "He'll never see the sun come up tomorrow."

Equally eager to retaliate, but a bit cooler in the head, Ike offered his advice. "It don't seem like a very healthy thing to go shootin' up a bunch of people right here at the fort. We might oughta wait till we pull outta here tomorrow, and then do the job."

"Ike's right," Garth said, cooling down a little. "We'll wait till we're on the trail again. Then, by God, we'll have us a funeral. In the meantime, we'll bide our time."

"Uh-oh," Jacob Freeman muttered under his breath.

Ida looked up to see the imposing bulk of Garth Leach approaching from across the way. She quickly glanced back at her wagon, where Cora was feeding the campfire with more wood. She immediately got to her feet and headed to the wagon. Seeing her ominous brother-in-law, Cora went to stand beside Ida at the wagon. Not waiting for Jacob to speak, Ida demanded, "What do you want here, Garth Leach?"

Garth didn't answer until he came to a halt almost at her feet. Glowering down at her, he said, "You got some gall to talk snotty to me, ain't you?" He glanced at Jacob before continuing, confident that he wasn't going to cause any trouble. "Kidnapping a man's wife, and you call yourself a Christian." Then looking past her, he snarled at Cora, who was clutching the wagon wheel as if afraid she would be torn from it. "Cora, I'm givin' you a chance to come on back to your husband, and you won't be punished, so come along, girl. Get your things."

"She ain't coming with you," Ida replied.

Garth glanced at her with a cold eye. "I ain't talkin' to you, am I?" Looking at Cora again, he said, "Come on, Cora. You've got chores to do."

Speaking barely above a whisper, Cora replied, "I'm not coming back, Garth. I don't want no more beatings. I'm gone for good."

Garth glared at the frightened girl for a long moment before giving his warning. "You're gonna be mighty sorry you said that." He turned to leave, barely glancing at Jacob, who had stood without protesting the whole time.

"Maybe I'd better go on back with him," Cora said. "I'm afraid he's gonna cause you some trouble."

"Nonsense!" Ida replied. "We ain't a'feared of that big ol' bear. Him and his brothers need to know a woman ain't something to beat on anytime they feel like it." Even as she said it, she cast an uncertain glance in her husband's direction.

Jacob said nothing, but shook his head slowly before turning away. Garth Leach was hardly the kind of bully who would take a tongue-lashing from a woman and then turn tail and run. There was going to be trouble ahead for the folks in the wagon train. He wished at that point that Jeb Hawkins had not taken it upon himself to avenge the girl's abuse. He also wished that Ida had simply kept her nose out of the affair. *It's too late to do anything about it now,* he thought.

Chapter 7

Jacob Freeman was still in the midst of establishing the order of travel when someone in the group of drivers assembled around him remarked, "Now, where in the world are they goin'? Ain't nobody told them they was leadin' today."

All eyes turned as one to see the two Leach wagons pulling out of camp, heading toward the trail, two of the brothers driving, and two on horseback. "Maybe they're settin' off on their own," Floyd said. "They said they might fork off before we reached Fort Dodge."

"Looks that way," Jacob agreed, at once relieved, although somewhat surprised that the belligerent brothers would simply leave without retaliation for Cora's desertion. Before he could comment further, someone in the small gathering issued an "Amen," which was followed by a chorus of similar sentiments. The general mood of the travelers seemed to rise in spirit with the thought that they might have seen the last of the Leach brothers. Jacob, thinking of the twenty-wagon, thirty-man restriction, quickly called out the order of travel. "We'd best get under way before the army decides we can't," he said. Then turning to Fred Lister, whose wagon was to lead that day, he said, "Once we get clear of the fort, haul back a little. I ain't anxious to catch up with them polecats."

As Jacob had anticipated, Lieutenant Puckett rode out to see the travelers off. Noticing the absence of a couple of wagons, he inquired about it. Jacob told him that two of their wagons had taken an early lead to make sure they identified the right trail to Fort Dodge, and would wait for the rest of the train a few miles out. It seemed to satisfy Puckett, although he questioned the party's decision to follow the Dry Route to Fort Dodge. "It's been a pretty dry season," he said, "and most folks passing on the trail have taken the Wet Route along the Arkansas."

"I reckon that's so," Jacob replied, "but we're lookin' to save a little time, and we're takin' plenty of water with us."

"Well, good luck to you folks," Puckett said. He wheeled his horse and loped to the top of a low ridge to watch the wagons move out, following the trail along the banks of the Pawnee.

Walking beside the Freemans' wagon, Cora Leach was more mystified than Jacob had been to find that her husband had ridden away without causing trouble. Still frightened, however, she knew it would be some time before she could rid herself of the shadow of Joe Leach, or the threatening look in Garth's eyes when he had warned her of the mistake in her decision to leave her husband.

Glancing toward the other side of the wagon, she tried to return Ida Freeman's smile with one of her own, but it had been a long sleepless night for Cora. She had been afraid to close her eyes for fear Garth would be standing over her when she opened them again. There had been some reassurance in knowing that Jeb and Tanner were bedded down right outside the wagon. But they were only two men, and probably the only two who might stand up to Garth Leach and his brothers. These innocent people, with whom she now traveled, had no idea how violent the evil clan could be. As she walked now, easily keeping pace with the slow-moving wagon, she could not help but continue to glance from side to side, half expecting to see Joe and his brothers suddenly appear.

Riding out ahead of the wagons, Tanner and Jeb served as scouts, primarily to make sure the main trail was picked up, but also to keep an eye out for the two wagons that had left earlier. There was not a great deal of conversation between them as they rode the almost treeless plain. Jeb, usually talkative to a fault, was uncharacteristically quiet, due, Tanner figured, to a slight feeling of guilt. He figured he was the cause of the uneasy cloud hanging over the folks in the train. But he could not in good conscience say that he would not do the same thing again. Tanner had assured him that he had acted properly. The girl, Cora, should not have been subjected to such brutal treatment—by her husband's hand, or that of any other.

The day progressed without incident. The Leach brothers' tracks were quite clear. They had stuck to the main trail, but it was evident that the wagon train was not gaining on them. Roughly an hour before going into camp for the night, Tanner pointed out that the two wagons they followed had cut off the main trail and taken a smaller track that led due north.

"You think those bastards might be doublin' back on us?" Jeb asked.

"Maybe," Tanner replied while studying the prints of the wagon wheels where they veered off to follow a small stream. "Might be they just decided to fork off here and camp a ways up this little stream. I expect it would be best for us to follow their tracks for a while and maybe see what they're up to. We'll ride back and tell Jacob where we're goin'."

When the train caught up to them, Tanner decided it might be a good idea to ask Cora a few questions. Jacob and his people had assumed that the brothers were heading west for the same purpose as everyone else in the train. Tanner was a little more curious now. Upon questioning, Cora enlightened them on Garth Leach's reasons for traveling west. Reluctant to say more than she had to at first, primarily because of a feeling of guilt for having been with them, she admitted that her husband had no intention of homesteading.

There were scant articles of furniture or tools in either of the two wagons driven by the brothers. Instead, they were loaded with whiskey kegs and rifles stolen from the army. Some of the whiskey was sold at Fort

Larned, but most of it, and all the weapons, were slated for trade with the Indians.

Jeb could hold his curiosity in check no longer. "How in the big blue-eyed world did you ever get mixed up with the likes of Joe Leach?"

Cora looked down in shame, as if she was somehow guilty for the union. "My daddy used to ride with Garth Leach," she replied, her words soft and halting. "He cheated Joe out of some money they took from a bank, hid it in his hat. Joe found out Daddy cheated him, and wanted Garth to kill him. Daddy begged him not to kill him, and Garth asked Joe what it would take to let him live. Joe said they'd be square if he could have me."

"Jesus Christ!" Jeb blurted out. "And your daddy gave you away?" He shook his head, amazed. "Didn't you have any say about it?"

"I wasn't but thirteen. I didn't know what to do," she said, ashamed.

Tanner shook his head and turned away. Speaking to Jacob Freeman then, he said, "Jeb and I'll follow their trail to see if they're thinkin' about doublin' back. I expect it would be a good idea to camp right here where there's water. This stream is the first one we've crossed all day. I reckon they don't call this the Dry Route for nothin'."

The trail that Garth Leach and his brothers had taken was one that had evidently been traveled a great deal. There were old and new tracks that followed the narrow path down a ravine and along the small stream. Most of the tracks were made by unshod hooves, indicating that the trail was a popular route of the Indians. Leading toward a line of hills in the distance, the trail never wavered in its northern course. "If they're thinkin' about doublin' back on us, they woulda cut back by now," Jeb remarked.

"I expect you're right," Tanner agreed.

By the time the sun started to sink below the hills to the west, they prepared to turn back, knowing that it would soon be too dark to follow the wagon tracks. "Hold on a minute," Tanner said. "I smell smoke."

Jeb stood up in the stirrups and sniffed the air. "Yeah, me too," he said.

They scanned the open range before them, finally deciding the smell came from a campfire beyond a low rise a little off to the west. Riding to the base of the slope, they dismounted and made their way up to the top of the rise, where they dropped to their hands and knees. On the other side of the rise, in a wide ravine, they saw the two wagons.

Lying on their bellies, they located all four brothers. Joe was tending the fire while the others were taking care of the horses. After watching for a few minutes, Tanner decided, "It doesn't look like they're thinkin' about anything but headin' north and sellin' their rifles and whiskey."

"I reckon they're done with the wagon train, all right," Jeb said. "Didn't figure 'em for that—not that mean son of a bitch Garth." After a moment more, he pulled his rifle up beside him and sighted it on one of the brothers. "We oughta do the world a favor and cut the bastards down right now," he growled.

"Maybe," Tanner said. "But I reckon we got the girl away from them. We might as well call it even, and get on back while there's enough light to find our way." Jeb shook his head and grimaced, reluctant to withdraw. It would have been a risky shot at that distance in the fading light, anyway. Tanner was right. Let the bastards go as long as they were headed away from the wagon train.

It was hard dark by the time the two partners rejoined the wagons. Had it not been for the campfires to guide on, Tanner and Jeb might have missed them altogether. The night did not remain cloaked in darkness for long after their arrival, however. Tanner paused as he pulled the saddle off Ashes' back to look at a full moon rising over the hills behind them.

"We coulda sure used that a while back when we were stumblin' around in the dark," Jeb said.

"I reckon," Tanner agreed. Then, hearing footsteps behind him, he turned to see Jacob and Floyd approaching.

"Well," Jacob said, "you two don't look like you're excited about anything, so I expect the Leaches ain't right on your heels."

"No, sir," Tanner replied. "We followed 'em till they made camp. They were still headin' straight north. Didn't look like they were thinkin' about doublin' back on us."

Visibly relieved, Jacob nodded, then turned to look at Floyd, who nodded in answer. "I'm mighty glad to see the last of that bunch," Jacob said.

"Me and Tanner was talkin' about our plans on the

way back here," Jeb said. "We figured we'd ride along with you folks for another day or so before we head north, maybe until you make Fort Dodge."

"We appreciate it," Jacob returned. "You sure you boys don't wanna tag along with us to Fort Lyon? Like I told you before, we're plannin' to turn north from there. We'd be glad to have you stay with us."

"I expect we'll head on alone," Tanner said. "We'll move a whole lot faster than the wagons."

"Might be safer with us," Jacob said, still trying to persuade them. "There's been a lot of Injun trouble north of here."

"I reckon we'll just chance it," Tanner replied.

"It's still early in the summer, Tanner," Jeb suggested. "I don't see where a couple of more days would hurt."

Tanner cast a sideways glance at his partner, and couldn't help but smile. There was little doubt as to why Jeb wanted to stay with the wagons for a while longer. The fact that the slender victim of Joe Leach's abuse had already seen a lifetime of man's cruelty in her young years did nothing to discourage his interest in her. Tanner knew that part of that interest was Jeb's natural empathy for someone that fate had treated so unfairly. Seeing a grin creep slowly across Jeb's face as he waited for his response, Tanner found it hard to refuse him. "I suppose we could hang around for a few more days after Fort Dodge," he finally allowed.

Breaking camp early the second day out of Fort Larned, Garth Leach pushed the mules hard until reaching the Walnut River. Then he turned the two wagons west, following the river until almost sundown. Riding up beside the lead wagon, he told his brother Jesse, "We'll make camp here." He turned in the saddle and signaled Ike in the wagon behind to pull up beside. They were joined in a few seconds by Joe, who, like Garth, was on horseback.

When Joe rode up and dismounted, Garth said, "Joe, you get a fire started and cook us some supper." When Joe's face screwed up into a pout, Garth cut his protest short. "Damn you, you lost us our cook, so, by God, you'll be the cook till we get her back."

"Damn, Garth, that ain't fair," Joe whined.

"That's right, Blue," Jesse teased. He had started calling his younger brother Blue since Joe's broken nose and cheeks were still a dark shade of bluish gray, a result of the smashing right fist of Jeb Hawkins. "Maybe when we get Cora back, I'll take her for a wife. I'll guarantee you, she won't leave me." He laughed then. "She won't wanna leave me, after she's been with a real man." The big simpleminded man threw his head back and roared with laughter.

Ignoring Jesse's innocuous prattle, Joe pressed Garth. "When are we gonna go back and get my wife?" Knowing that he was held in contempt for his failure to settle with Jeb Hawkins at the time, he was desperate to regain his standing as a Leach. "I've got a score to settle with that son of a bitch. He caught me when I wasn't lookin', and I'm gonna kill him."

"You shoulda kilt him when he done it," Ike commented dryly.

Garth continued to gaze at his youngest brother with

eyes filled with disgust. After a moment he spoke. "We'll go back when I say we'll go back," he growled. "I've got a score to settle myself. I want that whole wagon train rubbed out, and I expect Yellow Calf might just be interested in a little party—after we sell him these rifles."

Morning saw the four back on the trail again, following the river west. Upon reaching the junction where the Walnut forked, they took the southernmost. The afternoon found them approaching the Kiowa village of Yellow Calf. Garth rode on ahead of the wagons. Some Kiowa boys watching the pony herd gave the alarm that visitors were coming.

Yellow Calf walked to the center of the camp to see who was approaching. Seeing the huge man on horseback, he grunted, "Big Bear," the name the Kiowa had given Garth Leach. The two wagons behind Leach immediately caught his interest. Big Bear had traded whiskey on more than one occasion. On his last visit, Yellow Calf had insisted no more whiskey. Bring rifles, he said, or the four white men would not be welcome in his village. Yellow Calf went down to the river's edge to await Garth's crossing.

Garth permitted a smug smile to crease his stern features when he saw the Kiowa chief coming down to meet him. "Yellow Calf," he called out and raised his hand in greeting.

"Big Bear," Yellow Calf replied. "I see you have come back. What have you got in your wagons?"

"I remember what you told me last time," Garth answered. He turned to point toward the wagons, now approaching the riverbank. "Guns," he proclaimed. "Guns and ammunition, enough to arm half your warriors." Garth expected to trade the rifles for enough buffalo robes to fill both wagons. Yellow Calf's eyebrows lifted and his eyes grew large. Garth chuckled. "Your enemies will fear you now," he said.

"Ah," Yellow Calf replied, eager to see the weapons. "The guns that shoot many times?" he asked.

"Well, no, these ain't repeatin' rifles," Garth admitted. "But these is good rifles, the same kind the soldiers use—load fast, shoot straight." He didn't add that the weapons were surplus arms, some in various states of disrepair, but generally functional.

Yellow Calf was disappointed. He wanted the lightweight carbines the cavalry used, but he would not turn down the Springfields, for there were no more than half a dozen guns in his entire village, and they were old muzzleloaders. For the sake of the trade, however, he continued to display an air of disappointment. "Maybe I wait till I get guns that shoot many times," he said as he watched the wagons ford the river. When they pulled up on the bank, the drivers halted the mules and the wagons were immediately surrounded by Yellow Calf's people. The three brothers climbed down and stood aside, cautiously watching the Kiowa pressing close around the wagons.

Unperturbed by the chief's show of indifference, Garth said, "I might have somethin' else to sweeten the deal. I can lead you to a wagon train of white settlers, carryin' a lot of things your women could use, and more guns, too. No soldiers, just farmers and women. You'll have more guns than they have." Garth could see that the chief was thinking this over with a great deal of interest.

"You will lead us to these people?"

"Hell, yeah. I'll lead you there. Me and my brothers will fight side by side with your warriors. There is one woman that I want. Everything else is yours."

Chapter 8

Eleanor Marshall Bland carefully folded the dish towel and hung it on a hook by the kitchen window. She paused to look at it for a moment, not really seeing the towel, her mind wandering aimlessly. Feeling older than her years, she sighed as she removed her apron and hung it on the back of the pantry door. Breakfast over and the dishes done, she started down the hall to the bedrooms, barely glancing at her image in the hall mirror as she passed. She had decided to wash clothes today, since it promised to be sunny.

Stripping the sheets from the bed, she could not avoid thinking about the night just past. Trenton had attempted to make love, but failed once again to perform, which threw him into another fit of depression. She knew his despair was exacerbated by a suspicion that she was relieved when he could not achieve satisfaction. She tried not to show her reluctance to meet his desires, having made a vow that she would try to be a good wife to him. It was extremely difficult to hide even a little slip in her emotions, however, and she was afraid he was aware of every one, at times making comments that her mind was elsewhere. Although she always denied it, he was correct in his judgment, for she lived in her own world of despair, unable to forget what might have been.

Gathering up the sheets, she went to her father's room to strip the sheets from his bed. Trenton and Travis, along with their father, had gone to the lower end of the cornfield to work on a house for the newly married couple. Their own house. Eleanor dreaded the thought of it. An ideal setting for the house would have been the glade by the creek between her father's house and Trenton's father's house. No one could understand why she rejected it, favoring a site farther up the creek near the corner of the cornfield. Though he never spoke of it, she suspected that Trenton may have guessed the reason for her reluctance to build their home near the footbridge.

"The damn war," she suddenly heard herself exclaim. She blamed the war for destroying her dreams, dreams she had nurtured since she was a girl, slipping away from the house to meet Tanner Bland by the footbridge. The thought of Tanner brought a sense of longing that weighed on her heart like a stone, and she tried to send her mind elsewhere. But it kept returning to the image she carried with her of his face, frozen hard with bitter anguish as he confronted the wedding party. "I wish I was dead!" she blurted. Then at once contrite, she asked God for forgiveness for saying such a sinful thing. She returned her blame to the war—for her unhappiness, for a despairing husband who sought his solace in a bottle, and for her inability to forget the man she loved. Feeling guilty then for her grieving, she reprimanded herself.

Trenton was a good man. None of this was his fault. It was her responsibility to make their marriage work. "I'll try to do better," she said.

With the tallgrass country well behind them, Jacob Freeman's wagon train crossed great expanses of short-grass plains where wide trails left by migrating buffalo intersected their line of travel. The flat land before them seemed endless, with occasional hills and ribbons of cottonwoods wherever streams or creeks were found. Jeb seemed content to stay close to the wagons, most of the time beside Jacob's, where he could get occasional glimpses of Cora Leach. The frightened girl became a little less shy each day, even to the point that she would exchange a few words of conversation with the strapping young man who had defended her.

Unlike his carefree partner, Tanner was not entirely comfortable around a crowd of people. Feeling boxed in, even with folks as friendly as Jacob's company, he felt the need for room to breathe. Consequently, he contented himself with far-ranging scouting forays away from the wagon train where he could feel the country and study the game trails. As a result, he was seldom seen between dawn and dusk. Of particular interest to him were reports he had heard of the massive buffalo herds that roamed the short-grass plains. He had it in his mind to kill a buffalo, for up to this point, he had only heard tales of the great animal so important to the Indians' existence. He knew that Jacob and the others would appreciate a fresh supply of meat as well.

*   *   *

It was late in the afternoon when the train happened upon a small stream and Jacob decided to make camp. While the wagons were being circled and the teams unhitched, Jeb led his horse down to the stream to drink. It was by no coincidence that Cora happened to be there filling a bucket when he arrived. Hearing the horse's hooves behind her, she jerked her head around, alarmed. Met with his warm smile, she blushed, ashamed that she had reacted so.

"I declare, Miss Cora, when are you gonna stop jumping every time I come up on you?" He dropped the reins and stepped back to let his horse drink. "You've got nothin' to fear from me."

"I know," she admitted softly. "I'm sorry I jumped. I'm just . . ." She couldn't continue.

"I understand," Jeb assured her. "I'd like to show you that all men ain't like that no-good you were married to. Most men would appreciate a fine young lady like yourself."

His comments served to deepen her blush. She could not remember ever having been spoken to in such gentle tones. Shy and frightened before, she now found that she did not want to scurry away. She wanted to stay and hear more of his gentle talk. When he reached out to help her, she permitted him to take the bucket of water and carry it up the bank. "Thank you," she murmured.

"You're welcome," Jeb replied. "I'll carry it back to the wagon for you." She looked perplexed, as if what he offered was wrong. He realized that she had no earthly idea how a woman was supposed to respond to simple courtesies in a civilized world. Gracing her with a wide warm smile, he turned and started back. She followed along behind him.

Ida Freeman glanced up when the young couple reached the wagon. She paused in her preparation of supper to consider the two. Jeb Hawkins was paying a lot of attention to the troubled wife of Joe Leach. She could not help but notice, and now she stopped to consider whether or not it was a good thing. Jeb had made it perfectly clear that he and Tanner would be leaving them at Fort Dodge. She wondered if she should warn Cora against taking too strong an interest in the boyish charm of Jeb Hawkins. But maybe Jeb had more than a trifling interest in Cora. Who could say? In times and conditions like these, things happened awfully fast on the frontier. After thinking about it for a few moments, Ida decided that it was Cora's business. The girl was a good deal older than her years, and she had certainly known the rough side of life. If anyone deserved a fling with a handsome young man, it was Cora. And there was the possibility that Jeb might change his mind and go to the northwest with them. *Or,* she thought, *he might decide to take her with him to Montana.*

"You can just set that bucket down right over here," Ida said. "As scarce as water's been over the last four days, I don't want you to kick it over while you're staring at Cora." She favored Jeb with a knowing smile that almost made him blush. "Cora," she asked, "would you slice off some of that side meat and put it in the pan?"

"Yessum," Cora replied obediently, and turned at once to the task, leaving Jeb to stand there, awkwardly self-conscious.

With a mischievous twinkle still in her eye, Ida told Jeb, "If you're just gonna stand around, I'll find a chore for you, too."

"I reckon I've got my own chores to do," Jeb snorted indignantly, and spun on his heel to leave.

"Well, I don't see no buffalo ridin' on that packhorse," Jeb called out to Tanner as his partner rode into camp.

"Reckon not," Tanner replied. "The whole prairie is covered with tracks, but damned if I can find one buffalo."

"I ain't sure you can bring one of the critters down with a .52 Spencer cartridge, even if you do find one."

Tanner smiled and shook his head. "I'm not certain myself, but if the Indians can bring one down with a bow, then I figure I've got as good a chance as they have."

"Well, it's beans and bacon for supper tonight," Jeb said. "You're lucky I left you some." He watched Tanner unsaddle Ashes before asking, "You see any Injun sign while you were out there lookin' for buffalo?"

"Nope," Tanner replied.

Jeb nodded thoughtfully. "According to Jacob, we oughta strike Fort Dodge about noon tomorrow, so I reckon we're too close to the soldiers for Injuns to be nosin' around."

"Maybe," Tanner said, his attention drawn to the pan of beans warming on the coals. He had not eaten since breakfast.

It was a couple of hours past noon the next day when the wagon train reached Fort Dodge. Located on the north bank of the Arkansas, the fort was a dismal disap-

pointment to the party of travelers. A few lonely sod
buildings were laid out in a half circle that made up the
headquarters, shops, and officers' quarters. The enlisted
men lived in dugouts, carved in a twelve-foot clay bank
close to the river. Fort Larned now seemed luxurious in
comparison. The only positive aspect of the fort was an
unusually large campsite. The fort was at a point where
the Dry Route and the Wet Route met again at the
Arkansas. Consequently, it was a welcome spot for those
traveling the Dry Route to rest up after a long, dry crossing. Jacob decided to stay over an extra day before starting out again. Tanner decided it was a good time to rest
the horses. He had kept Ashes and the packhorse on the
move almost constantly during the past four dry days.
They deserved the rest, because he planned to go in
search of his buffalo as soon as the wagons rolled again.

In a reflective mood, Jeb sat down on the riverbank a
hundred yards or so from the fort, watching the sun sink
into the western prairie. He had persuaded Tanner to stay
with the wagons one more day before striking out to the
north. Tanner didn't argue against it. He understood Jeb's
reluctance to leave, but that was only part of his decision
to give in. He still had it in his mind to supply the party
with buffalo meat, so he welcomed one more day to
hunt. He felt confident that he would be successful in the
morning with his horses rested and the presence of fresh
sign the day before. He busied himself back in camp,
readying his weapon and saddle gear for the next day's
hunt while Jeb sat on the riverbank, staring thoughtfully
at the setting sun.

The afterglow would last for only seconds after the sun finally dropped below the horizon. Soon darkness would envelop the riverbank. Still Jeb remained. Deep, troubling thoughts worried his mind, thoughts of the girl, Cora, and why it bothered him that, after tomorrow, he would see her no more. He pictured her face, transformed in a few short days from the frightened, haggard countenance he had first seen to one of childlike innocence. It was a new experience for Jeb Hawkins. He had never before found it difficult to leave any lady friend or lover, but he suddenly felt the desire to protect someone. And he didn't know what to do about it.

Since he was unsure of himself, fate decided to lend a hand. Only minutes before dark, when he was about to get up and return to camp, she appeared beside the water. He watched her stepping carefully down to the water's edge before speaking. "Let me get that for you," he said.

Startled almost to the point of losing her footing, Cora couldn't suppress a squeal. Upon discovering that it was Jeb seated a few yards from her, she held her hand over her pounding heart and tried to calm herself. When she could speak, she said, "You scared me half to death!" After a moment more, when he scrambled to his feet and rushed to apologize, she regained her wits enough to joke. "Are you always gonna be around to fill my water bucket?"

"I'm s-sorry I scared you. I s-swear I am," he stammered. "I didn't know you couldn't see me settin' there. I wouldn't blame you if you hit me over the head with that bucket."

Calm now, she looked up into his face. "I wouldn't

ever hit you with a bucket," she said softly. "There's a lotta folks I would, but never you."

The moment was too overpowering for Jeb. His mind was caught in a whirlwind of emotions. "Doggone it," he sputtered, "I'm leavin' after tomorrow, and I know I'm gonna miss you somethin' awful."

Never suspecting before that moment that he could possibly have strong emotions for her, she was speechless for a few seconds. Just as he was about to sputter an apology for his brash confession, she whispered, "I'm gonna miss you, too. I'm awful fond of you."

Her response, unexpected, served to render him tongue-tied for a moment, a totally new condition for Jeb Hawkins. She gazed earnestly up into his eyes and, seeing his confusion, followed her instincts. Standing on tiptoe, she reached up to kiss him lightly on the cheek. "I'll never forget you, Jeb Hawkins," she whispered.

Ida Freeman's bucket dropped on the ground and rolled into the shallow water, unnoticed by the man and woman standing there. In the rapidly fading light of day, there was no one in the universe other than this man and woman—no thought of today or yesterday, or what might lie ahead. There was only this moment and the two of them. He took her in his arms, and she came to him eagerly, without guilt, knowing that what she did was right.

Lost in the sweet passion of their first kiss, they clung together for a long time before Jeb took her by the hand and led her to a willow thicket well away from the camp. There on a blanket of grass, they consummated their unspoken vows. Afterward, he held her in his arms, reluc-

tant to end the moment. It had never been like this before, and the one thing certain in his mind was that he did
not want her out of his life. He had to know if she felt the
same way.

"Cora," he finally blurted, "go to Montana with me."
Even in the dim evening light, he could see her eyes open
wide in surprise. Afraid that she was about to reject him,
he hurriedly said, "I'd take care of you. We could start all
over out there."

Everything had happened so fast that Cora's mind
was in confusion. She wanted with all her heart to say
yes to this decent man, but she feared that she came
with too much baggage from her past. What if, once
past the first blush of passion, he began to think about
her time as Joe Leach's wife and Garth Leach's sister-
in-law? She responded to his proposal in halting, carefully chosen words. "Are you sure you really want me
to go with you?" she asked. Before he could answer,
she reminded him, "I've had a lot of bad things happen
in my life, things I ain't proud of. I've been livin' with
bad people. You're the first good man I've ever known."

Jeb shook his head slowly, a faint smile on his face. "I
don't care about what you done before right now. I've
done a heap of things I ain't exactly proud of myself. You
and me can make it together. Hell, I reckon I love you."

"What about your partner?" she asked. "He might not
like you bringin' me along with you."

"Tanner ain't gonna mind," Jeb insisted. "He's always
backed me up, no matter what I got into." In all honesty,
he wasn't that certain that Tanner would react favorably
to the idea, but he was determined to convince him.

She hesitated a moment longer, then decided. "Well, hell, I reckon I love you, too!"

"You'll go?"

"I'll go," she replied, laughing as she pressed her slender body against him again, tears of joy streaming down her cheeks.

Tanner was fairly surprised to hear of Jeb's proposal. He'd known that Jeb was interested in Cora Leach, but figured it was like his partner's casual dallying with other women. Consequently, his first reaction was concern for the poor girl, but Jeb's fervent defense of his emotions convinced Tanner that he was truly in love with Cora. In truth, Tanner would have preferred to strike out for Montana without a woman in tow, but he understood Jeb's feelings, and it was not that long ago that he'd had the same feelings for a woman. "If that's what you want, then I reckon there'll be three of us heading out day after tomorrow," he said.

No one in camp was happier to hear of the young couple's plans than Ida Freeman. She felt justified in her assessment of Jeb Hawkins, and pleased at the abused woman's good fortune. Cora deserved a chance for happiness. Maybe Jeb was her answer. Ida and Janie Reece prepared a modest celebration that night for Jeb and Cora, which was attended by a few of the other families. There were some in the wagon train that were not sure the two young people were not without sin, Cora being a married woman. But as Ida put it, "The Good Lord's got to figure that Cora's already done her time in hell. I'm sure He approves."

Jacob was the first to declare it was time to end the party, since he wanted to get an early start the next morning. There was an air of goodwill and happiness as the evening drew to a close, at least in the Freeman and Reece wagons.

At sunup the next morning, the wagon company prepared to take the trail toward Colorado. Cora helped Ida pack the cooking utensils and bedding while Jeb helped Jacob hitch up the mules. It was to be their last day with the wagon train before heading north on the following morning. Tanner, his mind still set on supplying meat for the company before saying good-bye, had already left camp before sunup.

Chapter 9

"I was afraid we wasn't done with those devils," Jacob Freeman said.

Hearing her husband's comment, Ida looked up to see what had caused it. Ahead on the trail, sitting on his horse, awaiting them, was the ominous figure of Garth Leach. "I thought we were rid of him," she said, her tone laced with worry.

Jacob called back to Jeb, who was walking beside the wagon with Cora, his horse tied to the tailgate of Jacob's wagon. "We got company up ahead, Jeb." Jeb followed Jacob's pointing finger and immediately ran up even with the wagon seat when he saw Garth. "What do you suppose he's got on his mind?" Jacob asked.

"Whatever it is, it's bound to be somethin' we ain't interested in," Jeb replied. "I wonder where the rest of that pack of rats is." He glanced left and right, looking for signs of the other three Leaches, but there were no other riders in sight. For the last several minutes the wagons had been following the trail through a narrow ravine. The other three brothers could be behind either of the ridges that formed the ravine.

As the wagons made their way slowly toward the solitary rider in the middle of the trail, Garth raised his hand and waved it slowly back and forth. With no further sign, he continued to wait until Jacob's mules came to a stop before him. Then he nudged his horse and guided it around to stop opposite the wagon seat.

"When you left camp ahead of us, we thought you and your brothers had decided to go on alone," Jacob said.

Garth took note of Jeb standing on the opposite side of the wagon, then looked back at Jacob. "We decided to wait for you," he said. The wry smile that creased his dark face did little to ease Jacob's concern. "Afternoon, Cora," Garth said, nodding to the frightened girl, who had dropped back by the rear of the wagon. "You ready to come back to your family?"

"What do you want, Garth Leach?" Ida demanded. "Where are your wagons?" By this time, all of the wagons behind them had caught up and were now standing motionless in a line, waiting for Jacob to start out again. She was about to scold Garth again, when she suddenly gasped, "Mercy!"

Her gasp was followed almost instantly by similar sounds of alarm from the wagons behind her. Jeb looked toward the ridge to see what had startled her. There, along the crest of the ridge, a long line of Indian ponies had suddenly appeared and now sat quietly watching the wagon train below them. The blood drained from Jacob's face. Jeb, his rifle still in his saddle sling, dropped his hand to rest on his revolver.

Apparently amused by their sudden fright, Garth smiled. "No need to get scared," he said. "Them's Yellow Calf's boys, Kiowas. They don't mean you no harm. They just wanna say howdy, and maybe trade a few things. I told 'em to wait up there till I explained they was peaceful. We wouldn't want somebody to take a shot at one of 'em and start a massacre."

"They don't look so damn peaceful to me," Jeb interjected. "From here, it looks like they're wearing war paint."

Garth's smile immediately turned to a scowl. "Ain't nobody asked you for your two cents' worth," he snapped. Then just as quickly, the twisted smile returned to his face, and he turned back to Jacob. "Best tell them in the other wagons Yellow Calf is peaceful, and not to shoot off no guns."

"I don't know," Jacob started, not sure what he should do.

"Well, let me put it this way," Garth replied. "He's peaceable enough right now, but if you insult him, he's liable to turn mean." His grin grew wider as he locked his eyes on Jacob's.

Jacob glanced at Jeb for help, but Jeb could offer very little. He had already judged their odds as poor to middling, trapped at the bottom of a narrow ravine with no room to circle the wagons, even if there was time. Maybe what the black-hearted villain said was true, although he doubted it. If they told Yellow Calf to go to hell, they might be in for a fight, but at least they could make the savage pay with a few dead warriors. Of course, if the chief was peaceful, then no lives would be lost, white or red. Finally Jeb told Jacob, "I guess we ain't got much chance one way or the other, but maybe we'd best gamble on the odds that that damn Injun ain't as evil as Mr. Leach here." He caught the sudden spark of anger in Garth's eye, but the huge man made no comment. "I'll go tell the others not to shoot if the Injuns come down to visit."

Garth waited until Jeb returned before signaling his Kiowa friends. Standing up in his stirrups, he waved his arm back and forth. "Come on down, Yellow Calf," he roared. Then he backed his horse a couple of paces before halting again to fix his gaze directly upon Jeb.

Almost as if performing in a giant pageant, the line of Kiowa warriors moved slowly down the ridge, their ranks unbroken, feathers on their lances fluttering in the wind as they sat easily upon their ponies. There were so many that their line extended beyond both ends of the wagon train. A few paces behind the warriors, the other three Leach brothers followed. The warriors continued to slow-walk their horses as they came right up to the wagons. Jeb noticed that many of them carried Springfield rifles cradled in their arms. He realized at that moment that he had made a serious mistake. "Jacob! Get down!" he yelled, but it was too late.

On a silent signal, the Kiowa suddenly opened fire. The whole line fired as one, riddling the line of wagons with bullet holes. Those warriors without rifles attacked with bows. Two shots from Garth's pistol knocked Jacob over backward, dead. When Ida tried to come to his aid, he shot her as well, casually taking aim as if shooting for sport. Many of the doomed tried to dodge the deadly rifle fire by running for their lives. None escaped.

As soon as he had shouted a warning to Jacob, Jeb dropped down behind the wagon wheel, his pistol in hand. On his hands and knees, he scrambled back to find Cora. The terrified girl was clinging to the back wheel, afraid to move. "Come on!" he yelled, grabbing her by the hand and pulling her to his horse, which was tied to the tailgate. Their only chance was to try to ride out of the ravine.

"That one!" Garth shouted when he saw Jeb and Cora trying to make a run for it. "She's mine!"

In the midst of the horrifying sounds of the slaughter—gunfire, hysterical screaming of the women and horses, and blood-chilling war whoops of the Kiowa—Jeb tried to calm his terrified horse long enough to get his rifle from the saddle sling. With the weapon halfway out of the sling, he looked up to see Joe Leach charging through the milling mass of Indian ponies, straight for Cora. An instant later, Jeb was knocked back a step by the impact of a rifle slug in his chest. Grabbing the saddle horn to keep from falling, he managed to get off one shot with his pistol. The bullet caught Joe in the shoulder, causing him to howl in pain. He jerked on the reins, veering away to avoid a second shot from Jeb.

Fit to explode with anger upon seeing Joe wounded, Garth put another bullet into Jeb's chest. "Damn you!" he roared as Jeb released the saddle horn and slid to the ground. Cora, screaming in terror, dropped to her knees beside him. Her actions further incensed Garth. He had promised Joe that he would get her back, but seeing the girl lamenting so over Jeb infuriated him. "Get her!" he commanded as his brother, Jesse, rode up. Laughing like a child at the county fair, the simpleminded Jesse dragged Cora from the mortally wounded man. "Is he still alive?" Garth demanded.

Jesse looked at Jeb, then reached down and pulled the pistol from his hand. When Jeb made a feeble attempt to resist, Jesse grinned back up at Garth. "He's still alive," he said gleefully, "but not that much."

With the general roar of gunfire now tapering off to only random shots, Garth looked down the line of wagons, satisfied that the massacre was complete and no witnesses remained to tell the tale. "It's time for Cora and her sweetheart to pay up," he said. Spotting a gully cutting into the side of the ravine, he said, "Drag both of 'em over to that gully." A moment later when brother Ike joined them, Garth said, "Better go see how bad Joe's shoulder is." He hesitated a moment when he saw the Kiowa scalping the dead and plundering the wagons. There were more important concerns than Joe's shoulder at that time. Nodding toward Jeb's horse, he said, "Best grab ahold of that sorrel there before them crazy Injuns get it. I fancy that saddle."

Taking an ax from Jacob Freeman's wagon, Jesse busted a couple of boards from the wagon box and split them up for stakes. At Garth's direction, he staked Jeb and Cora out on the ground. "That oughta hold 'em for a while," Garth said. "Long enough for us to see if there's anything in them wagons we can use." Standing over Cora then, he said, "You be thinkin' about what you throwed away when you thought you could run off with this piece of shit."

In the saddle since well before daylight, Tanner figured he might have to ride a good distance to find buffalo, and he wanted to make it back to camp before dark. He was following a hunch that he would be successful in finding his prey south of the river. There had been obvious sign of buffalo in many areas that he had scouted north of the Arkansas, but no actual sighting of the massive animals. They were there, he concluded. He had just been looking in the wrong place.

The sun was already high overhead when he first saw the herd. Cresting a long ridge, he jerked Ashes to an abrupt halt, stunned by the scene below him in the shallow valley. All the tales he had heard about the sheer spectacle of a herd on the move failed to prepare him for the astonishing sight that met his eyes. The entire floor of the valley was filled with a black, bobbing stream of dusty grunting bodies, seeming to slowly flow like a mighty river toward the far end of the valley. There were so many that he laughed when he thought, *If I can get alongside, I won't even have to aim, just shoot in the general direction of the mob and I'm bound to hit one.*

He continued to sit there watching for a few minutes before making his move. The flow of heaving, bouncing bodies seemed endless, but finally the last of the herd moved into the valley. Now he loped along the top of the ridge, leading his packhorse, keeping pace with the animals below him. After deciding where he was going to intersect the herd, he stopped long enough to tie the packhorse's reins to a clump of sage, then jumped back into the saddle, drew his rifle from the sling, and gave Ashes a nudge. The big gray bounded down the slope toward the valley bottom.

The animals bringing up the rear of the herd started to run when Tanner pulled up beside them, causing a ripple in the dark stream of bodies as those ahead began to run in response. Tanner selected a medium-sized cow and, holding the reins in his teeth, leveled his rifle and took aim. Two shots behind the front leg brought the buffalo down and tumbled her, head over rump. It would have been easy to shoot five more with his remaining ammunition, but one buffalo was all he needed. He pulled Ashes aside, and headed back to butcher his kill.

Butchering his kill was not an easy task. It took him most of the afternoon to skin the animal and load as much of the meat as he could carry on the packhorse and Ashes. *There's gotta be a knack to this,* he thought, one he would have to learn. He felt certain the Indians must surely know a faster method. In spite of this, however, he felt satisfied with himself and the hunt. There was a lot of meat packed away. It would be well received by Jacob's company.

Taking a look at the sun, he set a course he figured to be a good bet to intersect the wagon train near the end of its day's travel. It was a long ride back to the Arkansas and the Santa Fe Trail, a lot of time to consider the recent change of events that had taken place in camp. He still found it amazing that Jeb had apparently found true love at last. The thought almost brought a chuckle—Jeb

Hawkins, finally tamed by a female. It was going to take some getting used to, having a woman along on the trail.

It was getting on toward dusk when he saw the smoke. It struck him as odd that there appeared to be more smoke than the campfires would ordinarily generate. Still at least a mile or two distant, he nudged Ashes to a comfortable lope, hoping to gain the camp with his fresh meat before the evening meals were prepared. Unable to see the camp after riding about a quarter of an hour, he realized that it was hidden from his view on the other side of a low ridge.

Driving Ashes straight up over the ridge, he pulled the horse to a sliding stop at the top, unprepared for the grim sight that met his eyes. Below him, in a narrow ravine, the wagons of Jacob Freeman's company sat idle, not in a circle as customary but still in line of travel. Horses and mules lay slaughtered in their traces. The ravine was strewn with the bodies of the company at various distances from the wagons, testimony to unsuccessful attempts to escape by some, while most were slain right there in the wagons. The smoke that had led him to the scene of the massacre had come from the smoldering ruins of several of the wagons.

The ghastly sight was almost too much for him to comprehend, and it took a few moments before he could realize the full meaning of it. When his mind began to function rationally again, his first thought was of Jeb. Kicking Ashes hard, he dropped the packhorse's rope and descended into the ravine at a gallop. At the bottom, the grisly scene only became worse. The dead were strewn everywhere, hacked and mutilated—men, women, and children. None had been spared.

Dismounting, he hurried to a wagon he recognized as Jacob Freeman's. Climbing up on the wheel, he was stopped abruptly by the sight of Jacob lying behind the seat, his bloody face sagging from the loss of his scalp. Behind him, at the back of the wagon, was Ida's body, a bloody clump of torn clothing. He felt a sick churning in the pit of his stomach when he thought of the horror the gentle woman had endured in her final moments. He looked around him, searching for Jeb, puzzled that the wagons showed no signs of bolting out of line. Wagon sheets were riddled with bullet holes and an occasional arrow shaft lay broken beside a wagon box. It was as if they had simply sat there to be massacred. He stepped down from the wheel and began a wagon-by-wagon search of the train.

It was a carnage he had not seen since Waynesboro, and it was magnified in horror by the inhuman mutilation, for the evidence pointed to an Indian massacre. Still, there was no sign of Jeb. *Had he managed to escape?* he wondered. He did not see the sorrel Jeb rode among the slaughtered horses, so there was some hope. As he searched the wagons for sign of survivors, he realized that he had not found Cora either. This fact served to encourage his hopes, for if Jeb had had a chance to escape, he would have taken Cora with him.

His hopes were destroyed a short time later when he came upon a gully near the head of the train. There he found Jeb and Cora. Both were staked out flat on the ground, Jeb with a dozen or more bullet holes in his body, Cora with her throat gaping crazily from the slash of a knife. From the slashes on Jeb's face and arms, it appeared that he had been subjected to a great deal of torture before his execution. The same could be said for the hapless girl.

Staggered by the brutal slaying, Tanner took a few steps backward and sat down on the side of the gully. "Damn, Jeb . . ." he moaned. "Damn. I wasn't here to watch your back this time. I'm sorry, partner." He sat there for a long time, until the fading light of evening stirred him to move. Trying to understand the reasoning God employed when allowing such things to happen, he was at a loss as to what to do. Revenge? That was his thought. But against whom? The Indians? Which Indians? Kiowa? Comanche? Cheyenne? He shook his head in sorrow. He couldn't seek revenge against a band of Indians.

With darkness coming on, he cut Jeb and Cora loose from the stakes. Finding a shovel in one of the wagons, he went to work digging a grave, determined to at least give his friend a decent burial. He dug it big enough to put Jeb and Cora in together. When it was finished, he tried to say a prayer over the grave, but ended it rather abruptly when he began to choke over the words.

With his friend in the ground, he paused to consider what he should do about the rest of the wagon train company. He wasn't prepared to dig graves for that many people, so he decided to gather all he could find, lay them in rows in the wagons, and set them ablaze. He decided it was the best he could do, better than simply leaving them to be eaten by scavengers. With a full moon ascending over the ridge, he set about his grim chore.

It was a sorrowful task. He couldn't be sure he had accounted for all the members of the train, and he wasn't familiar enough to know who was married to whom, or which children belonged to which adults. So he laid them all in the wagons, and set one wagon after another on fire. It was close to sunup when he lifted the last body he could find into the one wagon left to burn. Shaking the can of coal oil he had taken from one of the wagons, he was wondering if there was enough left to start a proper fire when he heard a faint murmur.

Grabbing his rifle, he dropped to one knee and listened. After a moment, he heard it again, but this time he identified it as a human voice, a woman's. Straining to see through the darkness outside the glow of the fires, he called out, "Where are you? It's me, Tanner Bland."

"Here," came the weak reply.

He quickly followed the sound to a gully grown up with sage. There, lying against the side of the trench, he found Janie Reece. Bloodied and battered, she had been partially scalped, and when Tanner tried to pick her up, she screamed in pain. More dead than alive, she protested, begging to be left where she was. Tanner saw no choice but to do his best to comfort her final passing, for it was apparent that her moments were short.

"Floyd," she forced painfully. "The others, anybody alive?"

"No ma'am," Tanner replied gently. "You're the only one alive."

"It was the Leaches," she gasped, each word seeming to require all her strength.

"What?" Tanner blurted in shocked surprise. "The Leaches? You mean they did this?"

"Them and their Injun friends," she answered in between labored breaths. "We thought they wanted to trade, but they just started shooting. We didn't have time to defend ourselves. They just started killing everything in sight." Exhausted with the effort to talk, she sank back against the side of the gully.

Burning with the merciless image of the massacre in his mind, he fought to remain calm. "You just lay still now. I'll go fetch some water and we'll see if we can't tend to your wounds." She said nothing in response, but her eyes opened wide, seeming to stare at him. He left her then and went down to the river to soak his bandanna in water. When he returned to the stricken woman, he found her still staring up at him with eyes no longer seeing. She was dead.

Janie Reece's body was the last one he laid in the wagon. When it finally caught fire after several attempts to start it, Tanner sat down wearily to consider what had taken place on that day. The early-morning light was eerily enhanced by the glow of the burning funeral wagons. He supposed it could be seen for miles, but he was too tired to care. He continued to sit there for a while, thinking about his carefree partner, lying with his new-found love in a shallow grave some thirty yards away. Then he turned his concentration toward the murderous creatures who were responsible for this massacre of innocent people. The thought of Garth Leach and his brothers turned his blood to molten lava in his veins, flowing hot for revenge. Montana goldfields would have to wait. He knew where his trail had to lead.

The incessant whinny of his horse reminded him then that he had left the gelding to stand saddled all night. Forgotten until that moment also was his packhorse, laden with fresh-killed meat. With his mind clear now, he got up to take care of his horses. After pulling the saddle off Ashes, he untied the buffalo meat, letting all but a portion of it drop to the ground. *The buzzards can feed off this,* he thought. He cooked some of the meat for his breakfast before closing his eyes for a few hours' sleep.

He awakened with the sun high in the morning sky. Irritated that he had slept so long, he saddled Ashes and hitched the lead rope for the packhorse to the saddle. After watering them, he left the horses to graze while he searched the ravine for tracks. It was not difficult to see that the raiders had descended into the ravine from the same ridge as he had the night before. He had not been looking for tracks, or he might have noticed. Now he was more intent upon seeing which direction the raiders had taken. The trail was easy enough, once he found which end of the narrow defile they had exited.

Judging by the multitude of tracks, it had been a sizable raiding party, and they had left the scene of the massacre to head north. On foot, leading his horses, he started out after the war party, closely scouting the trail until he found the confirmation he sought. Scattered among the many unshod prints were tracks left by shod horses. How many horses had been stolen was hard to tell, but he felt secure in speculating that some of the shod tracks were left by the four men he hunted.

He followed the trail for most of the morning before reaching a stream where the war party had obviously paused for a short time before changing directions and starting out again back to the east. Tanner started to follow, but then noticed that a small number of shod horses had split out a short distance from the main body. He interpreted that to mean the four white men had a tendency to ride together, apart from the Indians. In his mind, he pictured the four Leach brothers, the three youngest trailing Garth, a pack of wolves that even the Indians had best beware. With now only one purpose in life, to kill this pack of wolves, he followed the wide trail over the grass-covered hills.

Chapter 10

Garth Leach felt well pleased with the results of the raid on the wagon train as he rode back between Ike and Yellow Calf. Primarily instigated for revenge purposes, it had provided some surprising gains. True, he had derived a certain amount of pleasure in the punishment of Cora and Jeb Hawkins, but the real bonus came with the acquisition of Hawkins' saddle. Fine Spanish leather, it was too fine for the likes of a drifter like Hawkins. *He probably stole it,* Garth thought. *It fits my fanny just right, too.* The real surprise came with the discovery of the canvas sack in the saddlebag. *If I'd known that jasper was carrying a sack of gold coins, he'd have been dead a long time ago.*

"What are you grinnin' about?" Ike asked, noticing the unusual expression on his brother's face.

Garth gave him a wink. "I'll tell you later," he said under his breath. As yet, no one else knew about the gold coins, and he preferred not to tell the Kiowa chief riding beside him. Yellow Calf might want him to share the coins, and Garth knew the savage chief had no notion of the value of the gold. He might want them just because they were shiny. *Besides,* Garth thought, *Yellow Calf ought to be pleased enough.* The raid had resulted in horses and some additional weapons, as well as food supplies and tools. All things considered, everybody should be pleased with the raid, except Joe, who was shuffling along behind him, moaning over the bullet in his shoulder.

"Damn fool," Garth blurted, causing Ike to give him a puzzled look again. Before Ike could question him, he said, "Joe—damn fool for gittin' hisself shot."

"Well," Ike grunted, "he ain't got a helluva lot more sense than Jesse." He rode on in silence for a few minutes before voicing another concern. "I've been wonderin' about that other feller, that partner of Hawkins. I'm wonderin' where the hell is he? He oughtn't a'been too far away—mighta heard the shootin'."

Garth grunted, unconcerned. "Hell, what if he did? Even if he finds 'em, there ain't nobody to tell him what happened. He'll just think it was Injuns."

"Maybe," Ike conceded, "but I'da liked it better if he had been there, so's we coulda put his ass under with the rest of 'em. I don't trust that feller. He's too damn quiet and a lot more dangerous than his partner."

"Hell, he ain't nothin' to worry about," Garth scoffed. "I expect he'll hightail it outta these parts when he finds his friends layin' there with their topknots missin'."

When they approached the ribbon of trees that lined the banks of the river where Yellow Calf's village lay, the chief rode on ahead to join his warriors' triumphant return. As Garth had said, Yellow Calf was greatly pleased with the success of the raid. He had suffered no losses, and only a few wounded. The massacre added to his esteem as a war chief.

Holding their horses to a walk as the whooping Kiowa charged into their village, the four brothers took their time reaching the camp. "When are we gettin' the hell outta here?" Ike wanted to know. "We've got about all we're gonna get from Yellow Calf, and I don't cotton to hangin' around any longer."

"Hell," Jesse piped up, "I wouldn't mind hangin' around a while longer. Maybe we could go on another raid with Yellow Calf's Injuns."

"I swear," Ike replied, "I believe you got some wild Injun blood in you."

"We're leavin' in the morning," Garth said, settling the matter. "Just as soon as we load them buffalo hides in the wagons, we'll head on out to Fort Lyon and sell 'em. Then we'll head up to Denver City maybe."

"What about my shoulder?" Joe asked. Up to then, not one of his brothers seemed to care if he was suffering with the painful wound. "I'm hurtin' awful bad."

Garth did not harbor a great deal of compassion for his youngest brother. "Stop your bellyachin'," he replied. "You ain't gonna die from a little lead in your shoulder. When we get to Yellow Calf's, Ike'll dig it out."

"I wish there was a doctor around here," Joe complained.

"Ike's all the doctor you need," Garth said. "If you'da kept your eye on the man with the gun instead of lookin' at Cora, you wouldn't have a pistol slug in your damn shoulder."

"We could let the Kiowa medicine man take it out," Jesse teased, enjoying his brother's plight. "He'd probably wave an eagle feather over it a couple times, then chop it out with a war ax."

"I've a mind to put a bullet in *your* shoulder," Joe threatened, causing Jesse to chuckle again. The wound was no laughing matter to the youngest of the four brothers. It was painful. The shoulder was swollen and inflamed all around the bullet hole. There was no question that the bullet would have to be removed.

"Oh, sweet Jesus," Joe Leach cried out when Ike's blade probed into the hole made by Jeb's bullet, his back arching in an effort to pull away. The few Kiowa who had gathered around to watch the procedure grunted in response.

"Hold him, Jesse," Ike said as his incision caused a fresh stream to spread over blood already dried around the wound. He pushed the skinning knife in deeper, searching for the lead slug. To Joe he said, "This ain't nothin'. If we waited till this thing really got red and puffy, then you'd have somethin' to moan about."

"Your cuttin' is worse than it was to get shot," Joe complained. "Give me another shot of that whiskey."

Jesse released one hand long enough to reach the jug and hold it for Joe to take a long drink. He grinned as most of the fiery liquid spilled down Joe's chin. "You done drunk enough to knock most men out."

"I ain't had enough to dull that knife yet," he gasped. "Gawdam!" he yelled when Ike moved the tip of the blade, still probing.

"I felt it that time," Ike said. "Now, if I can just work it loose a little bit."

This proved to be the most painful part of the operation, for Ike kept working the bullet back and forth, trying to dislodge it from the muscle. It was too much for Joe. He actually enjoyed a ghoulish rush from watching others mutilated, but when it was his flesh that was being slaughtered, it was a different matter. "Hurry up," he pleaded. "I don't feel so good." It might have been better for him had he not watched the knife probing around in the bloody mess Ike had created out of the neat black bullet hole. As it was, however, the pain, the sight of his own blood, and the excessive quantity of rotgut whiskey he had consumed rendered him queasy.

"Uh-oh," Jesse warned, "I can smell it comin'." He released his hold on Joe and jumped back to avoid the disgusting gusher that erupted from Joe's mouth.

Ike was not so lucky, being the recipient of the major portion of his brother's stomach contents. Revolted by Joe's sudden discharge, he fairly thrust his knife in angry reprisal, cutting the muscle away from the bullet. Seeing the slug free then, he picked it out with his fingers and flung it at his patient. "There's your damn bullet," he roared. With only a glance at Jesse, rolling on the ground laughing, he stormed out of the tipi, heading for the river.

Pulling himself up on all fours, Joe yelled after his brother, "Don't leave me like this, dammit. I need a bandage or something. I'm bleedin' like hell."

One of the Kiowa spectators, like the other warriors, puzzled by the bizarre treatment of a bullet wound, turned and left the tipi. A few minutes later, he returned with a young Indian woman. Looking at Joe, he pointed to his shoulder. "She fix," he said. The woman immediately knelt down and began to cleanse the wound with a wet cloth she had brought with her. In a short time, the wound was cleaned and bandaged. She favored Joe with a faint smile, and quickly withdrew from the tipi. The Kiowa who had brought her nodded his head in approval before he turned and followed her.

At sunup the following morning, Garth was ready to depart the Kiowa village. The wagons loaded with hides stood ready to roll, with Jesse driving one and Ike the other. The only missing brother was Joe. Irritated, Garth stalked into the tipi to find Joe still in his blanket. "Get your ass outta here," Garth roared. "I ain't waitin' around here for your lazy ass."

Joe made no attempt to get up. "Dammit, Garth, my shoulder's hurtin' too much to ride. I need a day or two more, and I got a bad sick from that rotten whiskey I drunk last night."

Disgusted by his brother's show of frailty, Garth shot back, "Your shoulder's hurtin'? Well, I ain't waitin' while you lay around this camp. If you ain't somethin'— hell, you won't be settin' on your damn shoulder. Get up from there!"

Showing a stubborn streak himself, Joe replied. "I said I ain't fit to ride yet. I'm stayin' here for a couple of days."

Garth was about to grab him and drag him from his bed, but changed his mind. "Suit yourself," he finally said. "Me and the boys are leavin' right now." That said,

he turned on his heel, thinking of a three-way split of the
hides and coins.

"I'll catch up with you at Fort Lyon," Joe called after
him, but Garth made no reply. Joe thought about the wis-
dom of his decision, but he told himself that his shoulder
did need more rest. Besides, the young Kiowa woman
who tended his wound had a way about her that sparked
his interest. Outside, Garth and his other two brothers
said their good-byes, and soon Joe heard the sound of Ike
and Jesse calling the mules to their task.

As he had hoped, the young woman came to him in
the afternoon to look at his wound. Earlier, food had
been brought for him by an older woman. She spoke
enough English to tell him that the young woman was
Little Elk's daughter, Wren.

"Good?" Wren asked, nodding toward the bandage.

"It's sore," Joe said. "Not so good."

"Not good?"

Trying his best to converse with her with hand motions and the few words she knew, he finally made her
understand that he was weak and needed more rest.

"I come back," she said after changing his bandage.

"Yeah, you come back," he said as he watched her
leave, his eyes focused upon her slender behind. She was
little more than a girl, like Cora was when he took her
from her daddy. Joe preferred them that way.

He had several other visitors during the day, including
Yellow Calf. The Kiowa chief was more concerned with
the possibility of acquiring more ammunition for his rifles than the progress of Joe's healing. He was polite to

the youngest of the Leach brothers because of that need for cartridges. In truth, he had no respect for the shifty-eyed white man, primarily because of Joe's capitulation to a simple shoulder wound. A real warrior would have been ready to fight the next day after such a slight wound, instead of lying around the tipi being attended to by women.

As far as Joe was concerned, the shoulder was already feeling much improved since the bullet had been removed. In fact, he planned to leave the following day, but only after he had taken care of a little piece of business that had dominated his thoughts ever since Wren had changed his bandage that afternoon. He went to sleep that night thinking about the slender Kiowa girl.

The next morning, she came, just as she had promised. After examining his wound, she smiled at him, nodding for emphasis, and said, "Good, wound good."

"Yeah," he replied. "Wound good. Now I need to wash up, but I'm gonna need some help." She could not understand what he was saying, so he tried to convey the message with motions. It required several attempts on his part, but she finally understood that he wanted her to help him down to the river.

"Good," she said, although puzzled that he should need help. "I take."

He wasted no time strapping on his gun belt and following Wren out of the tipi. Several of the villagers nodded politely to him as he passed through the ring of lodges. He barely acknowledged their greetings, his eyes captured by the trim behind moving briskly toward the water's edge. When she turned to lead him toward a few men bathing in the river, he quickly took her arm and pulled her toward a willow thicket farther upstream. Making motions to show that he was shy, he was able to convince her that he sought privacy for his bath. She paused, finally understanding his message, and nodded up and down vigorously. Then she pointed toward the willows, a questioning look upon her face. He answered with a wide grin and nodded in reply.

Slightly amused by the strange behavior of the white man, she led him behind the screen of trees to a grassy bank, smiling to herself that it was the place where the women bathed. Once out of sight of the village, she stopped, pointed toward the riverbank, then turned to leave him.

"Wait a minute," he blurted, and grabbed her arm.

Though unsuspecting before, she recognized the leer now in his eyes as he pulled her toward the bank, his malevolent grin plainly conveying his intentions. "No!" she spat emphatically, shaking her head sternly.

"No, hell," Joe replied. "You little tease, lookin' at me so sweet. You knew damn well what I wanted, and you damn sure came back behind the trees with me." He clamped hard on her arm and tried to force her down on the ground. "If you think I'm gonna beg you for it, you're crazy as hell." Thinking to take what he wanted, he grabbed her skirt and tried to pull it up. She screamed for help, but immediately received a blow to her face from his fist. Stunned momentarily, she sank to the ground. "Damn!" he cursed when he felt a stab of pain in his wound as a result of the punch. It failed to deter him from his evil intent, though, for his desire for the slender Indian girl lying helpless at his feet was the only thought in his mind.

Dropping to his knees before her, he snatched feverishly at her skirt, pulling it up to reveal slender thighs above her doeskin leggings. Wild now with lust, he fumbled with his belt while she began to recover from the blow that had sent her reeling. Horrified, she looked up to see her assailant hurriedly pulling down his pants. She started to scream again, but it was quickly choked off by his hand on her throat. "You're just like Cora," he said. "Both of you pretend you don't want it."

Her eyes wide with horror, she struggled for breath as he forced his way between her legs. The bright morning sun seemed to suddenly fade over her, making her think she was losing consciousness. In fact, it was a shadow, caused by the formidable figure that suddenly appeared behind her attacker. In the next instant, the hand that threatened to crush her throat was released as Joe's head was yanked violently back. Pulling him forcefully off the girl, Tanner dragged the would-be rapist several yards by the hair of his head before slamming him to the ground.

His arms flailing helplessly, yelping in pain like a whipped dog, Joe rolled over and scrambled to his feet, only to be knocked flat on his back by a crushing right hand. Stunned for a moment, he reached for the pistol in his belt, forgetting that he had unbuckled his belt and his pants were down around his knees. Stricken with cold fear, he started whimpering, knowing that it was his executioner he was facing. Crying out fearfully, he tried to scramble up on his knees in an attempt to run. Tanner calmly stepped forward and, with a solid kick, sent him sprawling again. This time, Joe pulled his knees up like a baby and started moaning.

"I counted seven bullet holes in Jeb Hawkins' body," Tanner pronounced solemnly. "Was that before or after the knife slashes on his arms and face?"

"It wasn't me that done it," Joe blubbered between sobs. "It was Jesse and Garth. It's them you want."

"Is that so?" Tanner responded sarcastically. "Then you had nothin' to do with it. Right?"

"That's right," Joe quickly replied, seeing a glimmer of hope. "I had nothin' to do with it—killed Hawkins and Cora, too, they did, and then they went to Fort Lyon."

"Much obliged," Tanner said softly, his rifle still trained on the man cowering at his feet.

Joe's eyes opened wide with newfound hope. "I didn't have nothin' to do with it. You can let me go."

Tanner stared at the pleading coward for a long moment before speaking again. "I'm gonna let you go to hell," he said softly, cocking his rifle. "Jeb is waitin' for you."

The sudden crack of the rifle caused the terrified Kiowa girl to jump. Rendered almost paralyzed moments before by the drama taking place before her, she now backed away from the riverbank as Joe Leach's body slumped in death, a neat bullet hole in his forehead. Fearful of what might follow, she could only stare at the grim stranger, who turned now to look at her.

"Don't be afraid, miss. I ain't gonna hurt you."

She could not understand the words, but the look in his eyes and the tone of his voice told her that she had nothing to fear from the tall white man. She nodded in reply.

Knowing now that the other three he hunted were on their way to Fort Lyon, he had no more time to waste. It could only be a matter of minutes before someone from the girl's village would appear. If they had not heard her scream, they would surely have heard the rifle shot. He had less time than he thought, for before he could turn to leave, two men of the village appeared at the edge of the willows. They were followed almost immediately by a half dozen or more armed warriors. "Well, Jeb," he whispered, "I sent one of 'em your way, but I reckon I'll be right behind him."

Stopped abruptly by the sight of the broad-shouldered white man, standing solidly before them, his feet spread wide, his rifle held ready, one of the two Kiowa men held up his hand to halt the warriors. The girl ran to meet her father. Little Elk looked down at Wren, then at the body lying by the riverbank. Then his eyes were drawn back to the mysterious stranger, who stood watching him like a silent avenging spirit. He glanced down to see that the morning sun had cast the spirit's shadow toward his feet like a dark finger pointing directly to him. Thinking this might be a warning from the spirit of the sun, he cautioned the warriors behind him. "Wait. Let us find out what manner of man this is before we kill him."

Hearing what her father said, Wren spoke in Tanner's defense. "He saved my life," she cried. "The dirty one with the shoulder wound attacked me and was choking me." She pointed toward Tanner then. "This one killed him."

"Ahh," Little Elk murmured thoughtfully. Looking again at Tanner, he was still cautious. The sun behind Tanner caused his face to lie in deep shadow from the hat pulled low on his forehead. The effect was almost eerie. Little Elk decided it best to converse with the man in white man's talk. "You did not harm the girl?"

"I came for this one only," Tanner replied, pointing at Joe's body with the muzzle of his rifle.

"Ahh," Little Elk murmured again. Turning to the others, he spoke in the Kiowa tongue. "He did not harm my daughter. He came only for the worthless white man. I think he may have been sent from the spirit world."

Having heard the rifle shot, others came to the riverbank, led by the chief, Yellow Calf. Surprised to find the lone white man standing motionless and silent, his face absent expression, Yellow Calf immediately looked to Little Elk for explanation. Little Elk quickly spoke. "I think he was sent from the spirit world to save my daughter and to kill the wounded white man."

Little Elk's words jolted the Kiowa chief's sensibilities. Thinking of the murderous raid he and his warriors had just made upon the white wagon train, he took another long look at Tanner, still standing apparently fearless as if ready to battle the entire village. Speaking to Little Elk again, he said, "Maybe he has come because of the white people we killed."

"He said he came only for the white man," Little Elk repeated.

Yellow Calf was inclined to kill the strange man, but Little Elk was a wise man, and what he said might be true. It would be best to be cautious. Turning back to

Tanner, he asked in English, "Is it true you were sent to kill the white man?"

Tanner, standing patiently for the shooting to start, was confused by the apparent discussion between the two Kiowa elders. He assumed that, seeing him standing ready with his repeating rifle, they were discussing the number of lives that might be lost before he could be slain. Upon hearing Yellow Calf's question to him, he responded simply, "I came for this one." He pointed again at the body.

His answer caused a ripple of murmurs among the crowd of people now gathered. Yellow Calf looked at Little Elk and nodded solemnly. He, too, was convinced that, man or spirit, Tanner had been sent to protect the girl and rid the earth of a vile and evil white man. Speaking in English again, he said to Tanner, "We thank you for the girl's life. Go in peace."

Surprised, and completely confused by the chief's words, Tanner did not immediately withdraw. He hesitated for a moment while he thought the situation over. His mind, up to that point, had been dedicated totally to revenge upon those who had murdered Jeb and the others. This included the Kiowa warriors facing him now. Moments before, he was resolved to taking as many of the guilty warriors as he could with him to hell. His mind, now racing with thought, battled with the decision. Jeb's actual murderers were the Leaches, and his desire to punish them reigned above all others. If he walked away from this riverbank now, he could still hunt them down. These Indians, he decided, were only the instruments of murder. The guilty parties were the Leaches. It would be a sin to let them get away with the massacre they instigated. With that conclusion, he turned and walked slowly back down the riverbank.

No one stirred in the hushed gathering of Kiowa. Every eye was on the back of the mysterious stranger sent from the spirit world. Only when his head dropped below the steep embankment and he was gone did anyone speak. Little Elk put his arm around his daughter. "You must remember this, little one. In one moon, we will celebrate the Sun Dance. We must remember to dance for this day."

Out of sight of the group of Kiowa warriors, Tanner expected them to change their minds at any moment. In case they decided to come after him, he walked into the shallow water to a rock near the edge, then stepped from rock to rock before jumping back to the bank on a grassy plot. From there, he broke into an easy lope back to the bushes where his horses were tied.

In the few minutes that passed after Tanner's departure, the gathering of Kiowa gradually broke up with much talk about what had just happened. Most of the crowd moved over to examine the body of Joe Leach. Soon his body was stripped of weapons and anything else of value. Yellow Calf, Little Elk, and some of the others walked down to the river, following the path taken by the stranger.

"See!" Little Elk exclaimed, pointing to the footprints left in the soft sand next to the water. "They lead into the water."

Yellow Calf nodded solemnly. "He was sent by the spirit of the river," he said.

Chapter 11

"Gawdam, there's a whole lot of nothin' in this country," Jesse Leach exclaimed when Garth rode up beside the wagon.

"Seems that way," Garth agreed. They had been traveling for days with very little variation in the country before them, rolling hills of grass broken occasionally by ribbons of trees that told of the existence of a stream. They were approaching one such ribbon at the time. "I told Ike to pull his wagon over by yonder stream. You follow him, and we'll make camp there. It's gettin' late in the day, and God knows when we'll strike another stream."

"I'll be damn glad when we get shed of these wagons," Jesse lamented. "My backside is sore from ridin' this seat."

"We oughtn't be too many more days from Fort Lyon," Garth said. "The way I figure it, we oughta strike the river sometime tomorrow." They had decided to cut back toward the southwest a little more the day before to intercept the Arkansas and the Santa Fe Trail again.

From there, it couldn't be much farther to Colorado and Fort Lyon.

While Ike and Jesse pulled the wagons up side by side and unhitched the mules, Garth took the saddle off his horse and led it to the stream to drink. "We'd best hobble these horses," he called out to his brothers. They had taken care to hobble their horses every night, but the mules had shown no inclination to stray, so they just let them out to graze with the horses.

Later that evening, when they were finishing their supper, Jesse wondered aloud. "Reckon how come Joe ain't caught up with us yet? He shoulda caught us two days ago."

"Damn fool probably couldn't follow our trail," Ike commented.

"Shit," Jesse replied, "anybody could follow the tracks these wagons make. I bet he's found him a little Injun gal back there in that Kiowa camp."

"We'd better start watchin' our back trail a little more," Ike said. "You ain't lying when you say anybody can follow our wagon tracks."

"Shit," Garth snorted, "you're thinkin' about that partner of Hawkins, ain't you? Like I said before, I expect he's halfway back to Omaha by now."

"Maybe," Ike replied, "but he ain't the only one we've got to worry about. There's Comanche, Cheyenne, and Kiowa out here lookin' for scalps." Ike had concern for hostile Indians, but Tanner Bland was the one that worried his mind.

Garth paused to emit a loud belch, then said, "I don't

miss Joe a damn bit, but I do kinda miss Cora. She was a pretty good cook."

"Yeah, when Joe left her alone long enough," Jesse said. "Reckon why he shot her back there? Hell, we'd still have a cook if Joe hadn't kilt her."

"He coulda taught her a lesson with just a good hidin' with a stout stick," Ike offered, "but Joe's Joe. He couldn't stand the thought of anybody else dippin' in his sugar bowl."

Jesse laughed. "Hell, I dipped into that bowl a time or two. Cora didn't like it, but I told her I'd kill her if she told." He chuckled again at the thought of cheating his brother. "I miss that more'n I miss her cookin'."

Garth and Jesse were awakened the next morning by the angry swearing of their brother Ike. When Garth asked what had him so hot, Ike told him, "The damn mules, that's what!" he complained. "Two of 'em run off while we was sleepin'."

"They ain't ever done that before," Jesse said, rubbing the sleep from his eyes. "Maybe some Injuns stole 'em."

"You half-wit," Ike snapped. "If it was Injuns, they'da most likely took the horses, and probably scalped us in our beds to boot." He was plainly still angry over Garth's lack of caution. "If we'da took turns standin' guard like I said, we wouldn't be without two mules this mornin'."

"Fussin' ain't gonna get it done," Garth said. "Get saddled up. We got to find them mules. If we don't, we're gonna have to leave one of the wagons." Giving it further thought, he said, "Me and Ike'll saddle up. Jesse, you stay here with the wagons."

They split up to search, Garth to the northeast, Ike to

the northwest, since a few tracks were found heading generally in a northern direction. Jesse, content to stay in camp and drink coffee, made himself comfortable and awaited their return. Both riders were back by late morning, both giving up when there was no sign of the missing mules to be found. With no other option, they loaded all the hides into one wagon with what whiskey and ammunition they had, and set out again for Fort Lyon.

Riding away from the Kiowa camp, Tanner had put a sizable distance between himself and the Indians before circling to pick up a trail. He had not scouted much ground before he found what he was looking for—two sets of wagon ruts, still clearly etched in the short-grass prairie. He paused briefly to look far ahead in the direction indicated. Then, his mind focused on the task he had set for himself, he started out on his trail of vengeance. He rode for two days, following the wagon tracks over the endless prairie, from campsite to noon stop, to campsite again, stopping only when it became too dark to see. He could tell by the time of day he reached the campsites that he was rapidly gaining on his prey. Along his journey, he often sighted antelope in the distance, bounding away as he approached, but there was no thought about hunting, at least not for antelope. His life had been reduced to one purpose, and he went about it doggedly. If he had been able to follow the tracks in the dark, he would have ridden on into the night.

He had been in the saddle no longer than a few hours on the third day when he followed the wagon tracks toward a thin line of cottonwood trees that apparently marked a stream. Riding up over a low ridge, he pulled Ashes to a halt. There, by the stream, stood an abandoned wagon. The sight that made him hesitate to continue on, however, was the four Indian ponies beside it, their riders busily scavenging through the wagon.

His initial thought was that he may have been cheated. But there was only the one wagon, so it could have merely been abandoned by the Leaches, for whatever reason. He realized at that moment that he would not be satisfied to have the three remaining brothers dead. They had to be dead by his hand.

He remained stationary on the ridge for a few minutes longer, trying to decide what to do, whether to take a wide detour around the Indians or to ride down to see for himself that there were no bodies lying there. He hesitated too long, for one of the Indians suddenly stopped, and looking in his direction, pointed. Like him, they seemed undecided as to what they should do. The sudden appearance of a white man alone north of the Arkansas was certainly unexpected. Maybe he wasn't alone, and in fact was a scout for a large party of soldiers that followed. Maybe the wagon they had found was his wagon. There was good reason to be cautious until there were answers for some of these questions.

For several long minutes, white man and Indians stood transfixed, watching each other. Still cautious, the four Cheyenne hunters jumped on their ponies and withdrew a few yards from the wagon. There, they pulled up again, still watching the lone white man on the ridge. After a short discussion, they wheeled their ponies, rode

off through the cottonwoods beside the stream, and disappeared beyond the ridge.

Tanner remained still for a few moments after the
Indians had gone. When it appeared they weren't coming
back, he descended the ridge to have a look at the abandoned wagon. Upon walking around the wagon a couple
of times, he could see no apparent damage. It looked to
be a perfectly good wagon, causing him to wonder why
it had been left behind. *Had to be the mules,* he decided,
and peered inside to see a few scattered worthless items
that had been rejected by the Indians. There was nothing
that was of any interest to him.

Close to the stream, he saw the signs of a campfire. A
few yards away there were fresh droppings where the
horses and mules had evidently grazed. Extending his
circle a little farther out, he found tracks leading away
from the stream. The depth of the wagon ruts verified
that the one remaining wagon was now carrying both
loads. The tracks also told him that the Leaches had
changed their course to one of a more southerly direction, probably to strike the Santa Fe Trail, he figured.
Looking at the tracks, he felt a renewed sense of urgency,
for it was obvious to him that he was not far behind the
three murderous brothers.

"He is one man, alone," Burning Tree said as the four
Cheyenne hunters peered down from the western ridge
that bordered the shallow valley.

"With two horses," Walks Fast added. On hands and
knees in the prairie grass, he moved closer to the crest of
the ridge to get a better look.

Upon first spotting the white man on the ridge above them, they had been undecided on whether or not to run. At Burning Tree's suggestion, they decided to circle around to the east to see if there was, indeed, a cavalry patrol following the white man. He wore no uniform, but the army scouts were usually not soldiers, so he could have been a scout. Now, as they gazed down, watching him searching the wagon and campsite, they knew he was alone.

"I think he looks for the others who left the wagon," Crow Killer said. "I say we should kill him and take his horses."

Walks Fast nodded his agreement, emphasized with a grunt. The other two hunters quickly agreed as well, and all four crawled away from the top of the ridge to return to their ponies.

With one foot in the stirrup, and about to throw the other over the saddle, Tanner suddenly flinched when he heard the snap of the rifle ball pass over his head. Almost instantly, he heard the sharp report of the rifle that fired the bullet. Without taking time to think about it, he threw his leg over and kicked Ashes hard. The big horse responded immediately, charging full speed toward the end of the valley, with the four Cheyenne hunters racing down the opposite slope in an effort to cut him off.

Lying low on the big gray's neck, one hand holding the packhorse's lead rope, Tanner implored the horse for more speed as rifle balls cracked around him from behind. *Damn!* He cursed his carelessness. *I should have made sure they were gone.* It was too late to do anything but run now, for there was no place in the shallow valley to take cover. The trees bordering the stream would have been the only choice to make a stand, but they were too far away when the first shot was fired. He had to put his faith in the gray gelding's stamina.

Looking back at his pursuers, he realized that Ashes was losing the race. The increasing strain on his right arm told him that the packhorse was holding him back. With the Indians steadily gaining on him, he had no choice but to drop the packhorse's rope. Ashes responded by increasing his speed, but Tanner could see that the big horse was beginning to tire. Bullets began snapping closer around him, thumping the grassy plain on either side of him. Taking another quick look behind him, he saw one of his pursuers break off to chase the packhorse. The other three galloped after him, their fast Indian ponies continuing to close the distance between them and the tiring gelding. As the distance decreased, the Indians' accuracy improved, the bullets getting closer and closer until one finally ripped through Tanner's shirt, creasing his side with a fiery stinging that forced an involuntary grunt. He knew it was simply a matter of time before he caught one dead center. With no option left to him, he jerked Ashes' reins sharply over when he came to a narrow gully and pulled him to a sliding stop. Coming out of the saddle at once, he led his horse back into the gully. It was not deep enough to provide complete cover for Ashes, but Tanner figured the Indians hoped to capture the horse. Consequently, they would direct their fire away from him.

As quickly as he could, he grabbed the Blakeslee cartridge box from his saddle and scrambled up to the head of the gully. It was no more than knee-deep at the head, but it was enough to give him cover if he lay flat on his belly. Intent upon convincing his pursuers that he was not worth the risk of their lives, he took careful aim, waiting until he was absolutely sure of his target.

Crow Killer cried out sharply and tumbled over backward, landing wounded in the grass. Burning Tree and Walks Fast instinctively veered off to seek cover from the white man's rifle. Driving their ponies hard, they made their way over a high swale, where they dismounted and clambered back up to firing positions. Coming behind, their companion leading Tanner's packhorse stopped short when he saw Crow Killer lying wounded on the ground. The wounded Cheyenne's horse stood a few yards away, seemingly oblivious to the rifle fire now cracking back and forth between the man in the gully and the two Cheyenne behind the swale. Making a fatal decision, Black Eagle dropped the packhorse's rope and slid off his pony. Thinking to use Crow Killer's pony for cover, he ran toward his wounded comrade, keeping the horse between him and Tanner's line of fire. "I'm coming for you," Black Eagle called out to Crow Killer as he approached. Spooked by the man running toward him, Crow Killer's horse suddenly bolted, leaving Black Eagle exposed to the gully. In an instant the young Cheyenne lay dead beside his friend, a rifle slug in his forehead.

Burning Tree cried out in angry despair when he saw Black Eagle fall. He and Walks Fast immediately sent several rounds cracking toward the gully in response to the white man's deadly fire. Already, the price for the white man's horses was higher than they would have been willing to pay. In the gully, Tanner watched closely to pick up the muzzle blasts from the Cheyenne's rifles. As a result, his next shots were closer and closer to his attackers, sending dirt flying right before their faces.

The two Cheyenne slid back from the brink of the swale. "His gun is too good," Walks Fast said. "I don't have many cartridges left. I think maybe we had better leave this white man alone, and take Black Eagle and Crow Killer back to the village."

"I'm down to three cartridges," Burning Tree said. "I think you are right. We can't get close enough to get a good shot at him." He looked up at the sky. "It will be dark soon. I think we should wait till then, when we can get to Black Eagle and Crow Killer."

"Maybe we can't get a good shot at him, but we can get a good shot at his horse," Walks Fast pointed out. "I had hoped to capture his horse, but since we can't get close enough to kill the man, we can put him on foot."

Down in the gully, Tanner edged up closer to the lip in an attempt to keep the Indians from pinpointing his position. There had been a lull in the firing from the swale above him, and he was concerned that the two surviving warriors might be trying to circle around behind him. He looked up at the sky. The sun was already sinking low. If he could keep them at bay until dark, he would lead Ashes up the side of the ridge behind him. The thought had no sooner entered his mind when the shooting from the swale began once more. *Thunk, thunk.*

The sickening sounds of rifle balls impacting solid flesh jolted him, as Ashes screamed out in pain.

Close to panic, Tanner scrambled back to tend the wounded horse. Unable to stand because he, himself, would then be a target, he tried to pull Ashes down on his knees, only to hear two more shots rip into the horse's flesh. Mortally wounded, Ashes collapsed and rolled onto his side. Tanner, totally distraught with anger and disbelief, could do nothing to save the dying horse. He had counted on his attackers' desire to steal his horse. Unable to help beyond alleviating the horse's pain, he held his revolver to Ashes' head and ended his suffering.

Devastated by the loss of his horse, he sat there staring at the carcass for a moment before he called his mind back to the business of staying alive. Scrambling to the head of the gully again, he scanned the length of the swale across from him, searching for signs that the Indians had moved to new positions. There was no sign of them, but at least they could not approach his position without crossing fifty yards of open ground. *I guess we're just going to wait each other out,* he thought. All was quiet in the shallow valley.

When darkness finally descended upon the gully, Tanner thought about his previous plan to steal away in the night. The thought now of being out in the open prairie on foot, when his adversaries were on horseback, did not seem wise. He had to admit he didn't know enough about his enemy to predict what the Indians would do. He had shot two of their number. They might wait all night in hopes of finally killing him in retaliation. *Or,* he thought, *they might make a try at sneaking up on me at night.* In the end, he decided to risk the latter. When darkness set in, he made his way back down the gully to position himself behind his horse's carcass. With his back against the end of the gully, he sat with his rifle laid across Ashes' rump and his extra cartridges on the ground beside him.

The night seemed endless. With time now to attend to the wound in his side, he took a look at it. There was a long slash where the bullet had creased him, but he decided it was not deep enough to cause any concern. Most of the blood had already dried. His wound taken care of, he had a lot of time to think about the road that had brought him to this dreary gully in the middle of a vast prairie. There were many regrets that filled his mind, but the dominant one was the fact that he was now delayed in his pursuit of Jeb's murderers. He had been so close, and he blamed his lapse of caution for the predicament in which he now found himself. As soon as he'd seen the four Indians at the wagon he should have retreated to take cover instead of sitting there until they spotted him. Fear that Garth Leach and his brothers would escape his vengeance was the only fear Tanner had. Waiting in his fortress of horseflesh, he promised anew his vow to Jeb Hawkins that he would be avenged, no matter how long and how far. He thought of the girl, Cora, and the brutal way her wretched life had ended. The world would choke on the miserable likes of the Leach brothers if it was not rid of them. He had no other purpose in life than to exterminate them, and he was determined to do it, no matter how many Indians he had to kill in the morning. Just before dawn, thoughts of Eleanor Marshall Bland tried to creep into his sleepy brain. He immediately banned them from his mind.

Dark shadows turned to gray as morning finally approached the little valley. Soon first light dissolved the shadows, clearing the night away. Stiff and tired, he cautiously moved from his cramped position behind the carcass of his horse, lest someone might be waiting for him to show at the mouth of the gully. His rifle ready, he moved slowly toward the head of the grassy trench. There were no sounds. Scanning the swale across from him, he could see no sign of anyone. Then he discovered that the two bodies that had been on the valley floor were gone. They had been removed during the night.

The Indians had apparently quit the battle, although he found it hard to understand. Maybe he had made it too costly for them to pursue it. He could only guess. Maybe they were out of ammunition. He realized then that it was when they had shot his horse that they had decided to end the confrontation, choosing to leave him on foot in the middle of prairie. Now certain that he was alone, he walked out onto the floor of the valley and slowly turned all the way around. The prairie seemed endless in every direction. A man without a horse in this vast expanse had little hope of survival.

Walking up the swale, he found where the two Cheyenne hunters had taken positions to fire at him. Gazing back at the small gully across the narrow valley, he could understand the difficulty they'd had trying to target him. Down the other side of the swale, he found the place where their ponies had waited. Upon close inspection, he discovered the prints of more than their two ponies, and surmised that they had gathered the other three horses during the night while he sat waiting for them in the gully. Studying the ground further, he was able to pick up the Indians' trail as they left the valley. It was not as easy to follow as the deep wagon tracks he had trailed for days, but made somewhat less difficult by the presence of one set of shod prints. The thought of following the tracks on foot seemed a bit absurd, but he could think of no better alternative. "I've got to find a horse," he announced to the emptiness around him. "And the only place I know where there is one is in that direction," he added, looking north.

His decision made, he returned to the carcass in the gully to collect his belongings. It was a sad chore to leave Ashes to feed the buzzards, and he whispered a short word of thanks as he took from his saddlebags items of vital necessity—cartridges, flint and steel, and his canteen. His supply of food and coffee, along with the utensils to prepare it, had all been lost with his pack-horse. Taking the section of buffalo hide he had rolled up behind his saddle, he made a pack to carry the items, using the reins from his bridle to secure it. Deciding it was the best he could do, he paused to take a farewell look at his horse, the carcass riddled with four bullet holes, one almost directly below the "08" brand. He shook his head sadly, turned, and set out to the north at a trot, his rifle in one hand, his small pack on his back. The one thought that plagued him was that he was turning away from the Leach brothers' trail.

Chapter 12

A night without sleep and a day and a half without food began to take their toll on Tanner. With the sun directly overhead in a cloudless summer sky, he was no longer trotting, but still walking at a steady pace. He pushed on, doggedly determined to follow the trail left by the five horses. He was a strong man, but he realized by the middle of the afternoon that he must soon have food and rest. The pitiless Kansas sun seemed intent upon sapping him of every ounce of water in his body, and with his canteen less than half full, this became a serious concern. Still he pushed his tired body onward, for there was no alternative other than to sit down and die.

By late afternoon, his concentration had come to focus totally upon placing one weary foot after the other, and at one point he realized that he had lost his fixation on the hoofprints he followed. Instead, he had begun following the general contours of the prairie, taking the easiest and most direct route through the rolling plain. The realization stunned him for a few moments, and he paused to look around him in the short grass. Then he saw the faint print where his shod packhorse had mashed down the grass. The Indians had taken the easiest route as well. He was still on their trail, although it was a matter of sheer luck. He berated himself for letting his concentration stray.

As the sun began sinking toward the horizon, he spied a broken line in the endless prairie ahead. His weary mind was a little slow in registering the fact that the broken line was, in fact, a line of trees, which meant a stream lay ahead. It was a tired man that reached the little stream bordered by willow trees and berry bushes. After he made a fire, he sat down to give his feet some attention. The boots he wore were not made for walking, and they had already been showing signs of wearing out even before his forced walk. The stitching had worn through, allowing the soles to separate in several places. He couldn't help but wonder if he was going to be walking across Kansas barefoot before much longer.

"I think we have lingered here longer than we should have," Burning Tree lamented as he led the horses up from the river. The summer sun was not kind to the bodies tied across the backs of the two horses. Already, Black Eagle and Crow Killer were swollen, and Burning Tree was afraid that soon they would begin to smell. It was still a day's ride to their village on the Smoky Hill, and they would have already been there had they not stopped here on this tributary.

"You're right," Walks Fast replied. "I know we should have gotten back as soon as possible, but we could not ignore the good fortune sent our way." They had been a long time away from their village since starting out on this hunting trip. Their luck had been poor, causing them to ride farther and farther south in search of game. Then their luck had gotten even worse when they found the abandoned wagon. There was nothing of value in the wagon, and the time wasted there resulted in the chance encounter with the white man with the medicine gun. A fatal meeting, the encounter led to the deaths of Crow Killer and Black Eagle. Even though it was important to hurry back to the village with the bodies of their two friends, it would have been extremely hard to keep riding when they happened upon a large herd of deer near a tributary of the Smoky Hill. It was the first sign of good fortune, and in two short days, they packed all the meat and hides they could manage on the white man's horse they had captured. "I think the spirit of the deer felt sorry for our loss, and we would have insulted him if we had not accepted his gift."

"Perhaps you're right," Burning Tree said. "It's late now, though. We'll start back in the morning."

At first light, they were back on the trail again, following the river toward its confluence with the north fork of the Smoky Hill and their village.

By the look of the campsite Tanner came upon the next day, he was able to construct a picture in his mind. They had stopped here for more than one night to hunt, it appeared. The remains of several good-sized deer were discarded by the river and the scraps of meat and entrails were already being eaten by a flock of buzzards that ignored the man walking by them. Tanner stooped to check the ashes in the campfire, and found them still warm. "Two or three hours," he said as he stood up again and gazed upriver where the tracks led. He was close.

With his stamina somewhat restored after sleeping all night, and finding some nourishment courtesy of a careless muskrat, he had taken to the trail again that morning with sore feet but renewed resolve. The remains of the Indians' kill left no doubt that they had dined more elegantly than he. Muskrat was not to his liking. Encouraged by the knowledge that they had left this camp no more than two or three hours before, he immediately set out again. The tracks told him that they were simply following the river, so when darkness found him again, he continued following the river, feeling certain that he would overtake them by walking through the night.

Walks Fast stirred in his sleep—something had awakened him. He rose up on one elbow and listened for sounds. On the other side of the fire, Burning Tree was still sleeping. Thinking it was nothing, Walks Fast was about to lie down again when he heard the horses snort and move about restlessly. He *had* heard something— maybe a wolf or a coyote had caused the ponies to signal danger. Sitting up, he reached for his rifle and got to his feet. Suddenly he whirled around at the sound of a voice.

"Stand real still," Tanner commanded, his voice soft but forceful. "You understand white man talk?" Startled, Walks Fast nodded. "I just want a horse," Tanner said. Noticing that the other Indian was now waking up, he cautioned Walks Fast, "Tell your friend to stay where he is and he won't get hurt. Are you Kiowa?"

"Cheyenne," Walks Fast replied.

"Cheyenne, huh? Well, I got no quarrel with the Cheyenne, but you attacked me and shot my horse. All I want from you is a horse, and I'll leave you be."

Fully awake now, and aware of what was taking place, Burning Tree rested a hand on his rifle and slowly rose to one knee. "You killed two warriors," he said accusingly.

"You tried to kill me," Tanner replied. "So I figure we're square as long as I get a horse." He gestured with his rifle. "I reckon you'd best drop that rifle on the ground. If you hadn't woke up, you'da just lost one horse and I'da been gone."

"What makes you think you can kill both of us before one of us shoots you?" Burning Tree rose to his feet, still holding his rifle. "You are a foolish white man to come here. You will die here."

"Nobody has to die," Tanner insisted, "but if you raise that rifle, I'll cut you down where you stand."

A thin smile began to spread across Burning Tree's face an instant before he suddenly jerked his rifle up. Unprepared for the reflexes of the dark-haired white man, he bent over in pain with a rifle ball in his gut. As soon as he pulled the trigger, Tanner dived onto the ground and rolled over, cocking his Spencer as he rolled. In his haste to shoot, Walks Fast missed the sprawling white man. Tanner's second shot slammed into his forehead as Walks Fast fumbled to reload his single-shot weapon.

It had all happened in a matter of seconds, with no

time to think. Tanner's reflexive actions had no doubt helped cause Walks Fast to miss. Even though a repeating rifle, Tanner's Spencer was not fast enough to eject a spent cartridge and load another in the chamber faster than a man could pull a trigger. He had been lucky that the Cheyenne had not anticipated his evasive action. Knowing this, Tanner cocked the trigger guard, ejecting the spent cartridge, and cautiously rose to one knee, his eyes scanning back and forth between the two bodies on the ground. When there was no sign of life from either, he rose to his feet and walked over to Burning Tree's body. Expressing his regrets to the dead man, he muttered, "I didn't come to kill you, but you forced my hand. You coulda just given me a horse. That's all I wanted." Glancing then at the other body, he shook his head sadly. The killing was unnecessary. These men were not his enemies. The thought caused him to return his focus to Garth Leach and his brothers, and the urgency of his mission.

Looking over the camp, he wasted little time in making decisions. With five horses to choose from, he quickly picked a stout mottled gray pony as his first choice, since it had lines similar to Ashes'. Having no desire to bother with herding four horses, he decided to take his packhorse and a paint pony.

He stood before the remaining two ponies, still tied to a cottonwood limb and loaded with their grim cargo. "I ain't got time to worry about the dead," he offered apologetically, while cutting the ropes that secured them to the horses. Rigor mortis had already set in, causing the corpses to hang stiffly in place. Grabbing them by the feet, he gave each body a shove and dumped it on the ground. Then he removed the ponies' bridles and released them. Next, he dumped the load of venison from his packhorse, keeping only enough to eat before it spoiled.

The mottled gray pony was decidedly skittish when Tanner approached him, backing away while eyeing the strange white man cautiously. Afraid the horse might suddenly bolt, Tanner paused to consider the possibility that he might wind up chasing the horse on foot. The thought brought an instant memory of Jeb Hawkins chasing a Union sorrel across a creek in the Shenandoah Valley. It almost made him smile. Stepping back a few feet, he looked around to find a couple of parfleches near the buffalo robes that had served as beds. "That might do," he announced and picked up one of the robes. When he turned to approach the horse again, the sole of his boot flapped loose, and he almost tripped. Taking a moment to look at the worn-out boot, he decided to see if he could find replacements for them, figuring anything would be an improvement. The pair that came closest to fitting his feet was on one of the corpses he had dumped from the ponies. His feet were so sore that he didn't bother to be concerned about the source.

The buffalo robe held the odor of campfire smoke with a hint of something like green bark. He decided it was not unpleasant. With the robe in hand, he again approached the gray.

Moving slowly, he cautiously advanced toward the wary animal. Uncertain, the gray took another step backward as Tanner came near, but it did not bolt. Carefully reaching for the reins, which were no more than a rope looped around the pony's lower jaw with a half hitch, he held the horse steady. The gray did not fight him, but it still eyed him suspiciously. Tanner moved in close and rubbed the robe against the horse's muzzle, letting it smell the familiar odor of the Indian. Tanner had no idea which Indian the horse had belonged to, but the gray seemed satisfied to accept him as a friend. "Atta boy," Tanner said softly. "You're gonna be all right." He stroked the horse's neck for a few minutes before climbing up in the saddle made of wood and buffalo hide. The horse accepted its new master without resistance. "Good boy," Tanner uttered. "We'll see how you take to a real bridle and saddle."

He didn't take the time to ride his new horse before hitching a line between the paint and his packhorse. He figured he and the gray could get accustomed to each other on the way back to the gully, where he intended to pick up his saddle. With one last look at the scene of carnage he was leaving, he shook his head and muttered, "All I came for was a horse."

Retracing his journey of the past few days, he found his new mount to be exceptionally nimble, and certainly quicker than Ashes had been, an asset he was already aware of, remembering how the Cheyenne had steadily gained on Ashes during their chase down the valley. He could not say the Indian saddle was entirely uncomfortable, but he knew that he definitely preferred his own. The next day he introduced the gray to a bit, having kept his bridle to fashion a backpack with the reins. The horse fought the bridle, trying to expel the hard bit repeatedly but in the end accepting it.

There was no danger that he might have difficulty finding the little gully where he had held off the Cheyenne attack. The site of the battle was clearly marked when he was still a mile distant, by the ring of buzzards flying overhead. When he crested the last rise, where the Indians had positioned themselves before, he was revolted by the feast taking place below in the gully. Giving the gray his heels, he galloped down the slope.

The sudden charge of the three horses toward them was enough to cause the buzzards to take flight, but not for very long. Finding poor Ashes ripped and torn by the beaks and claws of the ravenous birds, Tanner was moved to strike out in anger at the first brave buzzards that returned to flop down again near the corpse. Firing his pistol, he shot two of the scavengers, sending the flock scattering noisily, only to land again a short distance away to watch the intruder upon their banquet. Tanner holstered his weapon and, working as quickly as he could, unbuckled the girth strap on the saddle. To pull the strap and the stirrup from under the carcass, it was necessary to use the horses.

He had plenty of rope from his saddle, so he tied one loop around the gray's withers and the other end to his saddle. Amid raucous jeering from the chorus of buzzards, he led the pony forward, pulling the saddle free. Unwilling to further witness the devouring of his horse, Tanner loaded the saddle on his shoulder and led the three horses up the valley, away from the noisy feast.

"You didn't care a helluva lot for the bridle," Tanner said to the gray. "I'll bet you're gonna fight like hell when I throw this saddle on you." The horse lived up to

Tanner's prediction. With the other two horses tied to a clump of sagebrush, Tanner attempted to introduce the gray to a western saddle. The horse bucked the saddle off before Tanner could buckle the girth strap. Tanner patiently threw the saddle on again while the horse sidestepped around in a circle, trying to evade the strange contraption. After two failed attempts, he managed to get the girth buckled, then had to hold on to the reins while the gray tried to buck the parasite off its back. Finally deciding that it could not rid itself of it, the horse calmed down enough for Tanner to tighten the girth.

The saddle in place, he stepped up in the stirrup, and the gray started to buck before Tanner could throw a leg over. Holding on for all he was worth, he managed to get his seat in the saddle. Letting the horse have free rein then, he held on while the horse galloped around the narrow valley in a wide circle. Finally, when Tanner began to think he was going to have to shoot the horse to make it stop, the gray suddenly surrendered and let Tanner guide it back to the other horses at a walk. He had to conclude that it was a relatively short adjustment period, and figured that it was because the horse was already broken to an Indian saddle. He hitched the other two horses on a lead rope and set out again to track down Garth Leach.

Chapter 13

"Looks like the cards just ain't your friends tonight, mister," the rotund man with the bald pate commented as Garth Leach lost another large pot to a pair of kings. "I didn't catch your name."

Glowering out from under bushy black eyebrows, Garth replied, "I didn't give it." The cards had not favored him with one winning hand since he'd joined the three men at the table. The round bald man on his right had enjoyed no better luck than Garth, but he had always folded early instead of staying in and calling the last raise on each hand. The bony dark-haired man in the frock coat, seated across from him, seemed to be the one Lady Luck was smiling upon this evening. The fourth player had won a couple of small pots, but was probably showing a loss for the evening. As the stack of gold coins grew across the table, Garth's anger continued to rise. He could not, *would not,* accept the loss of any of the gold coins he had taken from Jeb Hawkins.

While the bald man shuffled the cards, the man in the frock coat picked up one of the coins and examined it.

"I haven't seen coins like these around here," he commented. "How did you happen to come by them?"

Garth, his steely gaze riveted upon the cards being shuffled, shifted his eyes to lock onto those of the bony man. He continued to stare at him for a long moment before answering. "I don't see that as any of your business," he stated flatly. The spectators around the table grew very quiet. Looking back at the dealer, Garth demanded, "Are you gonna shuffle the faces offa them cards?" Baldy immediately offered the deck to be cut. "Deal 'em," Garth said, declining the offer.

All conversation stopped at the table as those in the game sensed the violent explosion that threatened, and no one was eager to test the huge man. The cards dealt, Garth watched with suspicious eyes as each man discarded. He discarded two, holding a jack, a nine, and a ten. Frock Coat discarded only one card.

Garth's brother Ike walked over to the table as new cards were dealt. He stood there watching for a moment, sizing up Garth's losses. "You ain't doin' too good, are you?" He received an angry glare in answer. "I'm headin' back," Ike said. "When are you comin'?" Ike wasn't pleased with the size of the pile of coins across the table, and he was worried that Garth might lose more than his share of the gold coins. He knew that Garth didn't have the brains to win at cards.

Garth didn't answer until he looked at his two new cards. "Right now," he said. "I'm done here." Without a word to any of the other players, he stood up and shoved his chair away from the table.

Fearful that some form of violence was about to

erupt, the round bald man leaned away from the table, figuring that if the huge man exploded, the force of the explosion would be directed at Garner, the man in the frock coat. Garner, equally concerned for his safety, had taken the precaution of pulling a double-barreled derringer from his boot as soon as Garth stood up. He held it under the table until Garth turned around and followed Ike out the front door of the saloon.

"Damn, Garner." Baldy exhaled. "You picked a helluva man to clean out tonight. I thought for a minute there that we was all gonna get shot. That man's got a mean streak in him a mile wide."

Garner smiled, relieved to see the two brothers go out the door. He held the derringer up for the others to see. "I was ready to use it if he came at me. He acted like I was cheatin'. Fact is, he just ain't a very good poker player."

The mood improved considerably after the gruff departure. Conversation that had been stifled for a few minutes resumed its volume. "I ain't sure you coulda done much damage with that little popgun," the third player commented. "Mighta just made him mad."

"You might be right," Garner said with a grin. "Might take a buffalo gun to stop that fellow." He picked up his cards again. "Whose bet is it?"

The three of them played a few more hands before deciding that they had all lost enthusiasm for the game. "Well," Garner said, "since I'm the big winner tonight, I reckon I can afford to buy you boys a drink."

After a couple of drinks of whiskey, Garner announced that he was heading back to his place. His bald fat friend offered a word of advice. "I ain't ever seen that feller before tonight, but I sure as hell don't like his looks. If I was you, I believe I'd go out the back. He's liable to be waitin' for you out front."

"I was thinkin' that myself," Garner said. "He probably stole these gold coins in the first place." He patted the heavy bulge in his coat pocket.

"I'll take a peek out front to see if he's out there," Baldy said. "If he is, I'll signal you like this." He made a motion with his hand. Garner nodded.

Baldy walked to the door of the saloon, a structure that was actually a long tent with a facade of boards, like most establishments in Denver City. He cracked the wooden door just enough to peer out. There, waiting by the hitching post, stood the huge man and his brother. "Uh-oh," Baldy uttered and quickly signaled Garner.

"I'm gonna use your back door, Jake," Garner quickly said to the bartender. Jake nodded. He had not heard all that passed between the poker players at the table, but he had caught enough of the last of it to understand Garner's concern for caution. Outside the tent, Garner stepped into the dark alley behind the saloon. There was a dank odor of urine hanging over the alleyway, as this was the place where most of Jake's patrons completed the final processing of his beer and whiskey. Garner sniffed contemptuously before turning and running headlong into the dark bulk of Jesse Leach.

At once terrified, Garner staggered backward, thinking it was Garth. "I was just lucky!" he pleaded in his defense before realizing that the imposing form before him was not the belligerent man at the poker table. He recovered his senses enough to explain. "Sorry. I thought you were somebody else." He waited then, wondering why the stranger remained standing in his way, a brainless grin plastered across his face.

"Just lucky, was you?" Jesse replied. "Well, your luck just run out." In the darkness, Garner had not noticed the long skinning knife Jesse held down by his leg. Striking like a rattlesnake, Jesse's arm came up hard under Garner's ribs, the force of the upward thrust lifting the slight man off his feet. Garner inhaled sharply as the knife ripped through his insides. "How you like this kinda luck?" Jesse chuckled as he withdrew the knife and thrust it deep into Garner's gut a second time. Withdrawing the bloody blade again, Jesse stepped back and let Garner's body crumple to the ground, where he lay whimpering pitifully as the life drained from him.

"Did you get all my money?" Garth questioned when Jesse appeared at the front corner of the saloon.

"All *our* money," Ike quickly corrected, still irritated that Garth had gambled with the sack of gold coins found in Jeb Hawkins' saddlebags.

Ignoring Ike's comment, Garth remained focused upon his simpleminded brother. "Did you get my money?" he repeated.

"Yeah, I got it," Jesse answered. "Them coins and more to boot. That feller had a sizable stash of paper money on him."

"What did you do with him?" Ike asked.

Jesse snickered, eager to impress with his originality. "There was a hook outside the back door. I hung him up by his collar. Won't that pucker the first feller's ass that walks out the door?"

"You dumb shit," Ike hissed. "Why didn't you drag him off in the bushes somewhere? When they find him, they're liable to come lookin' for us."

Garth answered for Jesse. "What if they do?" he demanded. "What are they gonna do about it? There ain't no law in this town."

"Maybe so," Ike conceded, "but a lot of these little towns have a vigilante committee that loves to have a necktie party every chance they get."

"You let me worry about that," Garth said.

Ike didn't reply for a moment, trying to decide if this was the time to spill something that had been on his mind for a long time. His mind made up, he spoke his peace. "That's just it, brother. I figure I'd just as soon worry about my share of things myself." His comment caught Garth's attention, and the big man cocked an eye in his brother's direction. Ike continued. "You lost a lot of that gold in there tonight—some of it my share, some Jesse's. What if that feller had slipped away somewhere where we couldn't find him?"

"But he didn't," Garth interrupted.

"But he coulda," Ike insisted. "Anyway, dammit, I'll be holdin' my share of the money from now on. We got a sizable sum right now, with them coins, and the sale of them hides. I don't want my share to disappear in no damn poker game." He paused then to see what effect his bold statement would have on his violent brother.

Garth said nothing for a long moment, his eyebrows lowered over dark eyes that glowered at Ike, causing Ike to drop his hand to rest on the handle of his pistol. Garth's authority had never been challenged before, although Ike quite often questioned his decisions. Garth was the oldest, the biggest, and by far the meanest. He had been the undisputed leader of the family ever since the brothers were boys. There had been many times when he had seen fit to administer physical punishment if his orders were not satisfactorily obeyed, but there had never been outright mutiny. Now, within a few weeks' time, Joe had split off to remain with Yellow Calf's Kiowa and Ike was threatening his authority. Finally, the intimidating man spoke, his words slow and softly delivered. "You sayin' you're the one to give the orders around here?"

Ike, matching Garth's deadly gaze with one of his own, responded immediately. "No, I ain't talkin' about givin' orders to nobody. I'm just sayin' I aim to have what's rightfully mine."

Garth glanced at Jesse, standing with mouth agape while his brothers faced off. Then he looked back at Ike, whose hand still rested on his pistol. If it had been Joe or Jesse, Garth would have simply kicked the hell out of him, and that would have been the end of the insolence. But Ike was different. Lean and hard, Ike was as lethal as a rattlesnake, and Garth knew he would not hesitate to draw that pistol if Garth, God Almighty, or anybody else threatened him. Garth considered his next move carefully before he spoke again. "All right, but let's get the hell back to camp before somebody finds that body." The time may have come for blood to be spilled between brothers. If this was to be, Garth preferred not to risk Ike's getting a shot off quicker than he could. He would wait for a better time.

Back in camp the two brothers resumed the discussion started outside the saloon. An interested and mystified spectator, Jesse busied himself with bringing life to the coals in the campfire, not realizing the seriousness of his older brothers' disagreement. With plenty of cash in their possession, they could have afforded to stay in a hotel, had there been one in the rough tent city near the confluence of the South Platte and Cherry Creek. After selling the load of buffalo hides at Fort Lyon, wagon, mules, and all, they had not lingered—too many soldiers for their liking.

There had been some minor discussion between Garth and Ike before this, with Ike ready to move on to a mining settlement thirty miles north of Denver City. But Garth favored remaining in Denver City. There was gold being taken from Cherry Creek, and the tent city was wild and lawless, an environment that suited Garth's nature. After looking the area over, Garth had picked a spot on the creek close to a mining claim run by two old men. Jesse still had to smile when he thought of the reaction of the two men when they got a look at their new neighbors.

Jesse was concerned that Joe had not caught up to them at Fort Lyon, but Garth had said they would wait for him in Denver City. It had been quite a while, and still Joe hadn't shown up. Jesse had to figure Joe was enjoying tipi living with that little Kiowa girl who had dressed his wound. His thoughts of his younger brother were forgotten when he was distracted by sounds of the argument heating up between his other two brothers.

"I say we stay here for a spell while the pickin's are good," Garth rumbled. "And, dammit, I'm the one who decides."

"Not anymore you ain't," Ike roared back. "Least-ways not for me. I'm headin' up to Black Horse Creek. They're just startin' to pull gold outta there. This place here ain't gonna last long. It'll be dried up before next winter." The two brothers locked eyes for a few tension-filled moments, and Jesse thought they were about to kill each other. Finally Ike broke the silence. "Dammit, Garth, you're my brother, and I don't wanna cause no trouble between us. But I wanna be my own man, and so help me, I'll not hesitate to put a bullet between your eyes if you try to stop me."

Garth studied the angry man for a few moments longer before deciding that maybe it was best for Ike to move on. It wasn't good for brothers to go against each other. "Ain't no use one of us gettin' killed. You go your own way. Me and Jesse'll stay here for a spell. We'll split the money up right now." He started to go to his saddlebag, but paused to add, "Joe ain't here yet, but he gets an equal share. I'll keep it for him till he catches up."

"That's mighty Christian of you," Ike replied sarcastically.

"When you plannin' on leavin'?" Jesse asked, genuinely disappointed by the outcome of the argument.

"In the mornin', I reckon," Ike replied. "I ain't in no hurry. You're welcome to go with me if you want to."

"I expect I'll stay with Garth," Jesse said. He had de-
pended on Garth to tell him what to do all his life. He
was mentally incapable of leaving the dominance of his
older brother.

Chapter 14

"I don't know about you, brother, but I think we put in a pretty good day's work." Travis Bland sat down on the step beside his brother. "I'm thinkin' another day or two and we'll have her done, plenty of time before the really cold weather sets in."

"Looks that way," Trenton agreed, though with little of the enthusiasm reflected by his brother. He reached down beside the step and picked up a jug that had been resting there. Bringing it to his mouth, he took a long pull from it before offering it to Travis.

Declining with a shake of his head, Travis said, "You oughta take it easy with that stuff. You've been hittin' it pretty heavy lately."

"I'm only drinkin' after the work's done," Trenton replied with a hint of agitation. "It ain't slowin' me down none."

"It ain't no way to go home to your wife," Travis lectured.

"Hell, she'd rather have me pass out drunk," Trenton replied.

"That ain't no way to talk about Ellie," Travis said. "You ain't still thinkin' about her and Tanner, are you? Hell, they were just kids then. You've got yourself a fine wife. You oughta appreciate it."

"Oh, I do," Trenton shot back, making no attempt to hide the hint of sarcasm. "I appreciate it a lot."

Travis gazed at him for a moment before shaking his head in exasperation and getting to his feet. "I'm ready for some supper. You comin'?"

"I think I'll sit here for a while," Trenton said. "I'll see you in the mornin'." He waited until Travis disappeared past the corner of the field before lifting the jug again. He welcomed the sting of the strong whiskey on his throat. He only wished it could burn away the agony he felt in his heart. Travis had said that Tanner and Ellie were just kids before, but they were not kids when they had become engaged to be married, before the war interrupted their plans. Trenton felt that he had cheated Tanner, although that was not what he had meant to do. He loved his brother, and he had stolen his wife. Although he had never confided this to anyone, this was the real cause for his bitterness. *If I was half a man, I'd go after him and set things right.* He feared that regret would curse him for the rest of his life. Tanner was gone, his father said to Kansas, and who knew where beyond that. He picked up the jug again.

Tanner Bland held the Indian pony to a steady pace, knowing he had lost a lot of time, but also knowing that time made no difference in his hunt. He was determined to track down the other three murderers no matter the time it took. After striking the Arkansas, he followed it west into Colorado Territory until he came to what he assumed was Fort Lyon. He was told by a soldier driving a wagon that the place was actually Bent's New Fort. Fort Lyon was a mile beyond.

"Much obliged," Tanner said, and continued on. Upon reaching Fort Lyon, he looked for the stables or a blacksmith, reasoning that the Leaches might have had need for one or the other.

"I expect I know the three you're lookin' for," Bill Bramble said in response to Tanner's inquiry. "A man ain't likely to forget them three—two of 'em as big as buffalos and the other'n lean as a whip." He eyed the dark-haired stranger wearing beaded moccasins and a flat-crowned hat pulled low over his eyes. "Buffalo hunters. At least I reckon that's what they was. They sold a whole wagon load of buffalo hides. Then they came over to my place and sold me their wagon and mules." He scratched his head as if finding his words hard to believe. "I give 'em next to nothin' for that outfit, but they took it, and I think I heard 'em talkin' about headin' to Denver City." He continued to study Tanner while he thought about what he had just learned. "Are they friends of yours?"

"Nope," Tanner answered.

"Well, I reckon you'll be lookin' for a place to board them horses."

"Nope," Tanner replied. "I'll be movin' on to Denver City."

*　　　*　　　*

Jesse Leach sat in the back corner of the saloon, his chair balanced on two legs as he drank a glass of beer and listened to Jake's wife torment the new piano. The woman was as lacking in musical ability as she was in physical beauty, but to Jesse the arrhythmic plinking of the keys was as sweet as the chords from an angel's harp. The smile on the simple man's face told of his satisfaction with life as he now knew it. Ike had ridden on to Black Horse Creek, and although Jesse missed Joe, his younger brother's continued absence increased the possibility that he and Garth would split Joe's share of the money. And Garth had even given Jesse some of his share as pocket money for beer and tobacco. As a result, Jesse was spending a good portion of his time in the saloon, looking at the customers and listening to the piano. Although there was a general suspicion about Garth regarding the murder of the man named Garner, no one could prove he had anything to do with it. In fact, there were more than a few witnesses that saw Garth talking to his brother Ike in front of the saloon after Garner had left for the evening. Jesse, on the other hand, had not been in the saloon until after the murder took place, so there was never any suspicion thrown his way. Jesse's grin expanded as he thought about it.

Slurping happily away at his beer, he decided it was time to refill his mug. Letting his chair lower back down to the floor, he was about to get to his feet when someone at the front door caused him to freeze halfway up. Jesse's simple brain misfired repeatedly as it tried to telegraph the message to his conscious mind. He was startled enough to know that the tall dark-haired man in the doorway represented danger, but his mind was too slow to identify him at once. When the connection was finally made, Jesse's reaction was to pull his revolver and open fire.

Oblivious to the few afternoon patrons in Jake's Saloon, Jesse blazed away, throwing as much lead as he could squeeze off in the seconds it took to empty his pistol. In his wild excitement to kill Jeb Hawkins' partner, Jesse's pistol found meat twice, once striking a man standing at the bar and then the back of a man playing cards at the front table. His other shots tore holes in the tent and the door. The man he had attempted to kill ducked down until Jesse's gun was empty, then calmly rose to his feet, his rifle leveled at the frenzied man fumbling in his effort to jam cartridges into his empty revolver.

Tanner advanced calmly toward the stricken murderer, his eyes cold and expressionless, a grim executioner with the sure confidence to complete his task. Trying to watch Tanner and load his weapon at the same time, Jesse could not control his clumsy fingers, dropping cartridges to fall and bounce on the board floor. With no show of haste, Tanner continued to walk through the panicked barroom with no sign of noticing the chaos around him of overturned chairs and people running for the door amid the shrill screaming of the piano player.

Giving in completely to his fright, Jesse finally threw the empty pistol at his stalker and bolted out the back door, running for his life. Still without a trace of urgency, Tanner stepped out the door after the fleeing brute. Raising the Spencer to his shoulder, he took dead aim and fired, cocked the rifle and sent another shot after the first. The two shots were spaced no more than a hand's width apart in the center of Jesse's back. The hulking man ran several yards after being hit before falling face forward in the dirt in almost the same spot where he had waited that dark night for Garner.

Cranking another round into the chamber, Tanner walked slowly over to the oversized figure now lying still in the filth behind the saloon. Standing over Jesse for a few moments, he detected faint signs of life as the simpleminded brute struggled feebly for breath. With the same regard he would have for a rabid dog, Tanner calmly pointed the muzzle of his rifle at the back of Jesse's head and pulled the trigger.

The few souls brave enough to have followed Tanner outside to witness the shooting stood speechless as the grim executioner turned and walked back toward them. They parted to give him plenty of room, no one anxious to speak until he disappeared inside the saloon again. "Where the hell did he come from?" someone asked. There was no answer to his question. "I guess it's a good thing he showed up when he did," another voice offered, "when that big feller went loco back there."

Inside the saloon, Tanner paused to witness the aftermath of Jesse's wild shooting. Two men were laid out on the barroom floor, one of them dead, the other waiting for the doctor to arrive. Over near the piano, the bartender was trying to calm the hysterical woman who was still crying. Calm, apart from the confusion, Tanner scanned the room, searching for Jesse's brothers. They were not there. Assuming the bartender was probably the owner, Tanner walked over to the piano. Both the bartender and his wife looked up when the tall stranger approached. Tanner's cold, dispassionate stare stopped the woman's crying at once. It was replaced by a look of alarm in her eyes.

"I reckon we owe you our thanks, mister," Jake said, although unsure if they did or not. There was a sinister look about the dark-haired stranger whose sudden appearance in his saloon had caused Jesse to go crazy.

"He's got two brothers," Tanner responded coldly. "Where are they?"

"I don't know," Jake replied.

A curious spectator who had inched up closer to get a look at the ominous man with the rifle spoke up then. "They had a camp over on Cherry Creek."

Tanner turned immediately away from Jake and his sniffling wife to face the spectator. "Where is Cherry Creek?"

"I can show you," the man eagerly replied. "I can take you right to their camp."

"I'd be obliged," Tanner said.

Excited to be part of the action taking place, the man led Tanner toward the front door, chattering as he went. "Yessir, I know where their camp is. I pass it on my way to town. They pitched a camp right up from my claim, and I tell you I didn't like the looks of 'em right from the first." He paused to look back at Tanner. "Rakestraw's the name." He paused again, waiting to hear Tanner's name. When there was no response, he went on. "Me and my partner's got a claim on the creek. We're gettin' a little out of it, not enough to pay off, but ever since that bunch moved in on us, one of us has to stay at the claim all the time to protect what little we've got."

Outside the saloon, Tanner stepped up in the saddle, and with Rakestraw leading astride a mule, he followed the excited little man through the tents and shacks and up Cherry Creek. After riding about a mile, Rakestraw pulled up and let Tanner catch up to him. "Yonder's me and my partner's claim, where you see that tent by the creek. The fellers you're lookin' for are camped straight up that slope behind them pines about halfway up."

"Much obliged," Tanner said, and started off straight for the pines that Rakestraw had pointed out, his mind set on finishing what he had started.

The man Garth Leach feared had never been born. Since the time of his father's death, Garth had always been bigger, meaner, and more ruthless than any man he ever met. Jesse was almost as big, and strong as an ox, but simpleminded. Ike was not as physically strong as either Garth or Jesse, but he made up for it with evil cunning. Joe seemed to have been shortchanged in both departments, brains and brawn. It was Joe who was on Garth's mind when he returned from the mining settlement of Auraria later in the afternoon.

Joe, the youngest of his brothers, had still not caught up to them. It was a matter of mild curiosity for Garth. He had no deep affection for Joe, but he was blood kin, and Garth wondered if he had decided to stay with the Kiowa, or if he had met with some treachery. He didn't trust Yellow Calf. *Maybe I oughta pay that double-crossing redskin a little visit,* he thought, *just to make*

sure he knows better than to mess with one of my boys.
Having thought about it then, he paused to consider if
Joe was worth the trip back into Kansas Territory.

Passing through Denver City, he decided to stop for a
drink of whiskey before returning to his camp on Cherry
Creek. He was stopped short of the saloon when suddenly confronted with a grim display before the barber-
shop. There, propped up in front of the tent like a
wooden Indian, stood the body of his brother Jesse. The
shock of seeing Jesse, stone cold and pale as a sheet, was
enough to cause Garth to back his horse up a few steps
without realizing he was even pulling on the reins.
Unconsciously, he roared in anger. The barber, who was
also the town's undertaker, heard the primal outburst and
came outside to find the source. When he saw Garth glaring at him like a crazed demon, he immediately started
to back away.

"Who did this?" Garth demanded, and pulled his pistol and aimed it straight at the undertaker's face.

"I don't know!" the terrified man cried, his brain momentarily addled by fear. "It was a stranger!" he blurted
as Garth cocked the hammer back. "Nobody ever saw
him before. He just appeared outta nowhere, and him
and this feller started shootin' at each other."

Garth hesitated for a moment, the anger churning bile
through his gut. "Where is he?" he demanded.

"I don't know, mister," the undertaker pleaded. "I
swear I don't. I'm just gettin' this poor feller ready for
burial. At no charge," he added fearfully.

Garth released the hammer and holstered his revolver,

having decided to direct his revenge entirely on this stranger that shot Jesse. "Where's his horse and saddle?"

"Down at the stables. Ain't nobody bothered his belongin's."

"Get him down from there," Garth commanded, "and get him off the street, or I swear, you'll be layin' beside him in another wood box." He jerked his horse's head around and started for the saloon.

"Whaddaya want me to do with the body?" the undertaker called after him.

Without turning his head, Garth replied, "Bury it," no longer interested in his brother Jesse's remains.

"Uh-oh," Jake remarked under his breath when the front door of his establishment was flung open and filled with the intimidating bulk of Garth Leach. He and his wife were in the process of cleaning up the blood left by the two shooting victims, and he was temporarily closed.

"Where is he?" Garth roared.

"Gone lookin' for you," Jake replied, without having to ask who, and trying to keep his voice from trembling. "Charley Rakestraw told him where your camp was, and he headed that way." The bartender could see that it would be useless to tell the menacing brute that Jesse had fired first and was responsible for the blood on his floor.

Jake's answer caused Garth to hesitate for a moment. He had said that this stranger had gone looking for him. *Who the hell could be looking for me?* he wondered. There was only one possibility that came to mind. It had to be the partner of that Hawkins jasper. *So he didn't turn tail and run,* he thought. *Well, by God, he's gonna wish he had.*

Tanner found the camp above Charley Rakestraw's claim deserted. Leaving his horses tied in the pines that ringed the ridge above the creek, he had worked his way carefully up through the trees and rocks until reaching a point where he could see the entire campsite. Impatient for the fatal encounter to occur, he considered the options available. Should he wait here for Garth and Ike to return? Or leave to look for them? Realizing that he had no idea where to look, he decided to wait them out. These last two were by far the most dangerous of the four brothers, so he deemed it a better risk to lie in wait.

Moving to a sizable boulder that afforded excellent cover from the campsite, he knelt down to wait. While he waited, he checked his rifle to make sure it was ready for use. Close to two hours had passed when his impatience caused him to become more and more restless. Thinking to change his location yet again, he rose to his feet. A solid blow to his back caused him to stumble and fall. Landing hard on the rocky soil, he rolled over and over, coming to rest against a pine tree. He didn't realize at once that he had been shot. He didn't remember hearing a gun fire. The fact hit him when he heard the next shot ricochet off the rock above him. Confused because he felt no immediate pain, he rolled over on his side, trying to see where the shots had come from. After a few moments more, he felt the beginning of a stinging pain, accompanied by numbness in his left arm. He cursed his carelessness for letting the bushwhacker get in behind him. His heart began to pound in desperate concern. He was shot, but he didn't know how bad it was. As he searched the ridge above him, trying to spot the gunman, he could feel the wet spot on his back as blood spread from his wound. Afraid to move, lest the movement might give his antagonist a target, he lay against the tree trunk with his rifle close and ready to fire.

Above the wounded man, Leach made his way cautiously down between two boulders. He had hit him. He was sure of it because he had a clear shot, and he saw the man go down when the bullet ripped into his back. Now it was a matter of making sure he was dead, and not playing possum somewhere. "Bland," Garth mumbled, just then remembering. "That was the son of a bitch's name." He had killed Jesse, and might be the reason Joe never showed up. "Well, you're messin' with me now, and if you're lucky, you're already dead. 'Cause if you ain't, I might take all night killin' you."

Arriving at the rock where Tanner had been kneeling when he was hit, Garth paused, crouching low while he searched for any sign of the wounded man. When he spotted him, his lips parted in a malicious grin. Lying back against a tree, with his shirt soaked with blood, the man looked helpless. Still exercising caution, lest Tanner wasn't as near death as he appeared to be, Garth took a step toward him, exposing half of his huge body. He stopped abruptly when Tanner tried to raise his rifle to his shoulder. Garth brought his weapon up to fire, but hesitated when he saw that Tanner could not bring his rifle to bear.

"Well, ain't that too bad," Garth said, gloating. "Looks

like you've about used up all your strength." He moved
down the slope toward the desperate man lying helplessly waiting. "I'm fixin' to kill you a little bit at a time,"
he said, pulling his skinning knife from his belt. "You
ever see a Kiowa scalp a man? I watched 'em scalp them
farmer friends of yours on that wagon train. I ain't as
good at it as they are, but I scalped that ol' son of a bitch
Freeman. Shoulda heard him holler."

Struggling desperately within himself to overcome
the pain and numbness, Tanner gripped his rifle, but he
could not seem to raise it. His effort amused Garth.
"Here," he said, "I'll just take that Spencer rifle out of the
way." He reached down and took the rifle by the barrel.
When he pulled it up, Tanner squeezed the trigger. The
weapon went off with the muzzle no more than a foot
below Garth's chin, sending the bullet ripping through
his jaw and into his brain. The huge man crumpled heavily to the ground, killed instantly. Feeling sick and exhausted, Tanner lay back against the tree trunk again,
wondering if Ike was coming behind Garth. This was the
way Charley Rakestraw found him hours later.

He blinked his eyes slowly, trying to bring them into
focus. "Look there, Mutt," he heard a voice say, "damned
if I don't believe he's alive after all." His eyes wide open
now, he looked up into the woolly face of Charley
Rakestraw. He immediately tried to sit up, but the sharp
pain that raced through the back of his shoulder forced
him to lie back again. "You'd best take 'er a little easy,
young feller," Charley cautioned. "You got yourself a
nasty-lookin' hole in your back, but you look a helluva

lot better than that big ol' grizzly you killed up on the ridge." He gestured toward the other hairy face peering down at Tanner. "This here's my partner, Mutt Springer. We found you up beside a pine tree when all the shootin' was over."

"Much obliged," Tanner managed to utter. He realized then that he had a clumsy bandage wrapped around him. "Ike?" he asked. When he received nothing in response but puzzled expressions, he said, "There was another brother."

"Oh," Mutt replied. "That other'n took off two, three days ago. He ain't here no more."

"My horses—" Tanner started.

"We found 'em," Charley said before Tanner had a chance to finish his question. "They're all took care of. We got the big feller's horse, too."

Tanner tried to test his shoulder again, but with the same results as before. "I've got to get movin'," he said.

Charley shook his head thoughtfully. "I don't expect you'll be doin' much movin' or anythin' else for a few days. We put a bandage on that bullet hole, but I ain't no doctor. I don't know if you need that bullet took out or not. Leastways, it didn't come out the front nowhere. You need a doctor. There's one over in Denver City if he's sober."

"I'll be all right," Tanner insisted. "I just need to rest for a little while."

"If you say so," Charley said. "This time of night, he'll be in the saloon, anyway, and he won't be much good to you. If you ain't no better in the mornin', I'll go fetch him."

*   *   *

Morning found him feeling a little better. The numbness in his left arm seemed to have improved, although the wound in the back of his shoulder was extremely sensitive. Charley wanted to go look for the doctor, but Tanner reasoned that if he felt improved after one night, he'd feel better as each day passed. His one thought was that he was losing Ike Leach, and he might as well heal in the saddle. The bullet hadn't killed him, so it was bound to heal eventually.

"I reckon I'll be on my way," he told the two partners. "I'd be obliged if you would help me saddle my horse."

"Be glad to, but you sure don't look in no shape to ride," Charley replied, then hesitated before broaching the subject that was burning his curiosity. "Mister . . ." He hesitated again. "I never did catch your name."

"Bland," Tanner replied.

"Well, Mr. Bland, I ain't got no idea why you was out to kill them two fellers, but if there was any two what looked like they had it coming, it was them." He glanced at his partner before continuing. "What I was gonna say is there's a bag of gold coins we found in that feller's fancy saddle pack that would take a year's pannin' in this creek. We—me and Mutt—figured that was maybe what you was after." He hastened to add, "Not that it's any of our business, one way or the other."

Tanner nodded and hesitated before commenting. He had all but forgotten the coins, having assumed weeks before that they were long gone. "That money belonged to my partner, Jeb Hawkins. The Leaches killed him for it."

Charley glanced at Mutt again before saying, "We figured it was somethin' like that. Reckon it rightfully belongs to you then."

"Tell you what," Tanner said. "Why don't we split that money half and half?"

Both pairs of eyes lit up at that. "Why, that's a mighty generous thing to do," Mutt replied. He wanted to say that they couldn't take payment for their help, but he couldn't bring himself to refuse the offer.

"Done, then," Tanner said. "And you might as well keep his horse, too."

The two miners stood watching as Tanner, sitting a bit uneasy in the saddle, led his two extra horses across the creek and climbed up the other bank. It was a brief encounter with the mysterious stranger, but it had certainly added to their gain. In addition to the gold, there was also paper money that had been generously split. They acquired a fine horse and a fancy saddle, plus they were rid of their menacing neighbors. They were left with the rewarding feeling that being a Good Samaritan paid off in spades.

"I believe this calls for a drink," Charley said as he watched Tanner disappear over the northern ridge.

"That's exactly what I was thinkin'," Mutt replied. "Let's take a little ride to town." They exchanged joyful grins, knowing that they could both go to the saloon without having to worry about the Leaches raiding their camp.

Chapter 15

Maybe I ain't as strong as I thought, Tanner speculated as he leaned forward in the saddle, trying to find a position that would ease the stinging pain in his back. The gray had a smooth gait, but as Tanner made his way up through the hills toward Black Horse Creek, it seemed he could settle on no pace that could free him of discomfort. *I reckon I'll just have to get used to it,* he thought, for the single force that drove him on was the knowledge that one remained. Of the four murderous brothers responsible for the massacre of an entire wagon train of innocent people, one was still free.

There were many small mining camps near Denver City. Ike Leach might have gone to any one of them. But Charley and Mutt told him of a sizable camp at a place called Black Horse Creek, so Tanner decided that was the first place to look for Ike. Tanner reasoned that Ike would more than likely gravitate to a place where there were more folks, for he felt pretty certain that the man wasn't interested in panning for gold. Ike was more likely to acquire his gold with his pistol.

As the sun began its climb over the hills behind him, Tanner guided the gray toward a long valley to the west. Mutt had told him to follow that valley for four or five miles and he would eventually strike Black Horse Creek. Follow the creek north, he had said, and you'll come across the mining settlement in a wide gulch, two or three miles from the valley.

He found the valley with no trouble, even though the pain in his back and shoulder seemed to be increasing with each mile. He kept telling himself to fight against a feeling of overwhelming weakness as he fixed his attention upon the rough valley floor before him. Soon a feeling of light-headedness descended upon him, accompanied by a spell of dizziness. Determined to outlast it, he commanded his brain to concentrate on the task he had set for himself.

He had no idea how long it had lasted. Suddenly, he was jolted awake when the gray was startled by a small rodent or possibly a snake. *Damn!* he thought and looked up at the sun, trying to determine how long he had been asleep. His head was reeling. Had he passed the creek he was looking for? As soon as he thought it, he dismissed it as not likely. His horses would probably have stopped to drink. He became aware then of the soggy bandage around his shoulder. The wound had started bleeding again. *I should have listened to Charley,* he thought, but the sneering, insolent face of Ike Leach flashed through his mind, driving him on. That was the last image he remembered.

*   *   *

Consciousness. A dim light penetrated the dark corridor that his conscious mind traveled to find its way to the light. With eyes only half open, he heard the soft murmur of voices. Puzzled, he blinked his eyes wide to discover a face staring down at him. It was a woman's face. His mind still struggling to free itself of the confusion between dreams and reality, he whispered, "Ellie?" As his eyes focused, he could see the face more clearly, and saw the puzzled expression his question had caused. More awake now, he could see that the face was that of a young woman, an Indian, and she smiled down at him for a few moments before turning away to speak to someone.

"He has come back," Willow Basket softly announced.

"I thought he was dead," a male voice replied with a hint of disappointment.

"No, I knew he would not die," Willow Basket said. "His wound was bad, but he is strong." She turned back to gaze at the wounded white man.

Fully alert now, Tanner realized that he was inside an Indian lodge. He had heard the exchange between the man and woman, but they spoke in the Arapaho tongue, so he did not understand what was said. Knowing something major had to have happened to find himself in an Indian village, he attempted to get up. A sharp stab of pain instantly reminded him of his wound. The woman immediately caught his arm and gently pushed him back on the blanket. She spoke to him then in English.

"You must rest. You lose much blood."

"How did I get here?" he asked, glancing from the woman to the man standing behind her.

She smiled. "Bear Paw found you on the ground beside your horses. He bring you here."

"My horses," Tanner asked, concerned. "Where are my horses?"

"No worry," Willow Basket replied. "Horses are here, all good." She glanced over at Bear Paw then and raised an eyebrow. He shrugged but said nothing. These Arapaho were friendly with the white miners, but he had found Tanner looking very much dead, with three fine horses. Had he remained dead, Bear Paw would have been a good deal wealthier.

"How long?" Tanner asked.

"Two days," she answered. "You lose much blood." She held up a lead slug for him to see. "Medicine man take out bullet. You get much better now, be strong again. Now you must eat, make blood strong."

"Much obliged," was all he could think to say at the moment as he examined the bandage that had been wrapped around his bare torso. "Where's my shirt?" he wondered aloud.

Willow Basket laughed. His shirt had been ripped in the side, had a bullet hole in the back, and the entire garment had been soaked with blood, some fresh, some crusted and faded. "Shirt no good, throw him away. I make you new shirt." Then something occurred to her. She pointed to his feet. "Cheyenne moccasins, Arapaho shirt." Then she pointed to herself. "Arapaho."

He smiled at her and nodded his head. "Arapaho," he repeated.

*   *   *

The days that followed saw Tanner recover rapidly. The medicine man was evidently skilled at his trade, for the wound healed nicely, and Tanner was on his feet a day after first regaining consciousness in Bear Paw's lodge. The Arapaho people made him feel welcome, and stopped to exchange pleasantries with him when he walked through the village.

During his days of recovery, he often spent hours with Bear Paw. At his request, his Arapaho host taught him to speak in sign language, a skill that Tanner figured might come in handy some day. Eager to learn, Tanner proved to be a good student, practicing each day's lesson on members of the village, sometimes to their gleeful entertainment whenever he used the wrong sign. Inadvertently, he picked up a few words of Arapaho as well. It was a gentle time for him, and for a short period he was able to push Ike Leach into the back of his mind. He knew that he stayed longer than he should have because of the peace he found there. He used as his excuse the fact that he had to wait until Willow Basket finished sewing a doeskin shirt for him. As he regained his strength, however, thoughts of his unfinished business began to find their way to the surface of his mind.

For what seemed like as long as he could remember, the one dominant thought that possessed him had been the vengeance demanded for the slayings of Jeb and the people who had befriended him. He reprimanded himself for lingering now in the peaceful environment of the Arapaho village. Who could say how long a man like Ike Leach might stay in the general area? By the very nature of the man, he robbed and killed, then moved on to the next place. Tanner knew it was time for him to move on. The decision was facilitated by the completion of his shirt.

"That's a mighty fine-lookin' shirt. I swear it is," Tanner remarked as Willow Basket held it up to him. She beamed in response to his praise. He had gone without a shirt, like the Arapaho men, during the time he had remained there. Willow Basket explained that the shirt she had fashioned for him was worn by the men of her tribe only for special ceremonies, but white men seemed to need one all the time. "Why, a shirt like this is too fine not to wear," Tanner told her, causing her to beam again. "I'm proud of this shirt. I wanna wear it all the time."

In payment for Willow Basket's gift, as well as the generous hospitality he had received, he gave Bear Paw the paint Indian pony. He also left him a few of the gold coins with the instructions that they were worth a lot to the white man. "So you make sure you get plenty for them at the tradin' post," he said.

Ready to go, he stepped up in the saddle. Bear Paw handed him the lead rope for his packhorse and said, "You find this man, you kill him. Then you come back here."

"Maybe I'll do that," Tanner said. "I thank you both." He turned the gray's head north. Looking back at the husband and wife, he gave a final wave of farewell.

Following the shallow stream up through the hills, he came to a split that formed a wide gulch with scraggy pine trees ringing the rim. Scattered along both sides, like toadstools popping up at random in a grassy meadow, were the tents of the fortune seekers. Tanner walked his horses slowly through the maze of canvas tents, ignored by the men he passed, as he searched each face for recognition. Near the center of the settlement, there were two tents, larger than those around them. One was a dry goods store, the other a saloon. He chose the latter to serve his purpose.

LUCKY DOLLAR, the sign scrawled in rough letters proclaimed. The board front of the tent still smelled of newly milled lumber, testimony to its recent establishment. Tanner stepped down from the saddle and tied his horses to the hitching rail. He stood at the door for a moment to look the customers over before entering. Failing to see the tall, gaunt figure he searched for, he pushed the door open and walked in.

"What's your pleasure, mister?" the bartender greeted him while giving him a good looking over.

Tanner looked around him at the tiny barroom with its two tables almost touching in the back half of the tent before answering. "I could use a drink of whiskey if you've got somethin' that won't take the hair off your feet."

"I don't serve nothin' but the finest," the bartender replied and reached for a bottle on the shelf behind him. "Dust or cash?" The stranger didn't look much like a miner, with his deerskin shirt and moccasins, so he held on to the glass until Tanner plunked the money on the bar.

Tanner tossed the shot back. "You're right, that ain't half bad. You can pour me another." When the glass was refilled, he swirled the dark liquid around a few times before tossing it after the first. His thirst satisfied, he said, "I'm lookin' for somebody."

"Hell, who ain't?" the bartender immediately rejoined.

Ignoring the curt reply, Tanner continued. "Name's Ike Leach—tall, lanky feller. I thought you mighta seen him around here."

The bartender's eyes immediately narrowed. "He a friend of yours?" he asked.

"No, I'm just lookin' for him."

"You a lawman?" the bartender asked, although thinking it highly unlikely that a lawman would be in these parts.

"No, I ain't a lawman," Tanner responded impatiently. "Have you seen him or not?"

"Yeah, I've seen him, all right. At least there was a feller around here for a couple of days that called hisself Ike. Never gave his last name, but he was tall and lean, and he knifed John Beasley in the side over a card game. Said he caught John cheatin'. It was a damn lie, and I told him so. He stuck a pistol in my face and woulda kilt me if I so much as blushed. Hell, I almost shit my britches. That's the meanest-lookin' man I've ever seen."

"Is he still around?" Tanner asked.

"He's long gone, and good riddance. If he'da stayed much longer, I expect we'da had to form a vigilante group. The only trouble is there ain't enough men around here willin' to stick their necks out to go after a man like that."

"Any idea where he mighta been headin'?"

"Hell, who knows? Away from here is all folks around here cared about."

Tanner nodded thoughtfully while he considered his chances of ever finding Ike Leach. "Well, I reckon I'll be movin' on," he finally said with a sigh. "Much obliged."

The weeks that followed offered little encouragement that he would ever find the man he searched for. He drifted from one mining camp to the next with no information on the whereabouts of Ike Leach, never getting more than directions to yet another camp. Midsummer turned into Indian summer with nothing gained, other than a more thorough knowledge of the country. Living by his wits, he hunted for his food—trading hides for coffee and salt whenever he found a store in one of the camps—hoarding his pouch of gold coins and cash against the day when he would need ammunition for his rifle. The Spencer took .52-caliber rimfire cartridges, and they were hard to find. He and Jeb had taken a generous supply of the cartridges from the field at Waynesboro, but the number was gradually dwindling. Cartridges for his revolver were much more common, but he couldn't hunt deer, elk, or buffalo with a pistol. As the summer wore on toward autumn, he knew he would soon have to make a decision.

The stitch was a little loose, gathering puckers along the seams, but he figured it was strong enough to hold together. Finished, he held the robe up to admire his

handiwork. Willow Basket would place a hand over her mouth and snicker if she could see it, but it would keep him warm when the first snows hit. The nights were already getting chilly in the Medicine Bow Mountains, where he had camped for the last two days while he hunted. Willow Basket had told him that she would make him some winter moccasins from buffalo hide, with the fur turned inside for warmth. The way things looked now, he doubted he would be back to get them, and he was not confident that he could make his own.

Laying the robe aside, he poured a cup of coffee from the pot resting on the coals. Taking a cautious sip from the cup, he sat back to think about what he was going to do. He had wasted two full days riding up in the mountains to find a camp that turned out to be long ago abandoned. And now he didn't know in which direction to start out come morning. The senselessness of his mission was beginning to undermine his determination to complete his vow to settle with Ike Leach. He was in the middle of nowhere with winter coming on, and he had no desire to spend winter in the mountains. Suddenly, his thoughts were interrupted.

"Hello the camp," a voice called out from beyond the pines on the far side of the stream. Caught napping, Tanner immediately grabbed his rifle and rolled out of the firelight. In the fading light, he could not see anyone. Before he could answer, a call came again. "Ain't nobody but me. I couldn't help but smell that coffee boilin'."

"Come on, then," Tanner called back, watching the dark stand of pines carefully.

A few moments later, a form materialized and separated itself from the darkness. One rider leading a pack-horse walked his mount slowly through the stream and approached the camp. Tanner got up on one knee, still in the shadows, his rifle still ready to fire. He watched his visitor carefully.

"Howdy," the stranger said when Tanner got to his feet to meet him. "My name's Jack Flagg. I could shore use a cup of that coffee I smell."

"Help yourself if you've got a cup," Tanner said. "This is the only one I've got." He stood back to let him get to the pot.

His visitor was a short man, no more than five feet tall, Tanner estimated. Scrawny as a monkey, he was well on in years, although it would be difficult to guess how old he was. His face was shiny and flushed, and framed with long bushy hair and beard, reminding Tanner of a wilted sunflower. Wasting no time, he pulled a tin cup from his saddlebag and helped himself to the steaming-hot liquid. With insides that must have been made of leather, he gulped the hot coffee down, emptying half the cup before he took a breath and wiped his mouth with the back of his hand.

"Dad-gum, that shore tastes good," he exclaimed. "I've been outta coffee beans for a solid month." He took another long swig from the cup, then brought it down to take a close look at his host. "I don't recollect seein' you in these parts before. Where you headed?"

"Hard to say," Tanner answered, still marveling at the man's indifference to scalding pain.

Jack cocked an eyebrow and grinned. "Are you lost?"

"No, I wouldn't say that," Tanner answered with a grin. "I just ain't sure where I am right now, and I don't know which way I'm headin' in the mornin'." He went on then to explain that he was hunting a man who had murdered innocent folks and was on the run. He described Ike, and asked if Jack had run into him.

"Can't say as I have," the little man replied. "But, hell, as big as this country is, it'd be one helluva coincidence if you did run into him. From what you tell me about the man, it don't sound like he's one to live in the wild like I do. There ain't no minin' camps in these mountains that I know of. My advice to you is to quit wanderin' all over hell and back, and go where the gold is." When Tanner's expression was questioning, he continued. "Alder Gulch, Virginia City, up in Montana Territory, that's where they're strikin' it big right now. You ain't too far from Fort Laramie. You might be able to find out if your man passed through there. Ever'body does that's headin' to Montana."

"Go ahead," Tanner said in response to Jack's questioning look when the curious little man held up the almost empty coffeepot. As Jack poured the rest of the coffee into his cup, Tanner considered his guest's advice. Alder Gulch made more sense than wandering around in the mountains hoping to run across Ike's trail. Jack was right, he decided. There were good odds that a man like Ike Leach would gravitate toward the goldfields. At least if he went to Fort Laramie as Jack suggested, he might find out if Ike had passed through there. His decision made, he asked, "How do I find Fort Laramie?"

"Can't miss it," Jack replied, his tone carrying a slight implication that any fool should be able to find Fort Laramie. He pulled a half-burned limb from the fire and used it to draw a simple map on the ground. "This is where we are right here. You ride across these ridges—oh, a half a day or so, dependin' on how fast you ride—and you'll come to a valley where you'll strike the Laramie River. Follow the river. It'll take you right to Fort Laramie. You oughta be there in two or three days."

"Much obliged," Tanner said. "How about you? Where are you headed?"

"Back toward Denver City. The nights are starting to get a little chilly. Won't be long before some honest-to-God cold sets in, and I'll be winterin' with a bunch of Arapahos that got a village near there. Been winterin' with them for the last two years."

Tanner told him of his recent stay in an Arapaho village, but it turned out to be a different village from Jack's friends. They talked long into the night about the country Tanner could expect to see if he proceeded northwest to Montana, the hostile tribes that he should avoid, and the brutal winter that he could expect.

"You must want this feller awful bad," Jack remarked. "What are you gonna do after you find him, considerin' you're the one still standin'?"

The question gave Tanner pause. The only conscious thought in his mind was to balance the scales of justice, to give Jeb Hawkins vengeance. It had replaced all others. Jack's question caused him to realize that he had no plans for life after his grim task was completed. The notion flashed through his mind that his life had been stolen. His brother Trenton was living his future—settling down with Ellie, running his father's and his father-in-law's farms. At once, his deep somber mood returned. He had no purpose in life beyond that of the cruel sword of the avenger. He glanced up to see Jack waiting for a response to his question. "I don't know what I'm gonna do," he said, then added, "if I'm the one still standin'." Jack made no further comment on the subject, but seemed to study Tanner intently, as if envisioning his host's probable future.

The next morning, both host and guest were up early, ready to depart. "I thank you for your hospitality," Jack said. "Maybe our trails will cross again sometime." Tanner nodded as he checked the cinch on his saddle, his mind already back on the hunt. Jack hesitated a moment more before deciding to impart some advice to his new friend. "You know, Tanner, I've been trackin' through these mountains, from here to the Bitterroots, for more'n fifteen years. And it's a generous country if a man has a sharp eye and a nose for danger. But the mountains can get into a man's head if he ain't careful. Some folks just don't take to bein' alone all the time. Especially in the winter, the wind whistling through the Rockies can sometimes make some strange sounds, almost like words. If you're alone long enough, and you don't watch yourself, you can start listenin' to them words, and sometimes them words can tell you to do some strange things."

Tanner paused to look at Jack before stepping up in the saddle, wondering what prompted the homespun advice. In his mind, he was already picturing the tall,

gaunt features of Ike Leach and the sneering countenance that seemed his trademark. "What are you tryin'
to tell me, Jack, that you think I might go crazy listenin'
to the wind?"

Seeing that his advice was lost on the determined
young man, Jack shrugged. "I'm just sayin' you seem
like a nice young feller. I'd hate to see you let this killin'
you're bound to do drive out the good things in your
heart."

"And wind up talkin' to the wind?" Tanner finished
for him. He laughed. "I'll try not to let it happen." He
swung a leg over and settled in the saddle as the gray
took a few steps to the side. Tanner pulled the reins to
turn the horse's head toward the north. "Take care of
yourself, Jack," he said.

"You as well," Jack replied. "Watch your scalp."

"I will," Tanner replied. He turned north and relaxed
the reins. The horse started out at a fast walk. He had not
ridden a hundred yards when he heard Jack Flagg calling after him.

"Wait up!" Jack called. Tanner looked back to see the
little man coming after him at a gallop. When he pulled
up beside him, he explained. "I changed my mind. Hell,
I'll ride to Fort Laramie with you. I ain't ready to lay up
for winter yet, and I ain't been to Laramie in a spell." He
paused. "If you don't mind the company."

Tanner laughed. "I don't mind."

The trip took less than two days with Jack leading
them. When they arrived, Jack suggested that Tanner
might find information on Ike Leach at the sutler's store.
Since Tanner needed to buy supplies and ammunition

anyway, he went directly there. Jack parted company with him then, telling him that he was going to visit a friend who had a little saloon on the road past the stables. "It's easy to find if you're ever lookin' for me while you're here," he said, "but if I don't see you no more, you take care of yourself."

Chapter 16

Seth Ward had been the post trader at Fort Laramie since 1857. During that time he had seen all manner of people pass through the army post; settlers heading for Oregon, gold miners heading for California, soldiers, Indians, trappers, mountain men, and many other opportunists. Most of these he could label as typical, none especially more memorable than the others until they had all melted into a single monotonous hash of humanity. But there was something decidedly different about the dark-haired, broad-shouldered stranger who entered his store on this early October morning.

He paused in the doorway for a few moments while he looked around the room. Tiny droplets of water glistened on his broad-brimmed hat and the roughly sewn buffalo robe draped across his shoulders. The few remaining snowflakes that had covered him melted in the heat provided by the stove and fell to create faint wet spots around his moccasin-clad feet. His right hand held a Spencer repeating rifle, hanging almost casually with the muzzle pointed toward the floor. It was not the man's combination dress of animal skins and wool that caught Seth's attention, however, for that was nothing out of the ordinary. Rather, it was the look in the man's eyes as he surveyed the store. Seth got the impression that the stranger missed nothing in his cursory glance. Two men, a soldier and a civilian standing at the counter, turned to see who had walked in the door. The stranger's eyes shifted momentarily to regard them before returning to focus on the post trader.

"Good morning." Seth greeted Tanner. "Look's like it's still snowin' a bit outside."

"A bit," Tanner agreed. He walked over to the end of the counter then, opposite the two men. The war was long since over, but he was still a little wary of Union soldiers. On their part, he was quickly dismissed as another of the many drifters who passed through Fort Laramie.

"What can I do for you?" Seth asked.

"Do you have any cartridges for a Spencer?" Tanner responded. Seth replied that he did, and produced a box from a cabinet behind him. He waited for Tanner to say how many he wanted, looking somewhat surprised when Tanner said, "I'll take the box." He was even more surprised when Tanner paid him with gold coins.

Pleased to receive the hard cash, Seth said, "You must be plannin' to start a war. Is there anything else you need?"

"Five pounds of bacon, a sack of those coffee beans over there, and something to keep my feet warm," Tanner replied.

Seth glanced down at the light summer moccasins

Tanner wore. "You might be in luck, mister. I think I might have some boots your size."

Tanner nodded as if thinking it over before speaking. "I've grown partial to Injun shoes," he said. "I don't reckon you've got anything like that."

"Reckon not," Seth said.

Overhearing, one of the men at the end of the bar, a husky man wearing corporal's stripes, interjected, "You can get some moccasins at that Crow camp up the river. There's an old woman there who'll make 'em for you if you've got the hides."

"I was just gonna tell you about her," Seth said, "but she'll take a while to make up some moccasins. I've got a stout pair of boots just your size."

Tanner turned to face the soldier. "Much obliged," he said.

"Shore," the corporal replied. "When you get done here, I'll walk outside with you and give you directions to that Crow camp."

"You think of anything else you need," Seth said, "you come on back, and I've probably got it. I don't get paid with gold coins very often. You're only the second one in a month."

Tanner felt the blood in his veins suddenly go cold. He turned his attention abruptly back to the post trader. "Who was the first?"

Seth shrugged, thinking back. "Some fellow on his way up to Virginia City," he said. "At least that's where I think he said he was goin'."

Tanner could feel his heart pumping against his ribs. "What did he look like?" he asked.

Seth stroked his chin as he recalled. "Tall fellow, taller than you maybe, but he was thin as a rail. Had a dark look about him. That's about all I remember about the man."

Tanner stood silent for a few moments, hardly believing he had at last stumbled upon Ike Leach's trail. Jack Flagg's advice had been good. "How far is Virginia City?" he asked.

"You thinkin' about goin' there?" Seth asked. "You're talking about two weeks or more, dependin' on the weather, through some pretty hostile Injun territory. And, mister, if you ain't ever been there, you're gonna need a guide. I doubt you can find one that'll set out this time of year.

Nodding to Seth, Tanner picked up his purchases and said, "Much obliged."

The soldier and his civilian friend followed him out the door. Outside, they gave him directions to follow the Platte for two miles west where he would find the Crow camp. "The woman you wanna find is Owl Woman," the corporal said. "She'll make you a fine pair of Injun boots."

Tanner thanked them for their help, loaded his purchases onto his packhorse, and rode out of the compound, his mind still spinning with the news of Ike Leach. Unwilling to waste another day, lest Ike not stay put in Virginia City, he was inclined to set out right away for Alder Gulch. He had two problems, however, the most important being that he didn't know the way to Alder Gulch. The second problem, only slightly less important than the first, was his feet were cold. Anxious as he might be, he knew that he couldn't set out blindly for a place where he'd never been, especially this time of year. And he knew the folly of starting out ill-equipped to handle the cold. So, he reluctantly decided, the first order of business was to acquire warm footwear.

Following the directions given him by the corporal, he had no trouble finding the Crow village. Owl Woman turned out to be an old woman who lived with her son and his wife. She made moccasins in exchange for hides, trinkets, and money, whatever she could trade for. When Tanner showed her the buffalo hide he carried on his packhorse, she said, "I make you fine boots, warm, come up to here." She touched his leg below his knee. "Two days," she said in answer to his next question.

"Two days?" Tanner questioned. "You mean you're gonna soften this hide and make up a pair of moccasins in just two days?"

She explained that she would take his hide to replace one she was already working on for a pair of boots for her son. Some minor adjustments could be made to change the size, and her son was in no hurry for his boots. Tanner considered this a real piece of good fortune, and the price was agreed upon—his buffalo hide and three dollars, paper.

Riding back toward the fort, he thought about Seth Ward's advice, that he would need a guide to take him to Virginia City. *I just might know one,* he thought, smiling. Jack Flagg had been careful to give him exact directions to his friend's saloon. The little man might have already been thinking that Tanner would need a guide. He couldn't imagine why the curious old man would want to go. Maybe he was wrong. *We'll find out, I reckon.*

As he guided the gray along the bank of the river, he decided he might as well start looking for a place to camp for a couple of days while he waited for his new moccasins. The path along the river dropped sharply as it doubled back around a large cottonwood that leaned out over the water. Rounding the trunk of the tree, Tanner pulled up sharply when he was suddenly confronted by a horse and rider blocking his path. Startled to find a pistol drawn and pointing at him by a man with a bandanna masking his face, he started to reach for the rifle in his saddle sling.

"I wouldn't if I was you," the man warned. "If you don't wanna die, you'd best just set peaceful there." The man nudged his horse up closer, the pistol pointing directly at Tanner's face. "Now, let's take a look in them saddlebags. Is that where you hide them gold coins? You could save me the trouble of tearin' up your whole outfit if you just tell me where you got 'em hid."

Feeling like a fool for being careless, Tanner quickly evaluated his situation. He couldn't see the man's face, but he had a strong hunch that it was the same man who had been talking with the soldier in the post trader's store, who had given him directions to the Crow camp. The thought of it made him angry, with no thought of fear. With a pistol in his face, he knew there was no time to pull his rifle from the sling. He was wearing a revolver on his belt, but he wasn't sure he could draw it fast enough to get a shot off before his assailant blew his brains out. Still, he was unwilling to meekly let this son

of a bitch have his way. After what seemed a long standoff, Tanner dropped his hand to rest on the handle of his
pistol.

"Get your hand off'n that pistol!" the man exclaimed.
"I'll shoot you down right now."

Ignoring the threat, Tanner spoke, his voice calm and
steady. "Mister, you're gonna have to earn anything you
steal from me. You might shoot me, but I can pull this
pistol in less than a half a second. So I'm gonna kill you,
even if I'm dead when I pull the trigger. You might
wanna think about whether it's worth the risk or not."

His unexpected threat caused the man to hesitate.
Tanner thought his bluff might have succeeded, but it
was only for a moment, for the next sound was a voice
behind him. "I expect you'd best get your hand off of that
pistol. I don't think you're fast enough to stop a bullet in
your back. Now get them gold coins outta them saddlebags like he told you."

Damn, Tanner thought, knowing he had no chance to
escape this standoff with no harm done. He was reluctant
to give them what they demanded, but it wasn't worth
risking his life. Still, the very thought of being robbed by
two surly scoundrels galled him no end, and they might
decide to shoot him anyway. He was seriously thinking
of telling them to go to hell, and letting the chips fall
where they may. Another voice made his decision for
him. "I got this Remington Rollin' Block buffalo gun
sighted right between your shoulder blades, mister. So if
the shootin' starts, this .50-70 cartridge is gonna leave a
right sizable hole in your back."

Even under such tense conditions, Tanner couldn't

suppress a hint of a smile, for he recognized the twang in the voice immediately. "Is that you, Jack?"

"I reckon," Jack Flagg replied. "You wanna go ahead and shoot these low-down snakes, or let 'em go?"

"I'd just as soon shoot 'em both," Tanner replied. He could see the confusion and uncertainty in his assailant's face. "I'm feelin' pretty generous today, though. Maybe we'll leave it up to them, live or die."

There was no indecision in the second highwayman. With the threat of Jack's buffalo gun at his back, he said, "I'll pick livin'." He wheeled his horse and retreated at a gallop.

Still reading the eyes of the man facing him, Tanner could see the confusion turn to panic. Instinct dictated his next move. Lunging sideways, Tanner suddenly dived from the saddle, just in time to avoid the pistol shot that whistled through the air where his face had been a split second before. As he hit the ground, fumbling for his pistol, he heard the solid report of Jack's buffalo gun, followed by the thump of the body on the ground. He was on his feet in seconds, his gun drawn, to find the man dead, a sizable hole in his chest.

A few seconds later, Jack rode up beside him. Looking down at the body, he said, "Damn fool." Then he looked at Tanner. "You all right?"

"Yeah," Tanner said, rubbing his backside. "Except where I landed on that damn root." He looked up at the curious little man. "Much obliged," he said. "Where'd you come from, anyway? I was in a helluva fix back there."

"I'd say you was," Jack said with a chuckle. "I was

havin' a drink with that friend of mine, and I happened to overhear them two fellers talkin' about some stranger buyin' stuff at the sutler's store with solid gold coins. I couldn't hear all their conversation, but I got enough to know they wasn't up to no good. You were the only stranger I knew that had just rode in, so I figured I'd best follow them two to see if they was up to somethin'." He grinned wide. "Good thing I did, warn't it?"

"I reckon," Tanner agreed. He reached down and pulled the bandanna away from the dead man's face. It was the same man who had been talking to the corporal in the store.

"Has he got anythin' on him that's worth anythin'?" Jack asked, and dismounted to see for himself. As he relieved the corpse of gun belt and weapon, he paused to ask, "Can you really pull that pistol of your'n in less than half a second?"

Tanner laughed. "Hell no. I haven't any idea how long it would take me to pull it. More like a half an hour, I guess. I've never had reason to time it."

"I figured you was just tryin' to bluff that feller."

"I suppose we oughta drag him outta the path," Tanner said. "We can dump him in that gully over there. I doubt if anybody's gonna miss him."

After the body had been disposed of, Jack took a long look at the deceased's horse and decided it was little more than buzzard bait. "Saddle ain't worth much, either," he said. "Might as well leave it here, and let the horse go free." Neither man felt any guilt over salvaging the dead man's property. There was no sense in leaving any useful items for someone else to find. "What did you find out about that man you're huntin'?" Jack asked when they were ready to leave.

"Like you figured," Tanner replied. "Leach came through here, all right, headed for Virginia City."

"That a fact?" Jack said. "How come you ain't on your way to Montana?"

"I'm havin' me some warm winter boots made. Then I've got to find a guide who knows the country." Suppressing a smile, Tanner waited for Jack's response.

"Hell, don't nobody know the country between here and the Judith better'n me," Jack proclaimed. "I hunted elk in Alder Gulch before they ever stuck the first pick in the ground, camped on Alder Creek and Stinkin' Water Creek before folks ever started tearin' up the soil in Daylight Gulch. Hell, when I warn't huntin', I picked gooseberries, and serviceberries, and chokecherries on the sides of the gulch. Lost a horse one year at Daylight Gulch—stepped in a stripped badger hole and broke his leg. Had to shoot him."

"I know you know the country," Tanner interrupted, lest the old-timer go on forever, "but you're goin' back to Denver City for the winter." He shook his head as if perplexed. "I need a guide."

"I'd go if you asked me," Jack quickly replied.

"What about all that talk I heard about you wantin' to winter with the Arapaho? I remember you said it was a bad time to start for the mountains. What changed your mind?"

Jack shrugged, looking a little embarrassed. "I don't know." Then he flashed a wide grin. "I just figured somebody oughta look out for you." In his heart, he didn't really know why he was eager to go with Tanner. He just had a feeling that he was getting ready to die every winter he gave in to the lure of a warm tipi in an Indian village. If he had delved deeply enough into his soul, he might have admitted that he was lonely, a lonely old man facing the end of his life. In Tanner, he saw courage and determination, and he felt a strong need to be part of it.

"A lot of folks would tell you it's the wrong time of the year to head up that way," Tanner reminded him.

"Hell, I've wintered up that way before," Jack replied. "Bitterroots, Bighorns, Wind River. Besides, it ain't even really winter yet." When Tanner didn't respond right away, Jack added, "You wouldn't have to pay me. I'll go for nothin'."

Tanner smiled. "How 'bout we go as partners, and I'll pay for whatever we need as long as the money holds out." Jack's wide grin more than adequately showed his gratitude. They shook hands on it.

Chapter 17

Ike Leach had wasted no time establishing himself in Alder Gulch. The first week after he arrived, he looked Virginia City over thoroughly. Although still sprouting plenty of tents, shacks, and log huts, the mining center was rapidly becoming a city with some houses built of stone quarried from the sides of the gulch. Stores, saloons, stables, bawdy houses had become commonplace. But even with these signs of permanence, there was already ample evidence of the town's coming decline. Gold discovered in Last Chance Gulch the year before was already drawing much of the town's population to that new strike. There was a nucleus of citizens who still saw real progress, with talk of Virginia City becoming the capital for the territory. But it was not a desirable situation for a cutthroat outlaw like Ike.

There was law in force in the settlement. Vigilante law, long a factor in Virginia City, did not trouble Ike. It was the coming of real law enforcement, territorial lawmen, that worried him. Unlike his older brother, Garth, Ike was a careful man. For these reasons, he decided to ride farther down the Gulch to seek his fortune. There were more towns to choose from in Alder Gulch— Junction, Pine Grove, Adobetown, Nevada City, and a few others, all in a fourteen-mile stretch of the gulch. The town that suited Ike best was Junction.

The first thing Ike did when he arrived in Virginia City was to have himself fitted for a fine suit of clothes. He could afford it, and he considered it essential for his planned occupation. When he moved down to Junction, he wanted to look well-heeled, so people would expect him to have money. Tall and lean in his dark suit, he was welcomed into the poker game at the Nugget on his first night.

The players, all miners, gambling with dust for stakes, welcomed the opportunity to win currency and occasional gold coins from the stranger. The fact that he did not always win made him welcome to the game, and right from the first he was there every night. At about the same time the stranger arrived, there began a series of claim robberies, all resulting in the murder of the owners. But no one suspected the gaunt dark man who worked for a big mining company soon to locate in the gulch. Besides, the claims hit were not in Junction. No one seemed to notice that, after a few nights, Mr. Leach played with dust only, and no longer with coins or currency.

At last the sun dropped below the hills to the west of the gulch. Soon the long afternoon shadows would disappear into the darkness of the evening. Bundled up in a heavy coat, Ike shivered in the cold snowy thicket where

he had been watching a lone miner load the last wheel-
barrow of dirt to take to his sluice box before darkness
forced him to quit for the day. "Get it all," Ike whispered
under his breath, which he could now see with each
breath taken.

Finally the miner combed the few flakes of gold and
emptied them into a pouch. Ike moved a little closer,
straining to see. "I'da been a while findin' that," he whispered, as he watched the miner remove a flat rock from
the edge of the creek. After the unsuspecting miner replaced the stone and went about the business of supper,
Ike moved back out of the thicket to retrieve his horse.
He then rode back up the creek before crossing over and
approaching the claim along the path.

"Hello the camp," Ike called out as he walked his
horse toward the campfire.

The miner quickly grabbed his rifle, and stood ready
to challenge his visitor. "Who the hell are you?" he
called back.

"Ike Leach," Ike replied. "I'm workin' with the law
enforcement committee. We're tryin' to track down some
of these claim robbers. You ain't seen no suspicious
strangers down your way today, have you?"

"Law enforcement committee?" the minor replied.
"Well, I reckon it's about time somebody done somethin'. It's got so you gotta sleep with your gun around
here."

"It's been a long day," Ike said. "Mind if I step down
and warm up a little by your fire? I've gotta ride all the
way back to Nevada City tonight."

The miner lowered his rifle. "Why, 'course not. Step

on down. I was just fixin' to boil a little coffee and fry up some bacon. You're welcome to share."

"Why, that's mighty neighborly of you," Ike replied. "I don't mind if I do."

The miner put the rifle aside and started to prepare his supper. "My name's Ellis. I'm sure glad to see some law around here. There's been killings up and down the gulch the past week or two. A man can't be too careful. I ain't had much luck myself, so I don't reckon nobody would waste their time robbin' me."

"Is that a fact," Ike said. "Well, maybe your luck'll change." Since his stomach had begun to growl, reminding him that he hadn't eaten for a while, he decided there was no hurry. He might as well let Ellis cook him some supper. "Anything I can help with?" he asked politely.

"You can get some water from the creek with that coffeepot," Ellis replied. Ike graciously complied. When he returned with the coffeepot, Ellis asked, "When did this law enforcement committee get started? I ain't heard a word about it."

"Just since I got here about a week ago," Ike replied, entertained by his charade. "I'm kind of a specialist, so they sent for me."

"Who did?" Ellis asked.

Ike cocked a suspicious eye at his host. Ellis seemed to be asking a hell of a lot of questions. "Some folks in Virginia City," he tossed off casually. Then attempting to change the subject, he asked, "Is that coffee startin' to boil yet?"

"It'll be a minute," Ellis replied. He busied himself slicing some strips of bacon from a slab of salt pork. "It strikes me as odd that I ain't heard nothin' about your committee."

Impatient, but still trying to maintain the charade, Ike said, "We try to keep it quiet. We don't wanna warn the folks doin' the killin'."

Ellis paused to think about that before continuing with the meat. "I suppose so, but it looks like somebody woulda heard about it."

A man of little patience to begin with, Ike finally reached his limit with the man's incessant questions. Moving around the fire to place himself between Ellis and his rifle, he pulled his pistol from his belt. "Here's your damn committee," he growled.

Already harboring suspicions about his mysterious visitor, Ellis immediately dived to the side, snatching a revolver from under the blanket he had been kneeling on. He was not fast enough to avoid taking a bullet in the chest, but he managed to fire once before falling back. His bullet grazed Ike's cheek, leaving a red trail across his face.

"Why, you son of a bitch!" Ike roared indignantly as he grabbed his cheek. "You shot me!" Furious at the man's sneaky attempt, he planted one foot on Ellis' gun hand and administered a stout kick to his ribs with his other boot. Ellis grunted with pain. Unable to free the hand grasping his pistol, he grabbed Ike's boot with his other hand in a desperate attempt to fight for his life. "Let go my boot!" Ike growled between teeth clenched in response to the pain in his cheek. He cracked Ellis sharply across his skull with the barrel of his pistol before pointing it directly at his forehead. "If you hadn'ta been so nosy, you coulda had a cup of coffee before you went to hell," he snarled as he pulled the trigger.

Jerking his leg out of the dead fingers that held his boot, Ike spat upon the corpse, fuming over the deviousness of the man. In pure anger, he wasted another bullet on the corpse, attempting to vent his ire. Then it occurred to him that others in claims down the creek would hear the shots and might come running.

Realizing a need for haste now, he turned toward the flat rock at the edge of the water. Feeling blood seeping down his neck, he paused to grab Ellis' shirt. He attempted to rip off a piece of the shirt, but he couldn't tear it. Frustrated, he picked up a corner of the blanket Ellis had been kneeling upon, and furiously mopped the blood from his face and neck. Permitting his anger to get the best of him, he almost fired another shot into the dead man. Checking himself, but still frustrated, he picked up the knife Ellis had sliced the bacon with, and with one forceful plunge, left it sticking up in the dead man's belly.

Working feverishly now, tugging at the flat rock, while pausing every few seconds to curse and blot the blood from the crease in his cheek, he uncovered Ellis' treasure. Taking a small canvas pouch from the hole under the stone, he hefted it, trying to estimate its value. Fifty dollars, he decided, maybe seventy-five. The man wasn't scraping a fortune from the claim, but he had more than he had let on. "The lying son of a bitch," Ike muttered. He was about to hurl more abuse at the corpse when he was stopped by sounds of voices coming from down the creek. "Damn!" he exclaimed. He had hoped to have some coffee and supper before departing.

Hurriedly climbing in the saddle, he rode through the creek and up through the thicket where he had watched Ellis' camp. He knew he would leave a plain trail through the snow, but he counted on the darkness to hide it until morning. By then it wouldn't matter. The night's work had not gone well. He could very well have been killed by the man. The miners were becoming much too alert to the possibility of being victimized by a claim robber. It might be time for him to think about moving on to Last Chance Gulch, a hundred and twenty-five miles away.

It had been a proper decision. Tanner was certain of that. The weather turned before they reached Bridger's Ferry on the North Platte, blowing in a light snow that left a thin frosting on the trail. And he shivered to think of how cold his feet would have been had he not waited for his new moccasins. Up ahead of him, Jack Flagg hunched his frail little body in the saddle, never wavering or hesitating before a fork or mountain pass. Both men wore heavy buffalo robes draped over their shoulders, Injun style, as Jack referred to it. He claimed that the tentlike style trapped in more body heat than a coat made from the hides would have. Tanner couldn't argue. He'd never had a buffalo coat, but he was beginning to believe his new partner knew a hell of a lot more about surviving in the cold than most folks.

They had already been in the saddle for over a week, and Jack figured they'd spend at least that much longer before they got to Alder Gulch. This was the easiest route, he explained, but the Sioux were not in a gracious state of mind after the so-called Powder River Expedition at the end of the summer.

"Some general name of Connor took a couple thousand soldiers or more up this way lookin' to punish the Sioux and Cheyenne," Jack explained. "All they found was Black Bear and Old Devil's Arapaho people in a peaceful village on the Tongue. They destroyed the village and killed a lot of Injuns that wasn't causin' any problems to anybody. Connor and his soldiers come draggin' ass back to Fort Laramie half starved and lucky to be alive after the Injuns got on their tail. The whole mess didn't set too well with the Sioux, so I expect we'd best keep our eyes open to avoid any Sioux hunting parties."

They continued cautiously, following the Bozeman route up through Powder River country toward the Yellowstone, camping a few days later at Bozeman City, approximately seventy miles from Virginia City.

Jack sat before the fire, cross-legged like an Indian, studying his young partner, who was absorbed in the cleaning of his rifle. Jack prided himself on being able to figure out most every man he met, but he found it difficult to figure Tanner. The dark-haired young man with ox-yoke shoulders was a quiet man who seldom wasted words. Tanner's silence didn't bother Jack, since he could do enough talking for both of them. What intrigued Jack was the feeling that Tanner was deep in thought about something far away, maybe something very serious. Yet he was not without a sense of humor. He could smile on occasion. *Of course,* Jack conceded, *when you're out to kill a man, it ain't much to giggle about.* Sometimes Jack would question his decision to partner up with Tanner, knowing so little about the man. It wouldn't make sense to a lot of people to team up with a man who was on his way to murder somebody. For want of a better reason, he decided that it was because he believed Tanner when he said Ike Leach needed killing. Besides, he was a nice young fellow who could benefit from Jack's years of experience in the mountains. Jack would never admit, even to himself, that he was drawn to Tanner because of the young man's strength of character and his quiet courage. And Jack was of an age where he needed someone strong to back him up.

Feeling the old man's gaze upon him, Tanner looked up from his rifle. "How long?" he asked.

"Two days," Jack answered. When Tanner turned his attention immediately back to his rifle, Jack pressed. "You sure as hell don't talk much."

"No need to," Tanner replied without looking up. After a long moment, he glanced up and gave Jack one of his infrequent smiles. "I've got you to take care of that."

"What are you aimin' to do after you find this Leach feller and kill him?" Jack asked.

"I don't know. I haven't thought about it."

"Well, maybe you'd better. In the first place, folks in Virginia City got tired of folks killin' each other in their town, so you'd best be particular about how you're gonna do it."

"When I find him, I'll kill him," Tanner stated simply. "Where I find him is where I'll kill him."

"Huh," Jack snorted facetiously, "That's a real complicated plan."

It was early afternoon when they stopped on a hill overlooking Alder Gulch. Below them, the winding creek made its way down the center of the gulch, staggering drunkenly out of sight, its banks crowded with men laboring to harvest the precious pay dirt. Before starting down the slope to Virginia City, Tanner advised Jack that they might want to separate, since he wasn't sure what was going to happen. From where they now sat, Virginia City looked like a sizable place, bigger than Tanner had imagined, even though Jack had told him it was a town of ten thousand or more. A town that size was bound to have lawmen. Tanner thought it best if Jack stayed clear of him.

"Shit fire, son," Jack scoffed. "I expect I'll ride right along with you. I'm too damn old to worry about the law."

Tanner looked at his partner for a long moment, thinking. Finally he decided he'd be wasting his time to try to talk the little man out of it. "Suit yourself," he said, and pushed off down the slope.

Tanner had never seen a busier town than Virginia City. There were people everywhere, and it appeared that there was not a shovelful of dirt left unturned in the whole gulch. They passed claim after claim with men shoveling, or pushing wheelbarrows of dirt, or feeding sluice boxes. The thought swept through his mind that he might never find Ike Leach in this mass of people. He pulled his horse to a stop to let a bull-train of sixteen horses, pulling three wagons linked together, rumble by on the muddy street. He glanced at Jack, a look of dismay in his eyes.

"I feel the same way, partner," Jack remarked. "Too damn many people."

Tanner shook his head, but having lost none of his resolve, he said, "Might as well start lookin'. We'll start with the saloons."

"Helluva idea," Jack said, smacking his lips.

For the next three days, Tanner searched every saloon and business establishment in Virginia City and Nevada City, but there was no sign of Ike Leach, and no one who remembered seeing him. Convinced that Ike had to be there somewhere, Tanner reluctantly left Virginia City to search the smaller towns along the gulch.

Chapter 18

"That's a right nasty-lookin' cut you got across your cheek there, Leach," Bob Gentry remarked. "Looks painful."

"It ain't nothin'," Ike said with a scowl. "Damn horse rode me right into a tree branch."

"I had a horse do that to me once," another man at the table said. "Rode me right into a spruce limb, tryin' to knock me outta the saddle. I got me a limb about the size of my arm, and broke it across that nag's face. It broke her of that trick."

"I expect that's what I shoulda done," Ike said. "Whose deal is it?" he asked, impatient to change the subject.

"Mine," Gentry replied, and picked up the deck to shuffle.

The card game continued, having started soon after Ike came into the saloon shortly after seven. It appeared to be his lucky night, as the cards kept falling his way. Outside, a lone figure moved among the horses tied at the rail, checking the front left hoof of each animal. He stopped when he found what he was looking for, a horse with a broken shoe. Knowing it to be the horse he had trailed all the way from Tom Ellis' claim, Johnny Becker went in the saloon to find the rider.

His attention was drawn immediately to the tall thin man seated at the poker table with his back to the corner. The fresh slash across his face looked like it could have been caused by a grazing bullet. Johnny studied the thin man's face. There was a menacing look about the man, enough so that Johnny was hesitant about confronting him alone. In his judgment it would be wiser to summon the group of miners who had descended on Ellis' claim when they heard the shooting. He sidled over to the bar. "How long do you expect that game'll go on?" he asked the bartender.

"Them fellers?" the bartender responded. "Hell, till I run 'em out. They'd play all night if I let 'em."

Johnny nodded, stood there for a moment, then moved casually toward the door. Once outside, he jumped on his horse and hightailed it back up the gulch.

The hour was late, but the game continued, even though no one at the table was enjoying it but the dark sinister-looking man with the slash across his face. With a smile of satisfaction never seen before by the others at the table, Ike raked in pot after pot. "Damn if I don't believe I've lost about all I can stand for one night," Bob Gentry complained as he threw his cards in.

"You ain't quittin', are you, Gentry?" Ike taunted. "I figured you for more guts than that."

Of like mind, the other two players threw their cards

in as well. "That's enough for me, too," one of them said. "It's time I was gettin' back to my place," the other chimed in.

"Ain't even gonna try to get your money back?" Ike was gloating. He leaned back in his chair, unable to suppress a wicked chuckle, as the three losers ambled toward the door. It was the biggest payday he could remember that he had come by honestly. "Come back tomorrow," he called after them. "Maybe your luck will change."

In the dimly lit doorway, a broad-shouldered man dressed in animal hides and carrying a Spencer rifle stepped aside to let the three cardplayers pass. When the door closed behind them, he stood searching the room until his gaze fell upon the gaunt man seated at the table.

Still chuckling to himself, Ike watched his benefactors until they went out the door. The smile on his face froze when he suddenly discovered the shadowy figure standing where there had been no one moments before. He couldn't see the face, but he immediately felt a sense of alarm. He pushed his chair back from the table as the specter stepped into the light. "Tanner Bland!" Ike blurted involuntarily, his eyes wide with terror. He grabbed for his pistol. Like the angel of death himself, Tanner calmly leveled the rifle and pumped a slug into Ike's chest before the horrified man could draw his revolver from his belt. Still alive, but mortally wounded, Ike fell back in the chair, his face a twisted mask of terror as the relentless agent of doom walked slowly toward him. Cocking the rifle, Tanner fired a second shot into the dying man's body, still walking forward until standing directly over him. The third and last bullet split Ike's forehead.

Tanner stood before the body, sprawled now in a grotesque posture in the chair, scarcely able to believe that it was finally over, and Jeb and the others could at last rest in peace. Aware of the total silence around him, as several pairs of eyes stared wide in frightened shock, he turned and slowly made his way toward the door.

Outside, he was startled to find himself facing six armed men, miners from the look of them—no doubt vigilantes—and all with rifles or shotguns aimed at him. "That ain't him," Johnny Becker said. "He wasn't here before."

A gray-haired man, who looked to be in charge, said, "Keep your guns on him, boys. He might be a friend of the other one. Johnny, go in and see what the shootin' was all about." He directed his next words toward Tanner. "All right, mister, you can just step down off that porch and drop that rifle on the ground."

Tanner stepped down to the street, but he did not drop his rifle. "You've got no quarrel with me. The man I shot was a murderer. I've done you no harm."

"Is that a fact?" the gray-haired man replied. "Well, I reckon we'll see about that. Cut him down if he so much as blinks an eye, boys." Glancing up at Johnny coming back out the door, he asked, "What did you find, Johnny?"

"The one I saw before's inside, deader'n hell. This'un shot him." He pointed to Tanner.

Standing patiently, Tanner said, "I told you that. He was a murderer."

"I don't doubt that he was," the gray-haired man said. "I don't know what you two were arguing about, probably over splittin' poor Tom Ellis' gold dust, but we don't stand for wild gunmen like you in Junction, and some-body's gotta hang for Tom's death. Now, drop that rifle like I told you."

Thoughts raced through Tanner's mind like lightning as he stood facing the six armed men. *So this is the way it's going to end,* he thought. One thing he knew for certain—he had no hope if he dropped his rifle. *I'd rather be shot than hanged,* he thought. After a long moment, he spoke. "I told you, I didn't have anything to do with your friend's death, but if you're thinkin' on hangin' me, then I'm takin' somebody with me. I expect I might be able to get two of you, but I'm sure I can get you." He nodded at the gray-haired man.

Not expecting to find himself in that situation, the spokesman for the lynch party hesitated. Not willing to back down in front of his neighbors, he blustered, "You're talkin' crazy, mister. We've got you outnum-bered six to one."

"I expect you'd best make that six to two." The voice came from behind the group.

Tanner almost smiled as the sudden announcement caused immediate concern within the citizen posse. They began to shuffle around in obvious discomfort. All par-ties were startled when another voice called out, "Maybe you'd best make that six to three."

Straining to see who had decided to join in his defense, Tanner looked beyond the hitching rail to see a figure emerge from the shadows. The walk seemed familiar, and when the man stepped into the lantern light, Tanner exclaimed, "Trenton!"

"Howdy, brother," Trenton replied.

Taking advantage of the hanging party's loss of resolve in the face of certain casualties, Jack Flagg took command. "All right, this little set-to is over. Tanner here didn't have nothin' to do with your friend's killin'. You fellers go on back and bury him. The man you needed to hang is in there dead."

There was little hesitation. The posse broke directly for their horses. The gray-haired man hurriedly said, "Justice has been served," and rode after the others.

Shocked almost speechless, Tanner moved to meet his brother. Equally speechless at that moment, Trenton stared into his brother's face, scarcely believing he had found him. Then as if on signal, they embraced in a big bear hug while Jack Flagg watched amazed. Tanner was the first to speak. "Trenton, what the hell are you doin' out here?"

"I came lookin' for you," Trenton said.

Tanner called Jack Flagg over. "This is my brother Trenton," he said before responding to Trenton's remark. "Lookin' for me? Is everything all right at home?" He looked around as if expecting other surprises. "Is Ellie with you?"

"No, she's at home."

"How in hell did you find me?" Tanner still found it hard to believe.

"I got to Fort Laramie a day after you left. The fellow in the post trader's store remembered you. I tagged along with an army surveyor's team. Otherwise, I don't know how I would have gotten here."

"You still haven't told me why you came all this way to find me," Tanner insisted.

"Why don't we get on our horses and mosey the hell away from here," Jack said interrupting the reunion. "Before them miners come back with a bigger posse."

"I expect that's a good idea," Tanner said. "Come on, Trenton. We've got a camp up at the other end of the gulch."

Back in camp, Jack announced that he was going to boil a pot of coffee, and discreetly excused himself in case the brothers had a private matter to discuss. Trenton joined Tanner while he watered the horses. He stumbled over his words at first, but was finally able to speak his piece.

"I came out here to find you because there's somethin' I've got to say to you. I can't live with myself any longer till I get it said."

"Why don't you just come on out and say it?" Tanner said.

"All right. Tanner, I feel like I stole Ellie while you were away still fightin' in the war. I swear, we all thought you were dead. Ellie wouldn't have ever married me if she thought you were still alive, and I can't make her a decent husband knowing I cheated you out of your life. I know I broke your heart, and I don't know what to do about it other than to say that she's rightfully yours and I'll step aside if you come home."

Tanner didn't say anything for a long moment while he thought about what Trenton had said. "I'll bet Ellie doesn't know that's what you came out here to say," he finally said.

"No. I told her I had to find you to sign some papers to make sure you were part owner of the farm."

Tanner turned his head toward his gray Indian pony, stroking the horse's neck while he spoke. "Well, brother, I'm glad to see you, but you wasted your time if that's all you wanted to tell me. You don't need to apologize to me for anything. You know, I was gone from home a long time. A man can change in that length of time, and that's what happened to me. I didn't know how I was gonna tell Ellie that I'd changed my mind about gettin' married. And I was just tickled that things worked out between you and her."

Trenton's eyes misted with the emotion he was experiencing. "You mean that? You and Ellie were always—"

"A long time ago," Tanner interrupted. "You go on back home and take care of that wife of yours. You've certainly got my blessing. I wasn't cut out for farmin'."

"You don't love her?"

"Of course not," Tanner replied. "Haven't for a long time." When he felt safe to turn and face Trenton again, he could see the relief in his brother's face, as if a great load had been lifted. "Me and Jack'll see you back to Fort Laramie. Then we've got some business to tend to in an Arapaho village down in Colorado Territory. Right, Jack?" he said as he passed by the rambunctious little man.

"That's right," Jack cheerfully agreed. When Trenton walked over to fetch something from his saddlebags, Jack said just above a whisper, "I overheard what you just told your brother, and I reckon I've been around you long enough now to know when you're lying like a blind dog."

"You ain't as smart as you think you are, partner," Tanner said. In his heart, he knew it was all a lie. He had loved Eleanor Marshall for as long as he could remember, and he would always love her. In this hostile world, that was the only thing he knew that would always be true.

Read on for an exciting sneak preview of
Charles G. West's next Western adventure . . .

RANGE WAR IN WHISKEY HILL

Available now from Berkley.

Like two old bulls, they stood eyeing each other. Two big men, determined and defiant, the gray-streaked manes of each bearing testament to a life of tests and survival. In Frank Drummond's mind, this confrontation was to be the final one. It was the third time he had made an offer to buy out Sam McCrae's Bar-M Ranch, a section of range that he needed and intended to have. Peaceful buy-out or otherwise, his patience was exhausted. He figured he had gone as far as he intended with the stubborn old son of a bitch, and it was time for a showdown. "Well?" he demanded.

"How many different ways do you have to hear the word 'no' before you get it through that thick skull that you ain't gettin' the Bar-M?" Sam McCrae replied defiantly. "You and that gang of outlaws who work for you have scared most of the smaller ranchers out of the territory. You even got to Sessions last year, but by God, you ain't gettin' the Bar-M or the Broken-M. Me and my brother were here before you ever saw this valley, and we, by God, plan to be here after you're gone. You've had your say now, so you can climb back on that buckboard and get the hell off my land."

Frank Drummond stood fuming, his heavy eyebrows glowering like dark storm clouds as he glared at Sam McCrae. Barely able to control his rage, he nevertheless spoke quietly but clearly. "You've gotten my final offer, McCrae. Now we'll see who stays in this valley and who doesn't." He turned away and climbed back on his buckboard.

Sam stood on the top step of his porch, a deep scowl etched across his weathered face, watching until the buckboard disappeared behind the cottonwoods at the bend of the creek. *I hope to hell he finally believes he ain't running me off my land,* he thought. Drummond already owned all the land from the north bank of Lodgepole Creek to the stream that formed the boundary at the beginning of McCrae range. That wasn't enough for Drummond. He wanted to control all the land between Lodgepole Creek and Whiskey Hill, more than fifteen miles of open range.

The price Drummond had offered was a fraction of the value of the land, which included both his spread and the free-flowing water of Crooked Creek. Even if the offered price had been reasonable, Sam had no intention of selling. He and his brother, Burt, who owned a spread adjoining his, had first come to settle here when the town of Cheyenne was known as Crow Creek Crossing. There was plenty of land north of Crow Creek Crossing for everyone then. Sam and Burt weren't the only settlers that claimed portions of the vast prairie, which was convenient to the proposed Union Pacific Railroad line.

There were a good many more, enough to establish a small town called Whiskey Hill, a half day's ride from Crow Creek Crossing. Drummond moved in a couple of years later with a crew of men more at home on wanted posters than tending cattle. His intentions were soon apparent—he was building a cattle empire, and he went about acquiring all the land one way or another. The smaller ranchers fell one by one. Some sold out to Drummond at desperation prices, some had unfortunate accidents; only the McCrae brothers and Walter Sessions had remained to stand between Drummond and Crooked Creek. But now Sessions had knuckled under after too many cattle had gone missing or been found shot.

With the completion of the railroad in November, 1867, Crow Creek Crossing was renamed Cheyenne, and had already earned a reputation as one of the wildest towns in Wyoming Territory. The little town of Whiskey Hill naturally inherited some of Cheyenne's undesirables. When the Union Pacific moved on to Laramie City, the construction workers and many of the riffraff that had contributed to Cheyenne's sinful ways followed along behind.

"I wish to hell Frank Drummond and his crowd had moved on with them," Sam mumbled as he stepped down from the porch and turned to go to the barn.

Vance should be back from the south ridge before supper time, Sam thought as he saddled the sorrel mare. *I'd best ride up as far as the north fork to make sure we ain't losing any more strays.* It bothered him that he had to tell Vance to check the south ridge. His oldest son should have learned by now to think of it himself. Sam shook his head, perplexed by the thought. Vance showed no evidence of ever being able to take over the management of the ranch.

"He needs a little more of his brother's grit in him." His muttered comment brought a familiar moment of regret to the gray-haired patriarch of the Bar-M. Vance's younger brother, Colt, the fiery young mustang, was as different from Vance as night is to day, and Sam blamed himself for the distance between father and son. In looking back to find a reason, he regretfully admitted that it was probably because Colt was clearly his mother's favorite. When Martha was taken by pneumonia, it seemed to change the thirteen-year-old boy. He missed his mother, and Sam knew he should have been more patient in his expectations for the boy to become a man. Colt seemed to be mad at the world for the senseless death of his mother, and consequently exhibited resistance to any form of authority.

Sam often thought about Colt while the boy was away these long years. He was convinced that if Colt had been allowed to sew his wild oats, he would have eventually settled down to run the ranch. "If 'if 'was a tater, we'd have somethin' to eat," Sam said, and sighed sadly. Sam's young firebrand son had been shipped off to prison at the age of eighteen, for a crime Sam faithfully believed the boy did not commit. Colt said he didn't have anything to do with it, and reckless and wild as he had been, Colt was never a liar. "Damn, I miss that boy," Sam whispered as he guided the mare toward a path that led up to the ridge.

His thoughts returned once more to Drummond. *I'd*

better go over and tell Burt that Drummond was here. *again,* he thought. "We'll probably start missin' some stock again." He had barely gotten the words out when the stillness of the late afternoon was suddenly shattered by the sharp crack of a single rifle shot. Sam McCrae stiffened, then, without so much as a grunt, slid to the ground, a forty-five slug embedded between his shoulder blades.

"McCrae, you've got a letter."

Colt McCrae looked up, surprised. The last letter he had received was two years before, when his father had taken the time to write. "Who's it from?" he asked.

"Burt McCrae, it says on the envelope," Bob Witcher replied, handing the letter through the bars. "Is that your daddy?"

"Nope," Colt answered. "That's my Uncle Burt." His curiosity aroused by the unexpected letter, he hurriedly tore it open, fearing it must hold bad news. Uncle Burt was not one to write letters unless there was a dire necessity.

Bob Witcher watched with interest. Of all the guards in the prison, Bob was the only one who had taken a personal interest in the solemn young man from Wyoming Territory. He had watched the wild-eyed, hostile kid develop from a skinny, tough-talking hothead into a soft-spoken man of few words. Bob had seen a strain of decency in the young prisoner, and after knowing him for a few years, became convinced that Colt really was innocent of the crimes with which he had been charged. He liked to think that he had been influential in Colt's maturing into a man. Aware of the bitterness festering in Colt's soul, Witcher had spent quite a few hours talking to Colt about the evil erosion of a man's mind when consumed with thoughts of vengeance. Over the years, as Colt grew in maturity, Witcher witnessed the silent strength of that maturity. There was little doubt, however, that the penitentiary's prisoner work program had to be given credit for Colt's physical development, turning the skinny boy into a strong, prison-hardened man.

Colt read his uncle's letter, then, without comment or even a change of expression, placed the letter on his cot. Witcher sensed a feeling of trouble. "Bad news?" he asked.

Colt looked up, his face devoid of emotion. "They killed my pa. Shot him in the back."

"Damn, son," Bob responded. "That is bad news. Do they know who shot him?"

"Yeah, they know," Colt replied, his words soft and measured. "Uncle Burt says nobody saw it happen, but there ain't any doubt who was behind it. Maybe they don't know who pulled the trigger, but they damn-sure know who ordered it done."

Witcher shook his head solemnly. "That is sorrowful news, but don't you go gettin' all riled up and cause the warden to order you into solitary for a few days. You don't wanna add no time on your sentence when you're this close to gettin' out." Witcher had seen it happen before when a prisoner received bad news from home that prompted an attempt to escape. It was the warden's policy to impose a cool-down period until he was convinced the inmate was no longer inclined to attempt some fool scheme to run. It would be a shame in Colt's case, when the young man had only six months to go.

Witcher cocked his head to one side, giving Colt a hard glance. "It's against the rules, but I won't report this to the warden if you'll promise me you ain't gonna do somethin' stupid."

Still with no show of emotion, Colt said, "I ain't gonna cause no trouble, Bob. I aim to do my time and leave this place in six months." He picked up the letter again and gave it a brief glance. "Uncle Burt wants me to come back to Whiskey Hill when my time's up. Says he and Vance need my help. There's a ticket in here from Omaha to Cheyenne, but I'd have to make it to Omaha on my own." He paused again. "Maybe I'll think on it."

Bob nodded. He knew that Colt had not intended to return to Whiskey Hill when he was released, having had his fill of the community that had stripped him of almost ten years of his life. Although he thought he had a limited window into the man's mind, Witcher could not know the depth of sadness the report of his father's murder caused. Colt had never been especially close to his father. He was closer to his Uncle Burt. Maybe it was because Burt McCrae's nature was closer to that of the wild young boy who felt more at home in the foothills and mountains than on a cattle ranch. A sad smile formed on Colt's face as he pictured his uncle—husky and rugged, bigger than life. Like Colt, Burt had been the black sheep of the family, a stark contrast to Colt's father, who was a man of few words and steady as a rock. Colt wondered how the years had changed his uncle. Then he reminded himself that nothing outside an act of God could change

Burt McCrae—Colt could almost see him, with his prized possession, a derby hat bought in Omaha, cocked jauntily to one side as he rode herd on his ranch hands.

The coolness between Colt and his father was now cause for regret on the son's part, for he felt it was his fault, and now the opportunity to atone for it was lost. It would have been better if he had been more like his brother. Then the gulf between him and his father might not have been so wide. Like his father and his uncle, Colt and Vance were miles apart as young boys. That, too, was a shame. Maybe now it could be fixed. As he had said, he would bide his time and think on returning.

Ready to find
your next great read?

Let us help.

Visit prh.com/nextread